Dear Reader,

Leave the everyday and journey into a magical realm with these three brand-new stories of breathtaking emotion and powerful enchantment.

In "Counting Crows," bestselling author Mercedes Lackey will take you to the court of Lady Gwynnhwyfar. Will this heroine's magic be powerful enough to survive threats to her kingdom, her marriage and her life?

Drusilla Morgan is a regular working woman, but at night...well, that's when her fantasies take over. In "Drusilla's Dream," *USA TODAY* bestselling author Rachel Lee explores one woman's nightly quests to battle evil and find true love.

Enter the world of "Moonglow," by Nebula Award-winning author Catherine Asaro, where kings must marry for magic and Iris Larkspur is forced into wedlock with a deaf, mute and blind prince. Will she find the power to heal her husband and claim her destiny?

We hope you enjoy this special collection of tantalizing, fantastical tales in which the greatest power of all is love.

The Editors
Silhouette Books

MERCEDES LACKEY
is the author of the Heralds of Valdemar series (currently at twenty-five books and still going), plus several other series and stand-alone books. She has collaborated with such luminaries as Marion Zimmer Bradley, Anne McCaffrey and Andre Norton. She lives in Oklahoma with her husband, Larry Dixon, and far too many birds. She is launching LUNA Books in January 2004 with *The Fairy Godmother.*

RACHEL LEE
I hate writing biographies because I think my life can't possibly be interesting to anyone but me. So I will say: I live to write, and I'm lucky enough to write to live. We have more than the usual number of children, all of whom are angels, of course. We have two dogs. One is an angel, too. The other...well, let's say I sometimes think he needs an exorcism. At present we have a yellow ribbon on our mailbox and candles in the windows for our son who is in the Persian Gulf. I'm a spiritual person, and I believe that life is all about love, all about the many kinds of love. My personal motto is: "Kindness is contagious. Infect the world."

CATHERINE ASARO
is known for her award-winning Ruby Dynasty series that combines futuristic adventure with strong romantic story lines. Her novel *The Quantum Rose* won the 2001 Nebula Award from the Science Fiction and Fantasy Writers of America, and many other awards from the romance and science fiction genres alike. Her novella in this anthology will be followed by her new novel, *The Charmed Sphere,* which is part of the launch of the new LUNA line. Praised for her ability to mix fantasy with character-driven romances, Asaro has been a writer, a Ph.D. physicist and a ballet dancer. Her husband is the proverbial rocket scientist at NASA, and her daughter loves math and ballet. They have three cats who are remarkably adept at eating.

Charmed Destinies

MERCEDES LACKEY
RACHEL LEE
CATHERINE ASARO

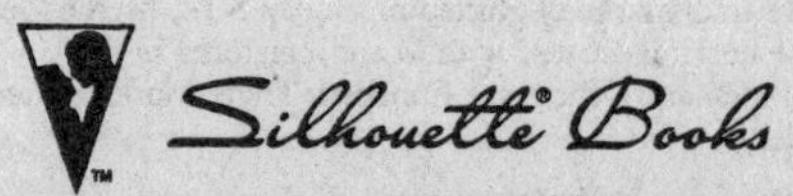

Published by Silhouette Books
America's Publisher of Contemporary Romance

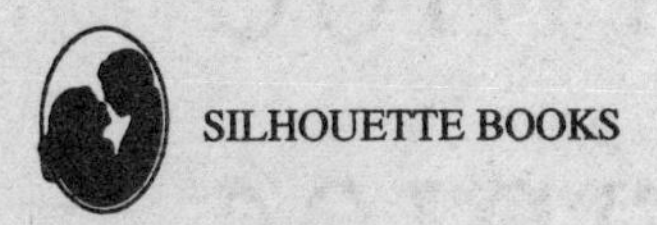

ISBN 0-373-21833-8

CHARMED DESTINIES

This edition published by arrangement with Harlequin Books S.A.

Visit Silhouette at www.eHarlequin.com

Printed in U.S.A.

CONTENTS

COUNTING CROWS 9
Mercedes Lackey

DRUSILLA'S DREAM 143
Rachel Lee

MOONGLOW 257
Catherine Asaro

COUNTING CROWS

Mercedes Lackey

Dear Reader,

This story was written as a little vacation for me from all of my other books, and what inspired it was a passage I read in a book on medieval history about something called a "glove marriage." Most marriages between noble houses were strictly matters of power brokerage and alliance; seldom was a young woman given any say in her fate, and even when she was, she generally let her loyalty to her house decide for her, rather than her emotions. Often enough she didn't even see her prospective husband until the day of their wedding, and sometimes, in a "glove marriage," not even then! In that case, she would go through an entire wedding ceremony with a glove standing in for the groom, and someone else, often one of her own relatives, giving the responses. So just how might a particularly resourceful young woman deal with such a situation? That was the genesis of this story.

Sincerely,

Mercedes Lackey

Chapter 1

The crow cawed morosely to himself; he had gotten separated from the rest of the flock when he flew off to investigate something shiny in the dead leaves, which had proved to be nothing more exciting than a bit of shiny ice. Now he was alone, cold and very hungry.

It was late autumn and most of the leaves from the tree on which he perched littered the forest floor. He balanced on the topmost twig, surveying the leafless forest and the leaf-strewn road below him, hoping to spot something to eat before he went in search of his flock. The squirrels had made short work of the acorns and other nuts; the crow knew that he could probably find some but it would be hard hunting in the fallen leaves and on the ground, where it was dangerous for him to linger.

While he was making up his mind about risking that hazardous descent, he heard something in the distance. He stretched out his neck and peered through the skeletal branches, down to the broad track that cut through his forest, a track made by men and their tame beasts. This was not the usual season for travelers, though, and it might only be a herd of red deer who sometimes ventured onto the track.

He cocked his head to listen. There were a great many creatures coming on that track, shuffling through the leaves—and there were other sounds besides those of footfalls, sounds that no wild things made. This sounded more like men and *their* beasts, a string of them, which often meant easy food.

He stretched his neck farther and waited impatiently for them to come into view. He was impatient, but he was also lazy and not inclined to fly to meet them when their own feet would bring them to *him.* Soon he saw them and knew at once that he had wasted his time; he cawed in derision and disappointment.

He knew the look of men like this. No food from *this* lot—or, at least, they weren't going to let anything fall to the ground while they were moving. These were the men-in-shells, the ones with hard, shiny skins who carried pointed things and commanded flying sticks—*they* didn't leave things on the road like the ones in carts did. There were eight of them; two of their kind were without the shells. Four rode in front and four behind the two who were different. There were also four beasts with burdens not riders. The burdens were far too tightly wrapped up for anything to fall from them. He peered hopefully at the different ones, but concluded very soon that they weren't going to let anything fall, either. There was nothing in their claws but the strings tied to the horses' mouths.

Still. He flicked his wings restlessly, feeling the urge to fly. They were men, and men were dirty by nature, always leaving litter wherever they went. They might not drop anything tasty here, but somewhere on their back trail they had probably nested overnight and there might be something there. Besides, it wasn't healthy to linger in the neighborhood of the men-in-shells. They were all too inclined to send their flying sticks buzzing after anything that moved, and that certainly included crows. He gave another mocking call, telling them what oafs they were and how inconsiderate for disturbing his peace without bringing anything to eat. Then he shoved off from his perch and beat a hasty retreat down the way that they had come, rowing his way through the sky, shouting insults and hoping to raid their nesting place before any of his numerous kin got there.

The sound of the horses's hooves, slightly muffled by all of the fallen leaves, was more than made up for by the rustle and rattle as they trudged their way through the scarlet, gold and brown drifts. The bitter scent of dead leaves permeated the air with its sad perfume of dying summer.

Gwynnhwyfar looked up at the sound of a crow calling overhead, shading her eyes with her hand. She just caught sight of him, screened by the bare branches, flying off into the grim sky, a sky in which the sun was visible only as a bright spot in the sea of gray. "One for sorrow," she murmured more to herself than to her companion as her palfrey ambled onward, hock-deep in yet another ridge of rustling leaves.

Her spirits were at their lowest since this journey to her new husband had begun. She was weary with dawn-to-dark riding, worn out with being cold. Every night had been the same: waiting on her palfrey's back until her well-armed, livery-clad escort pitched the dubious shelter of a tiny pavilion, then descending to dine on watery stew—featuring whatever they had shot while traveling—eaten with bread hard enough to build a wall. Then she would creep into a cold bed on the ground, to sleep fitfully until dawn, when she would be awakened to eat the same stew and bread, climb into the saddle and begin another day like the last.

She craved heat the most, at the moment. She might have huddled near the fire with the men when they all stopped, but she didn't like the way they looked at her with eyes as cold as the wind and as indifferent as the rocks. Her hands and feet were like those of a corpse, and she felt as if she would never be properly warm again.

Or clean. She stopped herself from self-consciously rubbing at the travel stains on her brown woolen gown and cloak. She had slept in her gown and undergown for the past week, without even a chance to wash her face and hands. Her hair, at least, Robin was keeping tidy. She could never have managed it on her own, as long as it was. But she wanted a hot bath so badly she could hardly bear it.

Her tiring-maid, who had been looking out suspiciously into the underbrush and had not seen the bird, shook her head. Robin was probably just as cold and weary, but she didn't show it. "One what?" she asked curiously, tucking the folds of her own gown of a coarser gray wool in around her legs. "What are you speaking of, my lady?"

"'Tis an old rhyme, Robin. A way of telling fortunes by counting crows," Gwynnhwyfar replied—but softly so that her words didn't carry past the ears of her maid. This was not something for the armsmen to overhear. "One for sorrow, two for mirth, three for a wedding, four for a birth—" She sighed. "I am not overmuch surprised, but meseems this is no good omen for what awaits us."

"Well, and you wouldn't get three, for you've already had the wedding, such as it was," Robin reminded her. She glanced at the scarlet velvet pillow that Gwynnhwyfar carried in front of her on the high pommel of the saddle. A rich, down-stuffed pillow upon which rested a single glove—that, of course, was as clean as *she* was travel-stained. Gwynn let her own eyes rest on it, as well, for all that she'd tried to avoid looking at it for most of the journey. That scarlet glove—elegant leather fashioned in the manner of a hawking glove but of finer materials and with the device of a blue boar inset into the wide cuff of it—represented her lord, husband and master, whom she had never yet seen. That device was echoed on the surcoats of the eight armored men who rode with her; the blue boar ramped across the fronts and backs of their scarlet tunics, in stark contrast with the gray cloaks and brown-and-gray gowns of Robin and herself.

"And all things considered, 'tis a bit early for a birth at Clawcrag Keep to get the four," Gwynn agreed, trying to make a feeble joke.

But Robin frowned, her swarthy face reflecting distaste. "Not," she answered darkly, "if all we've been told of Lord Bretagne be true."

Gwynn bit her lip to restrain her own too ready tongue. Lord Bretagne had no good repute—but she'd had no choice in this marriage, not if both she and her father were to survive the unhealthy interest of their own nearest neighbor.

Or the displeasure of His Majesty, for this was a marriage made in the King's Council Chambers, and the King greatly desired that Gwynnhwyfar's marriage portion from her mother, a rich dower of the income from certain vineyards, town houses and tanneries, should go to—

Well, to someone whose loyalty the King required and whose loyalty, to put it crudely, the King could purchase with the annual purses from those properties.

"It matters not," she said with resignation. "Repute—well, when did any man care for his reputation, so long as he's thought to be quick of wit and strong of arm? And good repute or bad, Father needs the

King's support to keep him safe against Baron Anghus. Thus, we gain it, and Father's safety."

"And you need to get from under the fat bull's eye yourself," said Robin with equal resignation. "He's been stretching his hand toward you for as long as I can remember. Still—is it better to flee the devil you know for one you know not?"

"Perhaps his reputation is a matter of envy or spite," she replied. "All that it takes is one ill-natured person within the Court to blacken someone's name."

"Milady—if you'd had the choice of husbands—*would* you have had a choice?" Robin asked suddenly, quite out of nowhere.

Gwynn blinked. Where had *that* question come from? "No," she lied quickly, for there was no point in giving Robin any more reason to feel sorry for her.

But there was someone, even though she had not seen him for a decade or more. Her first love, which fact surely must have embarrassed him, although he never gave her a hint of it. After all, few young knights in their twenties would find it flattering to have a little girl in love with them.

But Sir Atremus had been everything a little girl, raised on the tales of Arthur and his knights, would find irresistible. Tall, strong, skilled with sword and lance and unfailingly kind and courteous to his friend's importunate child.

Gwynn sighed and removed her own glove for a moment to rub at her weary eyes. Her glove smelled of horse and smoke. *She* smelled of horse and smoke. She supposed that she should be just as glad that she didn't smell of worse things and that the pennyroyal with which she had anointed herself liberally before she began the trip was keeping the fleas away.

A pity she could find no potion to repel Baron Anghus. No sane woman would care to find herself in the keeping of Baron Anghus; even had he not been uncouth, unkempt, loud, violent of temper and filthy. Three wives had already been laid to rest in the baronial chapel, under mysterious circumstances. Gwynn was not eager to find herself carried, bound and gagged, to the altar to become the fourth. That was how Anghus had "won" his third wife, as well as his first.

"I mind me what happened to Anghus's last wife," Robin continued with a shiver and a sharp glance with her bright, birdlike black eyes to see that their escort wasn't eavesdropping.

Gwynn just nodded; there wasn't much she could add to that. The Baron's last wife had been in the ground a bare three months and already he was sniffing around again, sending gifts of game and a herald to inquire of her health. When the King had proposed the match to Duke Bretagne, and her father had grasped at it with the desperation of a man with a pack of wolves on his doorstep, Gwynn had seen the marriage as a way to escape the danger of Anghus and to make her father safe again at one stroke.

It was only *after* she had agreed, the King had given the match his blessing and the contracts were signed that she realized she might be leaping from the kettle into the fire, as rumors reached her and her father of what her affianced was like....

Rumor claimed mistresses he had in plenty, both high- and low-born, and scores of bastards. Sure it was, that although he had given his solemn oath to support his monarch, the King felt he could not be certain of Bretagne's loyalty without binding him with a rich prize.

The King needed Bretagne's support to keep the Border Lords from revolt. Gwynn's father needed the King's support to keep Anghus from their own door. And Gwynn was the bridge between the two needs.

And she needed—well, what she needed was not to be thought of, for it was the stuff of minstrelsy, not of reality. There was no Gareth to her Lionors, and never would be. It would be enough if her husband would care for her and she learn to care for him.

She *was* going into this willingly and with open eyes. She and her father had discussed other options and, to her mind, there were none. "Plague," he'd said vaguely, grasping at straws. "You can feign plague, can't you? Or pox. Surely Anghus wouldn't want a pock-marked wife—"

But she had shaken her head. "Anghus would take me were I as old as Methuselah, squint-eyed and lame, without a tooth in my head," she had reminded him gently. "And you know what they say—that he has the blackest of black magic to help him."

Her father had shuddered, but he knew that she was right.

Robin frowned. "What are you thinking?"

"That at least, no matter what his repute, we've never heard that Bretagne is a black wizard," she replied *very* softly. Robin had been her friend as well as her servant since the child turned ten, for Robin was no ordinary servant. No, Robin was her half sibling, the result of her father's loneliness after Gwynn's mother was a year in the grave—and Gwynn certainly had not begrudged her father the solace of female company. *She* knew, none better, that he had not ceased to mourn her mother. Base-born Robin was a trusted member of the household in Gwynn's service; by now, she was privy to all of Gwynn's secrets.

Robin shivered at the reminder of Anghus's other—powers. "No, there is that. And with you away and gone, Anghus's quiver will be empty. He *can't* harm your father while milord stays on his own land. And by the time he learns you are gone, you'll be out of his reach. Right?"

"Out of his reach—yes, so far as I know. Fortunately, Anghus has nothing of mine to use to set his spells upon me when he learns I have escaped him." Of that, she was sure; she left nothing to chance in that regard, and never had. "And if he tries to find me and bring me back by force, he will soon discover that if the King's arm is weak along the Border, it is strong enough in the Marches. I have never heard that Bretagne ever let go of something that was his, and the King will have something to say about the kidnap of his liegeman's bride. One misstep and Anghus will find all the King's soldiers and all the King's men on his doorstep and all the King's priests, too. Let him try his black arts then.'' Her lips stretched in a tight smile. ''The King's priests are well acquainted with the ways of wizards, and I doubt not they have long wished for an excuse to deal with Anghus.''

''But milord...'' Robin said doubtfully, her thick, black brows knitted into a solid bar across her horsey face. ''There is still milord to face that evil magic, and all alone, too—''

''My mother ensured Father's safety with her own life,'' Gwynn breathed so quietly only someone with *very* acute hearing could have heard her. That made Robin drop her eyes for a moment. ''So long as he is on his own land, the land itself will shield him.''

''They say you're very like her, you know, milady,'' Robin replied after a long silence broken only by the crackling of leaves and the soft sound of hoof-beats on turf. ''That she was as beautiful as one of the Fair Folk and as kind as an angel. Mum told me she had green eyes, green as grass, like yours, milady, and golden hair, long enough she could stand on it when she let it down, like yours, also.''

Gwynn smiled, sadly, and felt her eyes sting. ''She *was* beautiful, and kind. I wish you could have seen her, Robin, you'd have been in love with her, just like everyone was. I will never be that lovely, or that good.'' She laughed a little. ''And I have too much of a temper to ever be that kind.''

Robin looked askance at her, as if thinking about disputing those statements, but held her peace.

''But I am my mother's daughter in this,'' Gwynn continued firmly. ''Whatever it takes to keep my father safe, I will do. All that I am, I owe to him, and 'tis a small sacrifice, this. Surely nothing worse than women have borne since Mother Eve. And belike, the rumors are mere air—"

"But if they are not?" Robin asked, even as her father had asked anxiously that last day together, holding both her hands in his and looking into her eyes. "I don't mean, what if he is cold, but what if he is cruel? What if he harms you?" She dropped her voice to a breath of a whisper. "What if he wishes to deal with you as Anghus would?"

"Then you and I will do what is both lawful and needful," she said firmly. Robin looked her square in the eyes and nodded slowly.

"Besides, if he were that bad, how could he keep drawing women to his bed?" she asked logically. "A man who makes a habit of murdering his light-o'-loves soon finds he sleeps alone. No, I doubt we need fear that, and all else—I will hazard."

And when it came down to it, this was a battle, quite as desperate as any battle of arms and men. Gwynn and her father were fighting for their land, for the folk who looked to them for protection and for, perhaps, their own lives. If the battlefield was the altar and the marriage bed, then at least it was a fight in which Gwynn could take part rather than stand on the ramparts, watching helplessly. She was not yet a match for Anghus's black powers; she might never be. And she could not afford to wait until she was. So she *would* be wife to Duke Bretagne and either make the best of it or—

—well, that would play out as the fates allowed.

At least, she reminded herself, he had not killed any wives.

At least, not yet....

It was certainly too late to turn back now. She was glove-wedded to Duke Bretagne of Clawcrag, a wedding as binding and as legal by every law she knew as if the man himself had stood beside her at the altar.

She had not needed the omen of the crow to feel plenty of misgivings. Her new husband had sent word with the glove and the men-at-arms sent to bring her north that she was not to bring her own guards, nor any more than a single tiring-maid with her. *We are simple border men, here, and there will be no need for a train of ladies,* he had written. And her father had not dared to object. For one thing, he could not spare any men, so Robin would have to be his eyes and ears for news of his daughter's well-being. For another—

Well, she had left her father as he had been for the past four years, with one side of his face slack and unmoving, one hand near useless, one foot dragging. He could not fend off Baron Anghus, because he could not have fought against a child and won. *She* was his protection as well as his heir now.

The eight grim-faced men had not spoken more than a dozen words in a day to her since this journey began. She didn't much like their look when they'd arrived, and her liking hadn't increased since. She'd seen how they had eyed Robin before they'd gotten a good look at her; like cruel dogs preparing to quarrel over a bone.

They seemed, to her, to be the sort of men who would have been brigands had they not come under the hand of a man stronger and more ruthless than they. She was grateful that Robin was anything but a beauty, stick-thin and stick-straight, with a long, homely face that reminded anyone who looked at her of a plowhorse.

Yet so far they had been strictly polite with her. Other than the initial rapacious looks, they hadn't offered any insult to Robin, either. And despite the omen of the crow, she had hope.

There was one weapon she could bring to bear in this battle that might change all, and that was her willingness to make something of this situation. Willingness? Nay, that was too mild a word—she was *determined* to turn this marriage of convenience and state into something more. If she could soften this man, if she could turn his heart to her, if she could win him—

Well, she would try. Her own mother had gone to her father as a stranger. She had not known what she would find, there on the Marches. And her father had been, if the tales were true, something of a hard man himself, but *he* had been won, by beauty, a soft word, a heart willing to create love, if she had not found it ready to her hand....

A chill wind suddenly whipped up the leaves around her in a swirl and sent an icy tendril down the back of her hood. She shivered and pulled her cloak closer about her.

"Captain," she called to the man riding just ahead of her. "You said last night that Clawcrag was near, but you did not say how near it was. Do we reach there today?''

The man looked back over his shoulder; she could not even see his face, only the glitter of his eyes in the slits of his round helmet. ''Before sundown, Lady,'' he replied curtly, then turned his attention back to the road ahead.

Before sundown! She didn't know whether to be glad or dismayed.

''Then...will we stop before then?'' she called again, determined to get something more than that bare word from him. ''I should like to prepare myself to honor my lord.''

''No, Lady,'' came the cold reply, and this time the man did not even turn to deliver it. ''I've my orders. No stopping between dawn and dusk for unnecessary nonsense. If primp ye must, do it in the saddle.''

She swallowed hard. It wasn't the first time that she had asked to stop while they traveled, and always the request had been refused, with no explanation of why those orders had been issued. This would be no exception.

So she would not be allowed to remedy her travel-stained state, and *this* was how her new husband would first see her. Not at her best, to say the least.

Not the way to captivate her new lord, showing up, looking as if she did not care how she looked to him, as if she could not trouble to make herself attractive for him and his people. He would wonder, at the least, just what sort of bad bargain he had made, for a slovenly, slatternly bride....

But on the other hand, tonight she would at least sleep in a bed—

Yes, but not alone.

She suppressed a feeling of panic. Not that she didn't *know* what went on with a man and a woman—but...well, that was for other people. It was the first time she had ever been faced with what it meant for *her*. And she had assiduously avoided the thought for this entire journey.

And she would continue to do so now.

"I reckoned something like this would befall," Robin said with a kind of grim satisfaction. "And I took some precautions last night. I've a cloth to clean your face, lotion for your skin, some of your flower scent, a jewel or two, and your handsome wedding cloak, all behind my saddle."

"Oh, Robin—" she gasped in gratitude. "You should be a commander of armies!"

"Mayhap, someday I will be," Robin said with a wink. "In the meantime, I'll command what I can. You, Captain!" she called ahead in her rough, imperious voice. "Have the courtesy to *tell* us when we're within a league or two of Clawcrag, sirrah, or if my lady's looks are not to her new lord's liking, I'll make certain to tell him *why* and who it was would not let her prepare herself to give him all honor."

"Robin!" Gwynn gasped at her temerity.

But when the captain turned around to stare, his mouth below the eye-guard of the helmet twisted into a ferocious frown, there was also a grudging admiration in his voice. "Well, enough, wench, and I will, provided ye plague me not with further chatter. Yon crows have voices more pleasing than yours.''

Gwynn bit her lip, willing Robin not to provoke him further. But Robin had never been a fool, and did not prove so now. She only traded him disdainful look for look until he turned back to the road, then *humphed.* But not very loudly. Robin might be bold, but she knew when not to press an advantage.

''You should have taken the upper hand with them when this journey began, milady,'' she said quietly. ''These are dogs that obey nothing but the whip and must see that your hand holds it.''

''If I had, would we have been let to pause in our travels?'' Gwynn retorted.

''Well—no,'' Robin admitted. '''Twas your lord's own orders—no stopping on the way, except when night fell. So they told me, as you will recall, when I badgered. Though they would not tell me *why,* and I should think 'twould be safe enough to stop on my lord's own lands...but perhaps, it isn't as safe as I'd have thought.''

''And would they have been more civil with us had I lashed them with my tongue?'' Gwynn continued. ''No, I think not. And I would not have them report to Baron Bretagne that his new bride was a scold and a harridan, hounding them with complaints and demands! Better they think me weak, soft and altogether womanish, and tell him so.''

''Humph.'' Robin raised an eyebrow and one corner of her mouth quirked up. ''Meseems I see your thought. Well, *I* have been the scold and harridan, and I will continue to be so. Such a path suits me.''

Gwynn nodded; she did not have to say anything more, not to Robin. Gwynn would be the milk-soft maiden and Lord Bretagne would underestimate her and her intelligence. If anything hard needed a heavy hand, it would be Robin who cracked the whip or demanded what was required as the rightful due of her lady. Gwynn would be sweet. Robin, sour. Both would play their parts to perfection. Gwynn's rank would protect her, Robin's sharp tongue would act with her looks to keep *her* safe.

And if certain actions proved to be required, no one would hinder Gwynn in the doing of them, for no one would suspect she had the intelligence, the courage or the deviousness—no, they would not suspect she had anything afoot at all. Those actions would require privacy, but if she seemed weak and tender enough, no one would in the least be surprised if she closed herself into her room to weep in private for hours at a time....

But that would be as the future ordered and only if all other recourses failed. If she needed to spend *that* arrow, truly, her quiver would be empty.

She shivered, and not from the cold wind that whipped her cloak flat to her body.

Those actions were lawful but only *just* lawful, and only if she herself was in deadly danger. So if she was forced to take that course—she would have found herself in a position that was as bad as if she had been in Anghus's clutches.

She would pray it would not come to that.

Chapter 2

The wedding cloak was a gorgeously impractical piece of clothing of heavy knotwork-embroidered satin in a wonderful blue lined with woad-dyed linen her grandmother had woven herself. Gwynn had worn it with the gown she had been glove-wedded in. A gown of lambs' wool dyed to match, with embroidered bands of the same satin at the hems of skirt and sleeve and forming a placket at the neck. The cloak had come down to her from her grandmother, and her mother had worn it for *her* wedding; so had the bands of embroidery, which each successive bride had applied to her own new gown. Unfortunately, the cloak could not be spread over the top of her traveling cloak without looking ridiculous. So if she had been cold before, she was freezing now.

But she and Robin had done everything they could

to make her look her best under the circumstances. Her face was clean, with lotion applied to her wind-chapped cheeks, an amber-and-silver necklet adorned her throat, a matching ring slipped over the glove on her hand. She had bitten her lips and pinched her cheeks to make them red, and she smelled of roses as well as wood smoke and horse.

As they rounded a curve of the road that brought them into view of Clawcrag Keep, she got her first sight of her new home and, despite her misgivings, she was impressed.

For she looked at it with the eye of a soldier, as her father had taught her, and not with the eye of a mooning romantic.

It loomed, tall, implacable against the sky and it was clear where the name had come from, for it looked like a powerful, blocky claw trying to grasp the heavens. There was not one thing that softened this structure, for not even ivy or moss had been permitted to grow upon the stones. Nothing could ever have been more imperious, more masculine, more martial.

This was a true keep, strong and eminently defensible. It stood on the top of a steep hill, well above the surrounding village. It was not moated, but with those slopes—on one side, not even a slope but an actual cliff that fell off directly from the right side of the keep—it did not need a moat. The outer walls were three stories high and in the very best repair; stout stone bulwarks that would require not one but many siege engines to break. The inner keep, which loomed an additional two stories above the surrounding walls, was just as strong and studded with arrow slits rather than windows. The inside would be secure from attack, but at the expense of being as dark as a cave, even in the brightest days.

A mooncalf maiden, of course, would have been horrified—Clawcrag was as harsh as its name, a thrust of cold, gray stone into the overcast sky, unyielding, unwelcoming. This was no graceful castle out of a ballad, all airy towers and balconies.

This was a Border keep and anyone who came here expecting a sugar confection was a fool living in a dream. She had anticipated nothing else.

So be it. This was a fighting man's stronghold, and a woman came into it knowing, as Gwynn had known, that the King did not wish Baron Bretagne's expertise in the laying out of gardens but in war. It was uncompromisingly masculine, built for the purpose of keeping the Border safe, both from the enemy without and unruly neighbors whose loyalty to the King was questionable. One commander and a handful of men could hold it against an army, especially if it had its own well. Which, she did not doubt, it did. Whoever had built this place had known his business and would not have neglected that detail.

But one thing did trouble her. As they passed through the village, it was ominously quiet. It might almost have been deserted but for the furtive opening of shutters, just a crack, as they progressed up the main road.

There were no villagers gathered along the main street to greet her—no evergreen swags decorated the houses, no children waited to serenade her—there was nothing to show that this was not an ordinary bleak day, not even a market day.

By the time they were halfway through the village and were passing the central square with the stone-walled well, it was very clear that no one was going to come out to greet them, either. The stone houses with their thatched roofs gone gray with weathering looked as uncompromising as the keep above. They presented the same blank gaze as Baron Bretagne's men-at-arms in their helms.

No one called out so much as a greeting. The few peasants in the street got hurriedly out of the way of the armsmen and did not even give her so much as a curious glance. This was in sorry contrast to the leave-taking through her father's village at the foot of *his* keep, where the streets had been strewn with red and yellow leaves, holly and ivy decorated the houses and the children had been brought to sing her a quavery song of farewell to a bride....

Robin frowned but said nothing for a long moment. Then, as they passed the last of the houses and started up the long, winding road to the keep itself, said grudgingly, "Well, and they could not have known *when* we would arrive."

And that was true enough. Though Gwynn could not help but think that *her* father would have had the village in readiness and a watcher on the road....

But this was the Border, and perhaps they did not have the time or the resources to spare on such fripperies. Still, shouldn't there have been *some* greeting for the baron's new bride?

Unless there was enough danger from the neighboring Border Lords that they had not wanted to present the opportunity to catch the village unawares in the midst of celebration. That was something that always had to be thought about, out here.

Nevertheless, from the watchtower the little procession could *clearly* be seen for many miles, and the road to the top was a long one. If there was no one to greet them at the gate, that would be a bad sign, indeed.

One crow for sorrow… Had they arrived at a bad time? Had there been a death? But if there had been, surely there would have been a sign, the baron's flag on the top of the keep flying upside-down.

Perhaps not a death in the keep—but perhaps the village headman had died, or some other important person in the village. Perhaps that would explain the closed look of the village.

The road to the top of the hill wound back and forth across the slope, a long, weary trudge not in the least relieved by the scenery. Gwynn supposed that it was a grand vista, and perhaps would be magnificent in the spring and summer, but now, with the gray village beneath, the brown fields beyond, the leafless forest beyond that, all surrounded by brown-and-gray hills covered with more dead grass and leafless forest, it was cold and bleak. The cold wind that had been with them all along now moaned along the edge of the road, sounding as if it was in mourning. The coming of snow would be a positive relief.

They reached the top just as the sun touched the horizon, still a dim disk behind the gray clouds, and had to follow the road halfway around the blank stone walls of the keep to reach the gate. There were probably guards up there on the top of the wall, but they weren't visible from the road and no one called down so much as a greeting. And there was no one to greet them at the gate, either—

But there was also no *room* for anyone to greet them. Clearly the purpose of the gate was to keep *out* as well as to let *in,* and there was barely enough room for a single cart to make the turn in to go beneath the walls. Certainly you could not bring an army to bear at the entrance, and there was not enough room to wield a battering ram effectively. The outer gate was a fearsome affair, a huge double door of wood a foot thick, and behind it, a portcullis gate of forged iron with sharp teeth meant to be dropped down by means of chains. And as they made the turn into the tunnel under the walls, she saw, with a sigh of relief, that there *was* to be a greeting party, after all. There was light in there, warm, flickering torchlight and a great deal of it. And now, at least, there was a sound other than the wail of the wind—the sound of men shuffling their feet, murmuring to one another.

They passed under the wall and emerged onto cobbles; their horses's hooves clattering on the stones. The outer bailey was lined with armed men, all clad in surcoats with her lord's blue boar upon them, like those of her escort. And there was someone waiting for her on the steps of the keep itself.

But her heart faltered as she drew nearer and saw that the man who awaited her was surely as old as her father. He was dressed in a slightly shabby, dark red surcoat with the baronial device upon it. Although he wore the white belt of a full knight, he had no golden chain, nor a coronet. He looked no wealthier than any of the men-at-arms, and considerably older than she had imagined. Could *this* be her husband?

Her escort divided and she and Robin rode straight to the steps. The knight limped heavily toward them and offered her his hand to dismount.

She took it, and with a care for her gorgeous cloak, slipped down from the back of her palfrey to alight on the stone cobbles of the courtyard. She was glad that it was dark, for her riding shoes were as ill-treated and dirty as her traveling gown. The knight bent to kiss her hand and rose quickly, smiling into her face; his hand felt very warm, even through her glove. He was clean-shaven, his brown hair going to gray at the temples, his nose had been broken and badly set at one time, and his complexion was weathered from being much out of doors. His eyes were a beautiful blue and yet inexpressibly sad—and somehow, familiar.

"My Lady Gwynnhwyfar," he said in a deep, melodious voice, which also woke the echo of long-ago memories that she could not bring to the fore of her mind. "It is my honor to welcome you to Clawcrag."

"It is my honor to be here, my Lord Bretagne—" she began.

"Alas, Lady Gwynnhwyfar!" he interrupted her. "I am *not* that happy man. And I am not surprised that you do not recognize me, my lady, for the years have not been kind to your father's friend. I am Sir Atremus. Do you even recall me at all? You were quite a little maid when I saw you last."

Gwynn gasped and her free hand flew to her lips. *Now* she most certainly *did* recognize him. The fact that she had not at first done so was that of all of the places she might have thought to find him, this would have been the very last! Recognize him? How could she have *failed* to recognize the man she had been in love with at five years old and had vowed to grow up to wed? Why, she had even made him promise to wait for her to grow up, which he, gallantly, had agreed to.

Her heart gave a great leap and then a spasm of utmost pain because—

Because she knew him so very well, knew his kindness, his bravery, his patience and nobility, and if it *had* been he who was her husband, she would have flown into his arms. Such a nature as that of Atremus would be so worthy of the mature love of a woman grown—

And she was wedded to his liege lord.

So she smiled tremulously and was very proud that her voice remained steady. "Sir Atremus, I beg you to forgive me—I have never forgotten my father's most trusted friend, and it is only because I never would have anticipated your being here that I did not know you at once. I am overjoyed to find you here, and pleased that you remember me. I will be very glad to have a familiar face, and that of a friend, among all of those both new and strange to me."

"And I—" He faltered, but covered it well and gave her hand a squeeze. "You will always find a friend in me, my lady. I would have known you among a thousand, for you have grown into the very image of your mother."

For the first time in a fortnight she was warm—*too* warm; she felt herself flushing from the top of her head to the tips of her toes, felt herself almost on fire—

—and in the next instant she was as cold as ice. Then flushed. Then cold.

She would have withdrawn her hand, but she could not seem to move it from his grasp. And he… He was turning with it still in his possession, to lead her with knightly courtesy and grace despite his limp, in through the massive wooden, iron-bound doors of the keep, out of the freezing courtyard and into the keep's Great Hall.

Which, though brightly lit with more torches and supplied with not one but two roaring fires in massive fireplaces to the right and left, was dark with smoke and nearly as cold as the courtyard.

The enormous room must have had a ceiling fifty feet above her, for it was so high that all she got were hints of roof beams when she glanced up. The smoke began a bit above her head and thickened as it rose, but there was enough of it lower down that her eyes stung.

She was the focus of the eyes of all the people

seated at their evening meal here, and there seemed to be hundreds of them. A central aisle divided the room into half, each side having two long, wooden tables with benches on both sides of it, the benches being crowded with diners. There were yet more folk serving them and some clustered about the two hearths, dishing up stew or pottage from enormous kettles or carving meat from the pigs roasting on spits above the fire.

Somehow she kept her head high, somehow kept her wits about her, as Sir Atremus led her between the first two tables, that were packed full of servants, men-at-arms and underlings. She thought that there were rushes under her feet, although it was difficult to tell for certain, since no good, clean aroma of dried rushes and sweet herbs came up when she trod on them. She suspected that it had been a very long time since they were last swept out. The hall smelled overpoweringly of smoke, of cooking meat and burned fat, with an undertone of unwashed bodies. There seemed to be dogs everywhere, every possible size of hunting dog, from the lop-eared brachts that coursed rabbits to a great deer hound that stood up and stared at her solemnly as she passed it.

Then she was past the first two tables, and paced past two more, packed equally thickly but this time with lesser nobles, hangers-on, a few shifty-eyed clerics and the baron's greater servants—all of them staring at her, a murmur of sound before and behind her, but nothing but silence from those immediately around her. She kept her eyes fixed upon the High Table on the dais, upon the seat at the center of that table; a great, high-backed chair as near to a throne as could be contrived without offense to the King.

She kept her eyes fixed on the man in that chair—because if she did not, she must needs *see* the blowsy, big-breasted redhead in the seat at his right, the seat for the baron's wife, the seat that *should* have been left vacant for her. And she dared not give her notice to that wench, dared not allow anyone to guess that she acknowledged her even though the tight, red-velvet gown the redhead wore was worth more than Gwynn's entire wardrobe and there was the glitter of gold at her throat and glinting on her hands.

She dared not see these things, for to see them would be to acknowledge them, and to acknowledge them would be to give her—whoever she was—the power of that acknowledgment. She was not the baron's wife; Gwynn doubted that she was his mother, unless she had given birth to him as a toddler. She could only be the baron's leman—who was occupying the seat meant for his lawful spouse, despite the fact that everyone here must have known for the past hour and more that the lawful spouse was on her way to the keep.

So she kept her eyes fixed on the man. Her husband. Who terrified her.

Not for his size, for he was no taller or more muscular than any of his best fighters. Not for his display of wealth, for he wore black leather, with his blue boar a modest design upon the left breast of his tunic, not silk and velvet like his leman, and no jewels at all save a coronet and the signet ring on his right hand.

Not because he was ugly, for he was not; in fact, many would consider his face—black-haired and black-bearded—strong and regular features, dark eyes and square chin, to be comely.

No, it was the look in his eyes that terrified her. She had seen such a look in the eyes of a greedy priest studying a fat capon he meant to have on his plate, in the eyes of a miser looking at a fee about to be placed in his hands, in the eyes of a shepherd assessing the fleece of a sheep he was about to shear. It was a look as cold as that in the eyes of his armsmen; measuring, weighing, assessing a possession and reckoning its worth.

And *she* was that possession.

Atremus led her to the foot of the dais and bowed. "My Lord Baron," he said into the silence—a silence that not even the dogs broke. "May I present to you the Lady Gwynnhwyfar, your consort and your bride."

Bretagne rose—then placed one powerful hand on the table before him, and vaulted over it. Then he leaped down from the dais, not troubling with the two stairs that led up to the platform upon which the High Table stood, landing with a *thud* right before her.

"Well come at last, bride!" he roared, and before Gwynn could think to make any sort of pretty speech, he seized her and bent her nearly double, planting his mouth on hers. She went limp with shock, as he forced his ale-bitter tongue past her teeth and nearly down her throat, crushing her to him until she could scarcely breathe, while the room erupted in raucous cheers and laughter.

She closed her eyes and forced herself *not* to bite down on his tongue, forced herself to remain passive, tried to breathe through her nose. This was a test. She knew it. He was trying her, wanting to see if she recoiled from him, if she showed any distaste for him and his embrace.

Now she was very glad she had not worn her new gown. It would have been ruined by the studs ornamenting his leather tunic, every one of which she fancied she could feel grinding into her own flesh. She was growing dizzy, he held her so tightly, and she felt her knees starting to buckle.

Finally he stood her up again, pulled his face away and let her go. She resisted the impulse to wipe the back of her hand across her mouth, somehow kept from gagging, and forced her lips into a smile.

His lips were smiling, but his eyes were still cold and measuring. "Good, my lord," she said with false brightness. "I had feared you would be reluctant to sacrifice your bachelor state. Had I known this would be my ardent welcome, be sure I would have urged your men to greater speed!"

"Ha!" He threw back his head and roared with laughter at her sally, laughter in which his men joined with spirit. "Good answer!"

Then he picked her up with both hands about her waist and lifted her onto the dais as if she weighed nothing. Leaping up beside her, he led her around the table—she'd been afraid he was going to vault it again—and summarily pulled the red-haired wench, who'd not had the wit to give over her seat, to her feet.

"Bartolemy!" he roared, and a fat, tonsured monk at the far end of the High Table started and looked up, wide-eyed, at him. "Take the bench down below! Ursula, get you to your place." He shoved the red-haired woman toward the now-vacant stool. She stumbled, gave him—and Gwynn—a vicious glare, but did as she was told. He manhandled Gwynn into the chair that the other had vacated, and flung himself down in his own place again. "Ursula has been in charge of my household in the stead of a wife," he told Gwynn, quite as if he expected her to believe him. "But now that you have arrived, you'll be taking your proper place, of course. I'll have her give over the keys in the morning."

"Of course, good, my lord," she murmured, bowing her head. Oh, Ursula had been tending *something,* she was sure, but it wasn't the household. Or if she was, it was in name only, for in the few moments she had been here she had seen nothing but the signs of an establishment so ill-regulated that she was surprised anything got done. There was a housekeeper somewhere who had those keys—well, Robin would find out who.

Robin! She realized in sudden panic that she had lost sight of Robin the moment she had passed the doors of the keep.

But as soon as she raised her head to look for Robin, she spotted her maid and saw with intense relief that Sir Atremus had taken her in his charge, getting a place for her at the end of one of the upper tables, seating himself beside her as extra protection. It pained her heart, though, to see how that good man was treated himself—completely ignored the moment that Bretagne had deigned to claim Gwynn, and clearly so poorly regarded that he barely ranked a place among the upper servants.

Now began Gwynn's wedding feast, if such it could be called. If she'd conjured a meal out of a nightmare, it could scarcely have been worse than this. The trencher bread that Ursula had used was brushed to the floor with a single sweep of Bretagne's hand, and a new one brought to replace it. At least she was not supposed to use Ursula's leavings....

She was expected to share her husband's cup, however, and one taste of the strong ale he clearly favored, so bitter with hops that it made her cough and her eyes water, was something that he seemed to find very funny. She was not so thirsty that it appealed to her at all, and she reckoned that she would do without drink at this meal.

Then came the parade of nearly inedible food. She was offered a cut of pork that seemed half raw to her, so she refused it. A page slapped a half-burned pigeon on the trencher in its stead. Well, better half burned than half raw—

But it was stone-cold as well as burned.

She picked at the bird as Bretagne ate and drank hugely of his ale, his cup being refilled three times while he feasted on the boar. The next course was a pie, the crust as hard as iron, the inside, watery, briny gravy with chunks of gristle and leathery carrots and turnips. Leathery they might be, but at least they were warm and brought a little warmth to her insides. Following that was a baked pike, which, though bony, was at least something with some flavor, though unfortunately there was not much of it. Then cheese, hard and dry and blue with mold.

One half-edible course followed another; she picked at what she could stomach and ignored the rest. There was entertainment of a sort: two of Bretagne's men stripped to the waist and wrestled three falls in the center aisle; then someone kicked a slack-faced idiot dressed in motley into the center when they were done, where the poor thing capered and wept until they were tired of watching him and allowed him to creep off to what seemed to be his usual post by the hearth. Then another of Bretagne's men got to his feet and roared out a bawdy song, which they all seemed to know, for every one of them joined in on the chorus.

It seemed to go on forever. Gwynn would have given almost anything for a draught of pure spring water, of cider, of watered wine or even a decent ale, not the stuff that Bretagne was drinking as if it were no stronger than water. The smoke made her eyes burn, her head ached and she was weary beyond belief.

But of course, the evening was not over—yet.

At last the "subtlety" came in, which wasn't subtle at all, merely a great mess of apples stewed in honey and wine, surmounted by a crust done with Bretagne's boar atop it in pastry dough. At least, she thought it was a boar. The blobby beast could have been anything, but truly looked most like a newborn bear cub that had not yet been licked into its proper shape by the sow bear. The apples she could eat, and with an exhausted gratitude, she did, while the men set two of the dogs to fighting one another in the center aisle. The juice eased her thirst, the fruit, her hunger and the honey managed to cleanse the tastes of the other courses from her mouth.

She began to feel a little revived and a little warmer, thanks to that final course. The dog fight was over, and she was licking her fingers clean of the honey, there being no other utensil supplied for her to eat with, when Bretagne stood up.

Instant silence followed. Bretagne looked down to the end of the High Table, straight at the sulky Ursula. "My lady and I," he roared, "would to bed!"

Chapter 3

Gwynn did not mistake Bretagne's words in the least; Ursula's face broke into a malicious smile. Meanwhile Bretagne's words froze Gwynn in her place, unable to move, hardly able to breathe.

Ursula rose and called out several names, which in her confusion and fear, Gwynn did not catch. But a dozen women came bounding up from the lower tables and, with Ursula in the lead, converged on Gwynn.

Ursula was nearly as strong as the baron, for all her apparent plump softness. She plucked Gwynn out of the seat even as she had been pulled erect by Bretagne. The women enveloped her in a mob and hustled her off the dais toward an archway that led to a stair and the wedding-night horseplay began.

Now Gwynn had participated in a milder form of such antics herself. The bride was supposed to be carried off, stripped naked and put into bed to await her groom. In the version in which Gwynn had played a part, the eager bride was serenaded with songs from the married women about the joys of the wedding night, and from the unmarried virgins, with laments about the loss of freedom. She had been gently disrobed and anointed with scent, her hair unbound and combed out, and put into a warmed bed, while the bachelors and married men treated her groom to a similar experience. Then, once both were bundled into bed together, they were pelted with nosegays of sweet herbs and rue, then locked into the chamber to consummate the marriage. The next day the evidence of the bride's virginity on the sheets was examined by both mothers and pronounced genuine, not that anyone had harbored any doubts.

Evidently the women of Clawcrag had a variant on those traditions in mind.

They rushed her up a darkened set of stairs, with Ursula hauling her on the right and another woman on the left, moving so fast that she stumbled over every other step, stubbing her toes painfully and barking her shins more than once. The songs they were singing were more akin to the obscene ditties that the men had been howling down in the Great Hall than the songs that Gwynn had expected; more than once she found herself flushing painfully at the graphic lyrics. They passed two torches and two landings before they finally paused at a third and one of the women in the front of the crowd flung open a door.

They all shoved her inside it and followed. The bedchamber that they crammed themselves into was as cold as ice but, nevertheless, they stripped her bare with such ruthlessness that a gown any less sturdy than her traveling robe would have surely been ripped. As it was, they snapped the laces that held it closed down the back in their callous haste to get her out of it. The gown they flung aside in a corner, followed it with the undergown and followed that with her hose and shoes. They actually tore the shift off her rather than pull it over her head, and left her standing on the hearth, on what felt like fur beneath her icy feet. They then attacked her hair. The careful braids that Robin had made were taken down and unbraided clumsily, more than once with a jerk at a knot they'd made themselves, making her eyes water with pain. No scents were offered, no lotions, no comforts of any sorts; she was shoved, stumbling, at the bed, then into it. It was like being enveloped in a shroud, so chill were the linens. Linens that were as coarse as canvas against her skin.

As she clutched the bedcovers to her chest and stared at her captors, who were now clustered around her, she did not see a single sympathetic gaze among them. There was no sign of Robin; Gwynn suspected she'd been taken off guard by the speed of Ursula and her cohorts. As the "ladies" stood around the bed, eyes sparkling maliciously, mouths working as they sang yet another obscene ditty, they were shoved aside by Bretagne himself.

"Out!" he roared. Cackling, they obeyed him. He

slammed the door of the chamber shut behind the last of them himself and dropped a bar across it.

Then he turned and stared at her, fists on his hips, eyes still full of that cold appraisal.

"Well, wife!" he said, his voice full of nuances she could not read.

She swallowed and pulled the bedcovers a little closer. "Well, husband," she whispered.

"Come out of there," he said. "I want to see what I have gotten of this bargain." He bent down, lit a rushlight at the coals of the fire, and threw a log upon the embers.

She would have been happy to disobey him, not just because of her own fear, but because the room was absolutely frigid. But she knew she dared do nothing of the sort.

So she eased carefully out from under the sheet that she had clutched and, shaking in every limb, walked to where he pointed, standing before him on that fur rug on the hearth.

At least at that point the fire blazed up suddenly, giving her a little warmth.

She would have liked to hide herself in her hair and her hands, but she sensed that would only make him impatient—and perhaps angry. He was full of drink and, in such a state, he could be dangerous.

So she stood with her eyes cast down, shivering, both hands limply at her sides. At least her back was protected from the icy drafts behind the curtain of her hair.

Bretagne held up the rushlight and peered at her,

looking her up and down as if she were a horse or a cow at a fair—which was precisely how she felt.

"No tits to speak of," he grumbled under his breath. "Thin as a reed. Fah. A milk-and-water bitch!" He prowled around her like a cat circling a mouse while she shut her eyes and waited for him to pounce. And waited. And waited.

After an eternity, she suddenly felt his hand seize her hair at the back of her neck, and her eyes flew open. Before she could think, once again his mouth jammed down atop hers, her lips grating painfully on his teeth as he first bit and sucked at them, then thrust his tongue inside her mouth. He tasted of that bitter, bitter ale, and she had to force herself not to gag, not to try to push him away, not to stiffen.

But try as she might, she could not force herself to put her arms around him.

It didn't seem to matter to him, anyway, what she did, so long as she didn't fight him.

He picked her up bodily and flung himself and her into the waiting bed. It was only then that she realized he was as naked as she, and it took every ounce of courage she possessed to keep from crying out and trying to curl into a ball.

One of his hands pawed and pinched at her breasts, making her gasp, not with pleasure but with pain. He seemed to enjoy that, and twisted her nipples cruelly as she whimpered in the back of her throat, the sound dying before it was born. Finally he tired of thrusting his tongue down her mouth and moved his attentions to her breasts, sucking and biting at the nipples while she writhed and gasped with the pain.

"Like that, do you?" he chuckled. And he bit down again, shoving his hand between her legs, parting them ruthlessly, spreading them so far apart she thought she was going to split in two.

He probed at her secret parts with his fingers and chuckled when she whimpered with the new pain. "At least you're the virgin they said you were," he growled, a horribly pleased tone to his voice. "Well, I'll be making a proper woman of you! When I'm done, you'll know what it is to have a real man!"

She knew what was going to happen next as he positioned himself between her spread legs and shoved both hands under her buttocks, holding her in such a way that she could not have escaped his grasp no matter how hard she tried, if she had dared to. She knew what was coming—but that didn't make it any easier.

She squeezed her eyes closed, and lay very still as he fell on her like a wild beast.

The first two thrusts failed to penetrate; he paused a moment and did something, she didn't know what, then she felt him fumbling at her again, felt something pushing—

And then he lunged a third time and she *did* scream with the pain of it, for she was certain he *had* split her wide.

He roared with laughter, then fell to sucking and biting her breasts again as he thrust and withdrew, over and over, while she shook and moaned in pain.

Faster and faster came his lunges, and then, suddenly, he lifted his head and made a strange sound—

And collapsed atop her, snorting like a pig. "Ha," he said thickly. "Ha. You're mine now. My mark's on you."

He was so heavy she wanted to push him off, and was afraid to. He rolled over a little, just enough that she could breathe again, and she lay with dumb tears leaking from her eyes and running into her hair above her ears. It hurt so much—

Slowly the pain ebbed as she wept, silently, because she hadn't died and, now that it was over, she wished that she had....

He said nothing more. At some point, as the fire burned low again, he rolled completely off her at last. She slid off the bed, moving slowly and painfully, and sought for a cloth, anything to wipe away the fluids and the blood that oozed down her leg. She finally used her own shift—the women had ruined it past mending. At least the old, worn cloth was soft; she cleaned herself as best she could. She knew what she *should* do—for of all things, she did *not* want to bear children to this beast in man's shape!—but she also had no idea of where her chests were and without them, she could not make the vinegar rinse that would flush away his seed.

When she was as clean as she could make herself, she huddled beside the dying fire and combed through her hair as thoroughly as she could with her fingers, making it into a single loose braid, tying the end with a piece of the lacing from her gown.

By this time she was as cold as a block of ice and Bretagne had rolled over and cocooned himself in all of the blankets on the bed, snorting like his namesake boar.

Still moving painfully, she looked about the chamber in the dim light of the dying fire. There was not much here; it wasn't very large, and seemed to hold only the enormous bed and a stool and a clothing chest. She didn't dare open the chest, which probably only held more of his clothing anyway. There didn't seem to be any other bed coverings, not even a spare blanket, and finally she decided that the rug on the hearth on which she had stood was the only thing left for her to use to cover herself. It appeared to be a full bearskin and though heavy, would make a more than adequate blanket.

The bed itself, though it made her flesh crawl to think of lying down beside him, was big enough that even Bretagne was swallowed up in it. She could lie down far enough away from him that they need not touch.

"You'd better get used to it," she whispered to herself as she stood beside the bed, staring down at the man within it with loathing. "This is your fate, until one or the other of you dies."

And it was, as she had said to Robin, no worse than other women had borne since the time of Mother Eve.

So she crawled onto the side of the bed furthest from him, rolled herself up in the bearskin that at least smelled of nothing worse than dirt and smoke, and her exhaustion was such that finally, as the fire burned down to coals again, she fell asleep.

It was to a less-than-friendly face that she woke the next morning, but at least the face wasn't Bretagne's.

Ursula shook her awake, as rough and rude as any of the baron's men-at-arms, probably as hard as the woman could manage. As Gwynn blinked confusedly up at her, the woman grabbed an edge of the bearskin and pulled, jerking her toward the edge of the bed.

Gwynn saved herself from a tumble only narrowly, getting her feet under her just as she slipped over the edge, grabbing the bearskin and taking it with her. As soon as she was out of the bed, the woman yanked the bloodstained sheet away and flounced off with it without a single word to her. Her expression was both sour and surly, suggesting that whatever had happened to her this morning, it had not been to her liking.

As Gwynn stood on the cold stone floor, pulling the bearskin around her, Robin and a blank-faced but strongly built girl came through the same door that Ursula had just used, bearing the first of Gwynn's chests between them.

Since Gwynn had packed them all herself, she knew what was in this one, and as they put it down on the floor and Robin turned to look at her with shock, she shook off her own numb malaise. "Bring the rest of my things, and quickly, please," she ordered in as firm a voice as she could manage. Only now was her body starting to wake up and ache; she hoped that none of her hurts were visible. At least this chest contained her underthings, her medicines, her herbs.

The moment they were gone, shutting the door behind them, she fell on the chest and pulled out a soft rag, pennyroyal and a soothing salve from her herbs and medicines, and then a clean shift from her underthings, and thanked heaven that it was this chest that Robin had brought first. By the time Robin was back with the second chest, she was decently clothed in shift and loose undergown and had soothed her own hurts as best she could. She had attended to the hurts of her father's folk often enough, the injuries from hunting, farming and fighting, to know that her own bruises weren't serious—but it was the first time she had ever been hurt herself, and that put an entirely new perspective on the injuries that she had tended on others.

"They're hanging the sheet over the battlements!" Robin said in a tone of utter disbelief and indignation.

Gwynn flushed and could find no words in her embarrassment. Oh, she knew that peasants made such displays, but never in her own experience had anyone of any rank done so.

Robin put her end of the chest down and looked at her closely. "Are you well?" she asked.

Gwynn bit her lip. "As well as may be," she answered after a long pause. "He *is* a fair match for Anghus, but—"

"But?"

"He has offered me no real harm." For probably, in *his* mind, what he had done to her last night was no more than his lawful right. Even though she had found livid bruises on her breasts and thighs, and his teeth had drawn blood in places. And, no doubt, most priests would *tell* her it was his lawful right, that she must submit to the wishes of her husband and lord, and counsel patience.

Well, she would be patient, but not because her spirit was going to submit.

"He has offered you no real harm. Yet," Robin said darkly.

"Robin," she replied in a tone of mild rebuke. Robin flushed, but set her chin stubbornly.

"They say that on the floor above this room is the solar used by the ladies of the keep, when there still *were* ladies here," Robin said after a long silence. "Mayhap we should see to it today. I've already had the keys of the slut they miscalled the housekeeper. It was that red-haired wench, and the baron took them from her himself and charged me with giving them to you."

Gwynn sucked on her bruised lower lip, more than a bit surprised at that. Well, so that was what had happened to Ursula to put her in a rage!

Then again, it was no great honor to be put in charge of a place that was clearly so poorly run.

"I suppose I must have them, then," she replied.

Robin pulled a long face. "So you must, but it's little enough use they'll be. There's no locks to the stores, and nothing worth having in them anyway. As to the household, so far as I can tell, keys or no keys, that creature Ursula calls the tune, and there's an end to it."

She nodded, unsurprised, and throttled down the urge to weep. "Then...well, do what you may with my hair. After that, see if there is aught fit to eat in what passes for a kitchen, then let us see the solar and what can be made of it. We'll make a start there."

Robin nodded, and when the last of the chests and packs had been brought to the bedroom, she sat Gwynn down on the stool and made short work of the tangles in her hair, impossible though that task might have seemed last night. There was a surprising amount of light coming through the slit windows, covered with oiled parchment in wooden frames to keep out the worst of the cold wind; enough for Robin to weave her clever braids.

When Gwynn's hair was neatly braided up and the braids themselves bound with strips of cloth to keep them neat and clean, she left Gwynn to rummage through her clothing chest to find a fresh gown, for her travel gown was too filthy to consider donning again. At the least, it would need an airing out and a good beating to shake out the grime. She much doubted that this place had anything like a laundry; washing it would have to wait until spring.

She picked the warmest gown she owned, and a thick woolen mantle to go over it, heavy stockings for her feet. And only when she stood up, dressed in clothing that was serviceable, but hardly the sort of thing that a woman intent on winning a man would wear, did she realize that she had unconsciously made her decision, at least about Bretagne. She would not try to woo and win him. There was nothing *in* him to woo or win; his heart clearly had room for a single object of devotion—and that object was himself. This was not the clothing of a woman who intended to find the soft heart of a man; this was the gown of one who intended, at the least, to survive without yielding her soul.

Well enough; the die was cast. She would give her husband nothing; let him take what he would, she would squander no tears on him, and allow him no part of her soul. Bretagne was a man of war and violence. Such men did not have long lives. She would do what she needed to do to outlive him.

And one of those things was to be certain he did not fill her with children, for that seemed to be the method of choice for a man to rid himself of a wife he did not care for. In that, he would find himself outmatched. She was not her mother's daughter for nothing. There were several things in her herbs and medicines that only she knew the use of, and she would begin as soon as Robin returned with something to break their fast.

Robin appeared with a…well, it could not be called a "tray" since it was more of a flat basket. But it held food and a flask and, much to her astonishment, Gwynn realized that she was famished.

There was bread, with the burned crusts sliced off, and a slab of raw bacon, a pannikin of salt and four eggs. The two of them knelt to mend the fire and actually get it burning brightly. "I stood over the idiots minding the kitchen fire and got them to boil these properly,'' Robin growled, handing her a warm egg to peel and dip in salt as the bacon crisped on a clean twig she held over the fire. ''And praise be to God! The well is spring-fed and they have not yet managed to befoul it.''

''Good.'' There was a small copper kettle in her chest; while they both ate bread and bacon, she put water to boil and brewed herself a potion. It was as bitter as aloes, but she drank it down quickly. Robin eyed it, and her, and the maid's lips thinned when Gwynn didn't offer any to share.

''Like that, is it?'' was all Robin said. Gwynn nodded; she needed to do no more. That potion, and her gown, told Robin all that needed to be told, without any need to exchange words.

Well, they had planned for this. They had laid many plans, and of all the ones they had made, this, at least, was not the most extreme.

Yet. It could come to that. They had only been here less than a day, after all. And if it came to that…well, she would need a place that was all her own that she could make private at need.

''The solar,'' she said when both of them had finished eating. Obediently, Robin got to her feet and Gwynn followed, suppressing a groan for her bruised and aching body.

There was no point in letting Robin know everything; at least, not yet. Perhaps not ever.

''It hasn't been used since the baron's mother died,'' Robin warned as they climbed the stone stair to the floor above—the very top of the tower. Thin sunlight came through the narrow arrow slits to weakly illuminate the stairs; unfortunately, so did a bitter wind, for these windows were not covered in parchment. Gwynn was glad of her mantle. ''But then again, maybe that's all to the good.''

The door was locked, but Robin took a key ring out of the pocket tied over her gown, and tried the largest in the lock and the door opened, creaking on rusty hinges. Robin pushed it all the way to, and the two of them stepped into the room.

The first thing that Gwynn noticed was that the slit windows had actual glass in them, rather than the oiled parchment of the bedroom. The second was that this room, though dusty enough to make both of them sneeze within moments of entering it, was clean. Or at least, cleaner than the rest of the keep.

The fireplace in this room was bigger than the one below and had a crane and a kettle, and an iron pot on the hearth. Evidently the baron's mother had been used to having meals cooked up here. This was more than a room that had been used only by day, though—there was a narrow cupboard bed to one side, and a wardrobe and two chests, as well as the expected spinning wheel, embroidery frame and loom. Evidently the baron's mother, or perhaps one or more of the mother's ladies, had actually lived up here, at least for a time. It looked as if—

Gwynn investigated the cupboard bed and discovered that what had looked like a drawer beneath it actually held a mattress, as well. So it was a trundle bed; two could sleep here, if they chose.

The wardrobe was empty, but the chests held soft bed linens and blankets, mercifully clean and with sprigs of herbs tucked in every fold to chase the insects. All the linens were made to fit this narrow, cot-like bed and the one beneath it, not the huge edifice in the baron's bedroom, so it was obvious why they hadn't been requisitioned to serve down there.

"Hmm," Robin said, looking significantly from Gwynn to that narrow bed and back again.

"There is every reason why you should make this bed up, Robin," Gwynn said firmly, "and why we should move all my belongings up here. I will want my tiring-maid near me, of course, and there is not room enough in Bretagne's chamber for my things. In any event, I will wish my things to be…safe."

"True enough, milady," Robin replied blandly. "Well, other than a good sweeping and warming and rushes to warm the floor, this place looks fit to your use. *I* shall find some help."

So it was Gwynn that made up both of the beds with the linens and plenty of blankets—then went down for the lighter packs herself. She had all of the smaller packs safely in the solar and was beginning to put her things away out of sight when Robin reappeared with a girl and two boys in tow. The girl had a basket of kindling and a broom, which Gwynn took from her when it was evident after a few moments that she was utterly unfamiliar with its use; the boys were both laden with logs. When they had unburdened themselves, Robin ordered them both downstairs to bring up the heavier things; Gwynn laid the fire and went to sweeping out the chamber, sending the girl down for a brand to light the fire with, and for water. The work kept her reasonably warm and when the girl came back with a rushlight instead of a brand, she lit the fire and had the satisfaction of seeing the chimney draw cleanly.

By noontide, the chamber had all the appearance of being properly tenanted. Gwynn's embroidery was on the frame, Robin had managed to find enough linen cord to string the loom and enough plain, undyed wool for a proper piece of cloth. Gwynn's clothing was put away in the wardrobe, and there was a good layer of rushes on the floor. Granted they were old and dry, but at least they were clean. Robin had found a clean barrel that had once held wine; now it stood beneath one of the windows, filled with clean water. And there had been much grumbling on the part of the boys about hauling water up all those stairs.

Robin went down to the kitchens again to find food, and returned with more bread and two bowls of pottage. "They haven't burned it yet," she said darkly. "Though it was a near thing."

The bread was stale; Gwynn dipped it in her pottage to soften it. She had to fight to keep despair from washing over her. "What are they saying, down below?" she asked. "About me, I mean."

A light tap on the door frame startled her and she turned with a smothered gasp.

"I beg you forgive me, for I did not mean to eavesdrop, my lady,'' Sir Atremus said apologetically. ''But I believe I can tell you what you wish to know. If, indeed, you truly wish to hear it.''

''Sir Atremus,'' she said slowly, ''you are welcome. And I do, indeed, wish to hear what you know, for it appears that I am faced with a thankless task at best and a hopeless one at worst. Please, come in.''

By the time the pottage was gone, Gwynn had a much more accurate picture of the situation she had been catapulted into, and in some ways, it was far less grim than she had thought. The neglect and decline within the keep dated from the time that Bretagne's father had died; something like six or seven years ago. Before that, his mother had properly controlled the household until her death, then the aged seneschal had at least kept things from lurching into the chaos it now lay in. But the moment that Bretagne inherited, he had installed the first of a series of mistresses in charge of the household and the rot had immediately set in.

''So,'' Gwynn mused, resting her chin on her fist, ''there are *two* sets of servants and underlings here—those that served under Bretagne's parents, and the new ones his lemans brought in.''

''Or that Bretagne himself took on,'' Sir Atremus said. ''That would be most of the men-at-arms and the bachelor knights.''

''But not you?'' Robin chirped.

Sir Atremus flushed. ''Nay, maid, not I. But when the baron's father was on his deathbed, he asked us, his loyal men, to swear fealty to his son, and so I have.''

Gwynn gave her a warning look; Robin was edging onto dangerous ground. A knight's honor was a delicate thing and not to be questioned. "The point is," she continued, "that I *might* be able to win the older servants to follow my orders."

"And they, in turn, can command those beneath them, whether they are the Lady Ursula's creatures or no," Sir Atremus agreed. "In the kitchen, there is much speculation upon what sort of lady you are—the frail and frightened sort or one such as the late Lady Anne."

She considered her options. "The kitchen, I think," she said at last, and got to her feet, concealing her winces from both Robin and Sir Atremus. "If any progress can be made, that is where we must start. If we can deliver edible meals, the men will be won to me. One does not lead a man by his nose, but by his stomach."

"Well said, my lady!" Sir Atremus applauded. "Now, if you will forgive me, I fear I have overstayed my welcome."

"Never that," she said warmly and, on impulse, took one of his hands in both of hers. He took the right one and bent to kiss the back of it, then turned and left. But she *thought* he was blushing, though his face was averted from her.

Well, so was she. Once again she felt herself growing warm as she flushed, and got annoyed at herself for it.

But there was work to be done, and little time to do it in if she was going to have any improvements in place by the evening meal.

Chapter 4

When she took her place on the dais that evening, it was with the weary satisfaction that she had accomplished if not a miracle, at least a measurable improvement. She half expected to find Ursula usurping her place as she made her way from the kitchen to the Great Hall, this time with no escort but Robin. But in fact the chair was empty and Ursula sullenly occupied the seat to which she had been demoted last night. Bretagne had been hunting—some said for something other than game—and had not yet come in from the stables. But she was not going to permit the meal to begin without him.

And therein lay a small part of the ongoing disorganization within his walls. It was, in fact, seldom certain *when* he would appear for the evening meal, which was the root cause of much of the inedible food that had been the norm at Clawcrag Keep, for he would have flown into a rage if a meal was begun without him. His father had always been precisely on time. The moment that the sun touched the horizon, he would be in his place. His cooks had gotten used to that and did not know how to cope with Bretagne's vagaries.

Well, Gwynn did. *Her* father could never be counted on to be ready for a meal when the meal was ready for him, and hence, their cooks had contrived some very clever ways of dealing with the situation. This afternoon, she had put several of them in play. Sir Atremus had helped, taking care to introduce her specifically to the oldest servants, and she to them with a warm word of how good a chatelaine her mother had been, and how he was certain that *she* could be no less skilled. She found herself flushing with pleasure when he made such compliments, but her blushes were soon forgotten as she'd set to work.

First, as people came into the Great Hall and took their seats, they found that there was bread already on the table—not the trenchers cut from day-old loaves from which they would eat their meals, but small crusty loaves the size of half a man's fist, and plenty of them, in baskets. There had been enough time to have these baked by the evening meal, and she had left orders that this was to be the case from now on. These bread "rolls" served to occupy those who were waiting and to blunt their appetite while they waited for the baron. If they wished—and many did—they could take their bread to the two hearths to dip it in the fat drippings from the roasting stag and boar that had been taken from the larder to cook on spits.

The rest of the dishes had been parcooked, then set aside until the moment he took his seat, to be finished when he finally appeared. They were still roughly made, and hardly seasoned at all, but at least they weren't burned, stone-cold or half raw. She couldn't do anything about the wretched cheese or the withered vegetables, but the burned crusts were cut from the bread before it reached the High Table. When Bretagne strolled in, he was presented with rolls and slices of venison and pork along with his ale—this served to signal the start of the meal, and while people were eating bread and meat, the rest of the dishes were finished and brought out in the order in which they cooked.

And if Bretagne didn't seem to notice the change, she could see that others at his tables did, and were reacting well, casting her glances of approval or sullen glares. The latter she put down in her mind as Ursula's creatures and probable sources of trouble.

Bretagne stuffed himself and was apparently just as pleased with the somewhat topsy-turvy order of his meal, which had begun with meat instead of soup. He just crammed himself with whatever was presented to him, as he had last night, and swilled vast quantities of his harsh ale. Gwynn got a decent meal, the first since she had left home, kept her eyes cast down, and hoped he would not notice that she had her own cup now, which was filled with the same ale cut with two-thirds water, which made it barely drinkable. The entertainment was much the same as it had been last night—and all through the meal, her dread of what was to follow grew.

But when the last of the dishes had been presented and eaten, Bretagne was engrossed in a cockfight and did not seem disposed to leave. The noise was such that she could not even get his attention, and so she retired without any fanfare—

She just hoped that he wouldn't be angry with her presumption.

No one else seemed to notice, either—well, except for poor Sir Atremus, whose eyes followed her as she sought the stair on her own. She felt his gaze on her long after she was actually out of sight. When she reached Bretagne's bedchamber, she took a stone she had left warming on the hearth and shoved it deep in the bed, while icy drafts made the hearth flames dance.

Tonight, however, was *not* going to be a repetition of her bridal night. She had taken certain precautions to make sure of that. From a certain little sponge steeped in vinegar and herbs deep within her secret places, to keeping her hair bound in its braids, from disrobing entirely, much though she shuddered at the thought of his hands on her, to that little cask of strong spirits she had discovered in the back of one of the storerooms....

That last would be her defense, at least, until her body had hardened itself to his assaults. She had left more herbs steeping in the cask, and now drank down a full goblet of the stuff, which burned like fire and left bitter lees in her cup.

Then she stripped nude, made her other preparations, and clambered quickly into the now warmer bed, where she waited, with the covers pulled up tight to her chin. And by the time he appeared in the door of his chamber, having finally noticed that she was gone, *she* was well and truly numb, both in body and in spirit.

She lay still and endured his attentions—but, thanks to her drink, with far less pain than the previous night.

And for his part, he was sodden enough with drink that he scarcely noticed, except to mutter curses and call her a "stone" and an "ice bitch" once or twice. And when he was finished, once again he rolled over in all of the blankets, leaving her aching and empty—

And horribly aware of a loneliness that took her entirely by surprise and made her force down tears that she *would* not shed.

She eased out of bed, gathered her things and, throwing her mantle over her nakedness, climbed the stairs to the solar.

Robin was there already, asleep in the trundle. *Now* she cleaned herself, donned a warm shift, disposed of the sponge back into its cup of vinegar and herbs, tended the new bruises with wormwood ointment, and climbed wearily into the narrow cupboard bed, to sleep, at long last, the exhausted sleep she had longed for since she had left her father's house so long ago that it seemed an age and not a fortnight past.

The next morning it was Robin who woke her; then began the work she hoped would occupy her time, if not her mind—returning Clawcrag to something like civilized surroundings.

It was a battle every step of the way, but at least each day saw some gains, in allies if not in progress. Bretagne was probably not aware that she had brought some moneys with her, over and above the dower price and her income, which was, of course, now his. These were dispensed with frugal care and much wrangling to get herbs and seasonings, some variety in foodstuffs, the wherewithal to set up a proper still-room. These things were not to be had in the village, of course, but somehow word that there was a new bride at Clawcrag had percolated to the countryside. Within two days, there were peddlers packing themselves up to the gate, and if they had herbs and spices, she left orders to let them in. Astonished servants found themselves down in the marshes cutting rushes, out in the meadows gathering the withered remains of lavender and rosemary ahead of the storms of winter. She was busy from rising to sleeping—but not so much so that she failed to notice Atremus or what he was doing for her, quietly, in the background.

When a servant was insolent or refused to obey her orders, if one of the senior servitors had not gotten to the miscreant, she could be sure that Atremus would be delivering a tongue-lashing or even a beating, if the occasion warranted. He saw to it that she was served by armsmen who did so with a good temper, even if it meant replacing them with those assigned by the captain's orders. By small deeds and careful intervention, he smoothed the way for her, until the results that she had obtained in the comfort level of the keep made everyone sensible of the fact that in obeying her, they increased their own ease. These little gifts of time and effort were like roses strewn at her feet....

By the time her courses came upon her—which, being a sign that she was not with child, relieved her so much that she spent an hour weeping as she had not done until that moment—the old rushes, filthy and greasy and full of garbage, had been cleaned from the Great Hall and replaced, the fireplaces cleaned, the chimneys cleared.

Her time coincided with the first great snowfall of the season, which had the unfortunate consequence of keeping Bretagne from hunting *or* riding out with his men-at-arms. As the snow piled up on the road, on the walls, and in the court, he glowered at it, and her, as if he thought she was somehow to blame.

He sat in his chair in the Great Hall, drinking from noontide on, looking more and more sullen as the day progressed. She ignored him, going about her duties, though she felt bloated, pallid and ungainly as a toad. At least there were friendlier faces now, even among the men-at-arms; as she had known, better meals won her supporters where soft words would have worked in vain. The hall filled early with men made idle by the snow, and as the storm worsened, the hall grew darker; she signaled for the torches to be lit and more wood to be brought in.

But as she supervised the laying out of the baskets of bread before the evening meal after making sure that the cooks knew there would be *no* putting back of dishes tonight, Bretagne suddenly came to life. He got to his feet and seized her arm, grabbing her so hard that he left bruises.

"My lord!" she gasped, choking back a whimper of pain. "My lord, what—"

He ignored her, dragging her by main force toward the stairs, and up them. She tried to keep up with him, but he took the stairs two at a time and she could not possibly match that with her skirts encumbering her, tangling in her legs. In a ghastly echo of her bridal night, she tripped and fell several times, only to be hauled abruptly to her feet and dragged onward.

When they reached his bedchamber, she was hurled inside to land on the hearth as he slammed and barred the door, then turned toward her with a face full of fury.

"Strip!" he shouted. "God's blood, you puny, puling milksop. If I can't have some sport out of doors, I'll have it within, poor amusement though you are!"

"But, my lord—" she whispered. "But—"

With a roar, he picked her up and threw her on the bed, then yanked her skirts over her head.

And that was when he discovered her state.

If he had been angry before, he was in a fury then, and for the first time, he showed what he was truly made of.

"Useless barren bitch!" he howled. "No good for futtering, and can't even hold a babe in the belly! I'll teach you—"

And he delivered a blow to the side of her face that knocked her off the bed and onto the floor. The first blow knocked her half senseless, so that she scarcely felt the rest of the beating, which was just as well. She had the wit to remain limp, a dead weight, so that when he tossed her about, she didn't break any bones. But when he finally wore his fury out, she throbbed and ached from head to toe, her lips were split and swollen, and she couldn't see out of one swollen eye. His last blow left her sprawled on the bearskin on the hearth, as he stood over her, panting.

She expected him to kill her then, she truly did. But he stared down at her, then abruptly threw open the door. "Out," he snarled. "Take yourself somewhere I can't see you. And don't trouble to be in my bed again until you're fit to plant seed in."

She didn't need to be told twice; she stumbled out of the door and somehow got herself up the stairs to the solar, to fall into her own safe little bed and curl up into a ball of misery and pain.

And Robin, faithful Robin, was at her side before she had begun to gather her wits enough to look for help.

She heard Robin's firm footsteps and raised herself up to turn toward the door, her vision a blur. Robin's hands grasped her shoulders and turned her toward the light.

The curse that the maid hissed out would have suited the crudest of stable hands. "A bucket of snow," she said to someone out of sight in the doorway, and she helped Gwynn to sit up. "What can I do?"

"A cup of my wine." She managed the words

through swollen, split lips. Her head spun; the pain was worse than anything she had ever felt in her life. Robin brought her the bitter, herb-laced wine, and put the cup into her hands; she would have liked to gulp it down but with her lips so swollen and bruised, she had to drink it carefully or it would be wasted, dribbling out of her mouth.

"Now what?" Robin asked as she took the empty cup from Gwynn's slack hands.

"I've the snow," said an uncertain and profoundly shocked male voice from the door. Gwynn was too far gone in misery to react or she would have been profoundly shamed, for it was Sir Atremus. Oh, she did not want him to see her like this, did not want him to know...

Half of her was afraid he would grow angered and attack Bretagne. Half of her was afraid he would not care....

"Bring it here, and get another," Robin ordered as briskly as if the knight was a mere servant. "And go to the kitchen and get some soup."

"I need...to go to bed," Gwynn said thickly.

"Then let me get you there," Robin said, and helped her to strip to her shift, then got her under the covers and packed hot stones in with her. She needed those stones, for the next thing that Robin did was to pack the snow in cloths to lay against her swollen, bruised face. Chill warred with warmth as she lay back in her bed, willing her wits to stay with her.

"I'll kill him," Robin muttered, bringing her a change of snow packs.

"No," Gwynn said flatly, forcing each word out between thick and uncooperative lips. "There is no way that we can touch him in the world of men that we can survive. You will not try, I order you not to. Stay out of sight, watch what you say, say nothing as much as possible. I do not want your true nature uncovered. And remember this, revenge is not our right, only justice."

"Then *surely* we'll—" Robin began, "surely *now*—"

"Perhaps," Gwynn replied slowly. "But I do not know. Remember the Threefold Law, Robin. If what we do is not just, it will rebound upon us threefold."

"At least let us make preparations!" Robin growled, her voice dropping nearly an octave with anger.

"That, we can do," she conceded, and dabbed at an icy trickle of water from the melting snow. "Tomorrow, Robin, tomorrow. And—beware your voice."

Robin made a little sound of satisfaction then and confined herself to changing the snow packs, helping Gwynn to eat the soup, and bringing her a second cup of her wine. That second cup had the desired effect of sending her, at last, into aching slumber.

She remained in the solar all the next day; the swelling had gone down in her face, but she was not minded to present herself to the curious gaze of Bretagne's people. She half expected the business of the keep to go to pieces without her supervision, but to her pleased surprise, a steady trickle of servitors came up to *her* for orders. These were, by and large, the older servants—the ones that predated Bretagne's rule, who had served under his mother and father. She made sure to sit with her back to the window, her face in shadow, a glare of light behind her; they kept their eyes purposefully averted. No one wanted to see what Bretagne had done, but they knew, and she knew that they knew, and it shamed all of them.

Robin brought her meals—and one surprise that touched her deeply, for one of the cooks had somehow contrived a dish of custard. Eggs, there were, of course, but for cream, someone would have had to go down to the village, in the snow. Evidently someone had, and she ate the gift, for gift it was, with gratitude.

She spent most of that day, when she wasn't sleeping or giving servants directions, in a careful mental inventory of what she had brought here beneath the secret bottoms of her chests, and in perusing a small, handwritten, leather-bound book. There were no mirrors in the keep, not even one of polished metal, so only Robin's descriptions told her how ghastly she looked. At least by the end of that day she was able to see out of both eyes clearly and able to eat something other than custard and soup.

Robin went down for more solid fare at the evening meal and came back with bread, dripping, slices of meat and a dish of apples stewed in honey. And news.

"Ursula," Robin said crisply, "is in your place."

"And she may have it," Gwynn countered. "At board *or* bed. Wife and lady, she *cannot* be, which leaves her only—" She shrugged.

"Unless..." Robin said darkly.

"Which is why we will begin with preparations this night. If our cause is just, we will know, and we will be ready." Gwynn said nothing more, and Robin knew better than to pursue the subject any further.

She ate her meal, with a care when chewing, for her jaw still ached abominably. And then, they waited, waited for the keep to settle for the night, and for everyone—especially those in the room below—to fall asleep.

Only when the last sounds from below had died away, did she motion to Robin, who got quietly to her feet, moved silently to the door and closed and barred it from within.

Then, together, they moved all of the furniture against the wall—the beds, of course, were built into the wall itself—then cleared the rushes away from the floor, piling them in a heap to one side. Then both chests were opened, the contents set aside, and from the bottom of the first, Gwynn took up a length of black cord. She tied a piece of chalk to one end, and as Robin stood in the middle of the room and held the free end, Gwynn used the chalk to inscribe a nine-foot circle on the stone flags of the floor. Then Gwynn sat down with a mortar and pestle, ingredients from the chest and a mixing bowl.

It was not so much the ingredients, though several of them were uncommon, and probably unobtainable here, as what Gwynn whispered over them that was important....

An hour later she and Robin were on their knees,

carefully following the chalk-line, painting in the line of the chalk with a very special paint.

And doing so with extreme care. Robin laid in the first coat; Gwynn followed along behind, making certain that there was not so much as a hairline crack that was not coated with the paint, and whispering under her breath. When it dried, it would be a color just slightly darker than the stone, so that even if someone kicked the rushes aside, it would not be immediately obvious, and yet the outline of the circle would be easy to see when the rushes were taken away. Together they painted the initial round of the circle, then began to widen it, making it a band as wide as her thumb was long, until they used up the last of the paint. They left it for an hour or so to dry, then spread the rushes back over the floor and moved the furnishings back. By morning, when the paint had cured, it would be impossible to take it up without scouring the first layer of the stone away.

Gwynn had done her best to keep Robin from guessing how very much she hurt as she worked. She felt every bruise, not as a fresh injury, but as a bone-deep, grinding ache now. When they finished the night's work, she was glad enough to fall into her little bed and to leave Robin to clean up, conceal her things in the bottoms of the chests again, unbar the door and extinguish the lights. If she had not hurt so much, she probably would have been asleep immediately. As it was, she drank down her potion and watched Robin busy herself with putting the room to rights, until darkness encompassed the room and she heard Robin settling into the trundle bed.

She might have remained awake anyway, for what she had just set in motion was not to be taken lightly—but she could not.

And perhaps that was all to the best.

It was easy to tell now who were her friends here and who her foes—and who were disturbed by their lord's actions, but too afraid of him to make any move that might be construed as a challenge to what he had done. Those that were her friends, or were afraid, pretended that nothing was wrong, that her bruises did not exist, while those who were pleased to see her so humbled smiled slyly whenever she passed.

But as yet, no one disobeyed Gwynn's orders when it came to the household matters, though Bretagne's actions could well have signaled the time to revolt. The kitchen staff, perhaps, was responsible for that; the first time that a serving man had sneered and ignored what Gwynn had told him, the cook clouted him across the back of the head with an enormous ladle, and since then, any order she gave belowstairs was obeyed with alacrity.

Ursula sat in Gwynn's seat at meals now, beside Bretagne, and rather than challenge the woman, Gwynn took *her* food in her room. Which was not so bad when it came down to it; she didn't have to sit through Bretagne's gobbling, the shouting, the wrestling matches and cock and dog fights. And as for that other duty—once her courses were over, she presented herself dutifully in her husband's bedchamber, only to discover that Ursula was there ahead of her.

She stood regarding the interloper gravely; Ursula was stark naked, curled up indolently in the bed. As Gwynn stared, the creature smiled maliciously and let the blanket she held to her chest drop, tossing her hair back over her shoulder, displaying her breasts proudly.

Gwynn noted without dismay that they were vastly larger than her own—and beginning to sag. With the same insolence that Ursula displayed, she ran her gaze over everything that was visible, refusing to be intimidated, making her regard cool and analytical.

If she was any judge of such things, Ursula's days were numbered. Either she would get with child and be discarded, or someone younger, with a firmer body and the advantage of novelty, would take her place. There had been, so rumor claimed, a long line of women in Bretagne's bed before Ursula, and there would be a succession of them to follow, unless Ursula was more clever than Gwynn thought. But there could only be one wife.

She let some of that come through in her expression, and Ursula's face began to change, to grow petulant and a little angry.

And perhaps, just a little afraid.

When Bretagne arrived a few moments later, he looked from one to the other and roared with laughter at the sight of wife and leman confronting one another like this. "Out for a moment, wench," he ordered his leman. "This won't take long."

With a smirk, Ursula slid from the great bed,

wrapped herself in a blanket and flounced out the door. Bretagne slammed it behind the wench, but Gwynn did not doubt that Ursula lingered on the landing, waiting, trying to hear what went on through a crack in the door.

Bretagne did not even bother to get Gwynn to disrobe, and his attentions were mercifully brief. He bent her over the bed, pulled up her skirts, and was quickly done. The act was so full of anger that there was no room left in him for anything else, and as for her, she endured the ordeal, sustained by her loathing. She was bound to this man in law, but nothing could make her submit anything but her body to him. When he was finished with her, he stood up and stared down at her with a loathing that must match hers.

"Be here every night that you're fit," he said with a sneer. "I'll plant a babe in your belly yet. But I won't share a bed with a cold stick this winter, by God, so get you up to that nun's cell you've taken over."

"Yes, my lord," she replied without any expression whatsoever. She got up, straightened her gown and walked out.

Ursula had been waiting on the landing. The woman laughed as Gwynn went past, on her way up the steps, and it would have been humiliating if she had not been so grateful. For once she had escaped Bretagne's attentions without much injury, and with all of the precautions she was taking, it would require a miracle for him to get his wish.

It did occur to her somewhat later that it was odd

he hadn't cautioned her against taking a lover...but perhaps it hadn't occurred to him that she would, or that any man would find her attractive. Or perhaps he knew very well what would happen if she did—there would be a hundred tongues more than willing to tell, and it would be drowning for her. Whatever the reason, she vowed to give him no excuse to accuse her. Any time there was a man in her chamber, she would be chaperoned, and the door would be open.

Ursula was *not* minded to usurp her place as housekeeper, apparently, for she made no move to countermand the orders that Gwynn gave. Gradually the keep returned to a place that was fit to live in—gradually, for she was careful not to pile too much work on the younger servants who were only obeying her because Bretagne apparently still gave her support for *this* position. The rest, the older ones, she was determined not to overburden, either—first, it was not fair, and second, she was not going to do anything to make them regret supporting her. And even though her lord appeared not to notice the changes in his surroundings, Gwynn noted that even her foes were not trying to undermine her work. Perhaps that was Ursula's doing, after all; even if Bretagne didn't notice, Ursula was sufficiently luxury-loving to be enjoying the improved state of things. Fireplaces that had ceased to smoke, fires that burned hot and clean, decent food, rushes underfoot that didn't stink like a midden—yes, even Ursula was not going to cut the neck of the goose that had laid that particular golden egg.

Chapter 5

As the keep settled into a routine, and as the weather tended to close everyone in within walls for days at a time, she could not help but be thrown into Sir Atremus's way more often. In a way, the manner in which he was treated was a parallel to her situation. The younger knights—more numerous than the older—regarded him with unveiled contempt. But the older ones gave him full deference, even though in years he was more their junior than she had thought. And the pages and squires—*all* of them, though there were fewer of them than there should havc been, given the number of knights—turned to him and not their own knights for help or guidance. Now that was curious. She had thought at first that it might have been because he was serving in part as the seneschal, and it was part of the seneschal's duty to see to the discipline of all the pages and squires in the keep. But no, in fact, that was not the case at all, for there was no seneschal, only a steward, who oversaw the affairs of the lands belonging to Clawcrag. Atremus ordered the boys, not because it was his duty, but because it was in his nature. When one was ordered to do a task beyond his strength or skill, Atremus saw to it that he had help, and somehow did it without making the younger feel inadequate, or the older helper feel put-upon. And she could not help but think that it should have been the lord of the keep who was doing all this and not one of his knights.

And Gwynn noted something else that was curious. For all of Bretagne's swearing, and all of the clerkly types at his table, he was remarkably lax in his observances of holy days. The keep's tiny chapel was usually empty but for a few old servants, her, Robin and Sir Atremus, nor did the fat priest who officiated there do more than mumble his way through his Latin to get the service over with as quickly as possible. She often wondered if the priest was a true priest at all, or only a self-taught charlatan, eager to claim a place where the living was easy. There was no change at Christmastide, either; in fact, curiously enough, that festival came and went with next to no difference to the keep. No Yule log, no caroling, no feast, no Christmas Eve Mass, and no orders for any such thing. It could have been any other of the dark days of winter; Gwynn would have suspected that she had missed the day altogether, but the stars told her that she had not.

She and Robin made an exchange of small gifts, and that was all.

Except that, the day after Christmas, when Gwynn's courses came on her again, she celebrated the season with a second beating.

It was not so violent as the first, but only because she had taken the precaution of serving ale mulled with spices to the High Table—spices that covered the taste of the additional distilled spirits she put into Bretagne's cup. Much though she would have liked to have poisoned him, all she dared to do was to impair his abilities temporarily. As a result, he was truly drunk by the time he discovered her state, and more than half his blows landed on something other than her body.

He ended his beating by aiming a great clout at her head, overbalancing and falling over onto the bed, where he lay snoring like a rooting boar. At least she had the satisfaction of leaving him that way for Ursula's pleasure.

This time she was able to go up to her room under her own power. She came away with another blackened eye and split lip, however, and Robin glared at her with anger and dismay as she entered the solar.

Since she had known what would happen when Bretagne discovered the signs that she had failed to quicken, she had gotten a bucket of snow ahead of time. Robin made snow packs and helped Gwynn treat her injuries and fumed the entire time.

"Now?" Robin demanded when Gwynn said nothing except to thank her for the pack.

"Not yet," she replied, applying the pack to her lip.

Robin glowered and sulked for the rest of the evening. But she was not too angry to take part in the evening's painting, however.

It was progressing slowly, but that was not bad; whatever Gwynn decided to do, the diagrams would have to be perfect, or it all might go awry. Better slow and careful now.

The outer circle was complete, and Gwynn had found true north to bisect it into the four quarters, so the inner square was done, as well. The circle that fit within the square had been completed last night, and tonight she began the pentangle that lay within the inner circle. When those figures were done, the real work would begin, work that Robin, willing though she might be, could not help her with. Magic took talent as well as learning; many who had studied long and hard could not master it, and a few, a very few, who never studied it at all could call upon it with concentrated will alone, though the cost was very high. Certain signs needed to be inscribed in the points of the square and the pentangle—and more pentangles would have to be painted on the walls. These, however, would be laid out in the white of an egg, invisible to the naked eye, and they would not have to be so perfect. She would lay them out with a string, following the line of the string against the wall rather than a charcoal-drawn outline, for she would want to leave no trace of her work to be discovered.

She remembered her mother, also, drawing pentagrams like these, late at night, when she thought that no one was watching. Her mother, also named Gwynnhwyfar, with green eyes and golden hair....

Her father had willfully pretended that nothing of the sort was going on. He loved his wife so deeply, and he was so afraid that what she did was rooted in deviltry and shadow, not light, that he simply elected not to see, not to know. And so, in the end, he had not known why his wife died, for he had not known she had died to protect him and her little daughter. But Gwynn knew...Gwynn knew.

Well, she was her mother's daughter. She would have been so happy to discover another such as her father in Bretagne. Why was he as he was, anyway? What had turned him into a brute that beat women, allowed his court to degenerate, lived like a pig? *His* parents, by all accounts, had been decent folk—the little she had heard of them from the old servants gave her no reason to think otherwise.

But he had been the unlooked-for child of their old age, and they had fostered him, early, to another Border Lord, keeping his older brother at home and training *him* to become the next baron. Only when that young man died of a fever, had they brought Bretagne, now fully of age, home again. Perhaps it had been when he was in fosterage that the damage had been done....

Or perhaps there was some truth to the tales of changelings, and he was a demon in human guise. God, He knew the truth of it; it was too deep for her to unravel.

All this tumbled through her thoughts while she and

Robin painted. She kept Robin awake a'purpose until her half sibling was yawning, then sent Robin to bed first and did the cleaning and straightening herself. Much more of that resentful silence and she would have been tempted to say something she would later regret. *She* fully intended to sleep through the worst of the aching on the morrow, for the servants had had their orders before she went up to Bretagne—she could tell by the looks that they gave her on getting those orders that *they* had known what was coming, as well.

She ached, but did not need her potion, only wine and willow; bitter, but not as potent. This she drank down and put herself to bed, locking herself inside the shelter of the cupboard bed with the shutters closed so that daylight would not wake her.

But sleep eluded her and her blackened eye and battered head hurt worse, once she was lying down, than she had thought they would.

That was when, with Robin lying asleep, and the shutters and the pillows muffling her sobs, she wept for the pure grief of her situation for the first time since she had come here.

Oh, she had wept before, but it was with physical pain rather than heartsickness. Now, though—this one hour she claimed for herself and for her grief.

So many hopes, dead, since she had come here! So much she had given up, and for what? The only difference between this beast and Anghus was that Bretagne was no magician! And she had been so completely willing to make something of the situation! If

Bretagne had shown her the least kindness, had given any indication that he saw the work she had been putting into his comfort and appreciated it, if he had shown that he cared for *any* thing other than himself and having his lusts satisfied, she would have fought to find whatever scrap of heart he had and nurtured it.

So why had there been nothing there for her to nurture? All things happened for a reason; she had to believe that, or go mad, but why was she suffering so?

Was this how her life was to be from now on? An endless series of beatings and loveless, brutal couplings while she fought to keep from being brought to bed with a child that, given his lord's behavior toward her, would surely kill her—and while she labored like a serf in what should have been her own household?

She wept, her whole being an aching, empty cry of *Why?* to the heavens, until she had no more tears left, and lay, wretched and feeling utterly alone, all emotion spent.

Now, if ever an answer was to come to her, she would have thought that it should have come then. But there was nothing, only the sound of the wind whining through the myriad crevices in the keep's walls, wailing softly like the lost soul that she had become.

And finally, the only thing that came was sleep.

She woke to voices, one Robin's, one muffled. The second one sounded like a man's voice, but it could not have been Bretagne's for Bretagne would have bellowed and this man spoke in low and reasonable tones. She wondered, sleepily, if the cook could have come up, needing more orders about some minor kitchen or household emergency.

But if it was an emergency, it was not sufficiently imperative that Robin came to wake her, and she fell back asleep again, for the dreams she had awakened from were disturbing and not at all restful.

She woke a second time feeling more like herself and opened the shutters. Robin was not there, but her dress was waiting, warming by the fire, and she was not so helpless that she couldn't get it on by herself. She felt stiff and sore, and without doubt her blackened eye was swollen, but she was better, much better, than after that first beating.

A quick wash in the cold water from the basin made her feel more awake, and she dressed herself quickly and warmly. Robin came in with a flat basket of food after she had sat herself down at her loom, for she had not felt up to trying to manage the fine detail of her embroidery.

"Bretagne has a head like a lightning-struck oak," Robin reported with grim satisfaction. "And a stomach that can't hold more than dry bread. He spent half the morning abed, moaning about his gut and now lurks in the hall, complaining about the agony in his skull. He doesn't blame the ale, though—"

"Typical," Gwynn replied blandly, coming over to the fire and taking up a bowl of soup and some bread. "What does he blame, then, since his guzzling is not to be considered?"

"The eels. He swears he'll never have eel pie again."

Gwynn shrugged. "'Twas he who demanded it. Cook did his best, but he made a right mess of it, and swore at every eel that went into it. That receipt I did not have, for you know that never there was an eel in any river of ours, and I could not help him. Mayhap that was what made it disagree with Bretagne."

"Mayhap," Robin agreed just as blandly. "As to aught else, Sir Atremus presented himself after breaking fast, while you were still asleep. He wished to present his Yuletide gift, and wondered if you had ever made good your vow to get your father to teach you chess. I told him that you had. He said then that he would give you his gift in person, this afternoon."

"Really?" Now that had her interest and roused her curiosity. She well remembered *why* she had made that vow—she'd watched her father and Sir Atremus spend long hours over the chessboard, ignoring everything around them—including an increasingly impatient Gwynn, who wanted stories. That was when she had told the amused knight that she would *make* her father teach her chess so that the next time Atremus visited, he would have to spend all that time with her....

Odd of Atremus to have remembered that. And what on earth could he have gotten her for a Yule gift?

"Get out that shirt that I made before we left," she told Robin, making a hasty decision. She had sewn a handsome linen shirt as a wedding gift for Bretagne—needless to say, she had not presented it to him, nor did she intend to now. But from the sorry state of Atremus's garb, he badly needed a new shirt, and if he was going to give her a gift, she wanted to be able to reciprocate.

Robin's face lit up with pleasure and mischief as she instantly understood what Gwynn intended. ''Happily, milady,'' she murmured, and dug into the bottom of the chest to retrieve it, still folded and bound with a bit of bright ribbon. She laid it aside on the stool beside the embroidery frame at Gwynn's nod. Gwynn finished her soup and went back to her loom, losing herself in the hypnotic passage of the shuttle, the thud of the beater, as she continued to weave a length of simple twilled wool. This, she decided, would also go to Atremus, as a new surcoat or tunic. That Bretagne allowed one of his knights to be so shabby was a sad comment on his neglect of his men. Though it was not *all* of his men who were neglected, but since Atremus was the least regarded of any of his knights, no one seemed to care what he looked like. She spent the time at her loom, lost in happier memories of the time when her mother had still been alive and Atremus had been their welcome guest. Odd. At the time he had seemed the same age as her father, but then all adults seemed the same age to a child. Could he have been her father's squire, and knighted by him before her father had wedded and become lord of his own manor? It was certainly possible; Atremus *was* younger than her father, though the years had not treated him kindly.

Atremus presented himself in midafternoon, tapping politely on the frame of the open door and observing the niceties by waiting for Robin to come to the portal to admit him formally. Gwynn set her shuttle in the warp and turned toward him, her hands folded in her lap. He was carrying a basket, and something bulky, wrapped in a cloth, beneath one arm.

She noted, a little sadly, how his eyes went to her blackened one, and how he quickly averted his gaze. "My lady," he said in that gentle, deep voice, "I beg you forgive me for making this somewhat of a Twelfth Night gift rather than a Yule gift, but my fingers are not as nimble as they once were and this took me longer to carve than I had hoped."

Carve? Now she was alive with curiosity. "Please, Sir Atremus, show me! You find me as greedy for your gift as a little child!"

He smiled at her sally and nodded to Robin. "Please, child, if you would bring me that small table, and by your leave, lady, a stool to sit on?"

Robin brought both, set the stool down near Gwynn, and put the table between them. Only then did Atremus wait for Gwynn's permission, and on getting it, sit down to reveal that what was beneath his arm was an inlaid wooden game board, alternate squares being walnut and white birch, upon which he began to set out handsomely carved chessmen in the corresponding woods.

Gwynn laughed for pure joy, the first time she had done so since setting foot in this place, and clasped her hands beneath her chin. "Sir Atremus! They are wonderful! However can I thank you?"

"By playing a game or so each day with me, my lady," the knight said with a pleased smile. "No one else here plays the game, and I miss your father's skill.

One grows weary of dicing and wagering, particularly when one has little to wager with.'' He seemed resigned and yet accepting of his poverty, to be able to make even a feeble jest of it. Gwynn was embarrassed for him.

''Then I hope you will not wager my gift to you away,'' Gwynn replied, lifting a finger to Robin in signal, more pleased than ever that she had decided to give Atremus the shirt. Robin brought it and at Gwynn's nod, gave it to him. He looked surprised, then pleased that she had thought of a return gift, and carefully unpicked the ribbon. He unfolded what, to him, must have looked only like a bit of cloth, and shook it out.

''Good my lady!'' he exclaimed, partly in pleasure, partly in shock. ''My gift is as naught to this!''

''Oh, I wager there are an equal number of hours in each,'' she said casually, but delighted with his reaction. ''But enough of that! Come, let us put your gift to good use—but I warn you, ere I left, I was trouncing my father three games in five!''

They played until the afternoon light began to fade. Gwynn, despite her boast, did not trounce him; he might have won, but that game ended in a stalemate caused at least in part because Atremus clearly underestimated her early on and was caught in check from which he extracted himself only with great difficulty and by sacrificing a knight.

''I see I have found a worthy opponent,'' he said when they both declared end game. He winked. ''I should have known better than to be deceived by a lovely face. I do believe, my lady, that we will not find our afternoons a bore any longer."

"Oh, but I must not neglect my duties," she said reluctantly. "It is only because I am...unwell...that I laze about here this afternoon." Then she felt her face brighten as she thought of an idea. "Come at evening meal. Robin can bring enough for three and we may eat and play out a game at the same time. I cannot believe that you find the company below to be congenial, as I have always known you to be a man who prefers lighter amusements to blood sports and would rather take his meals seasoned with conversation than conflict."

"No more do I," Atremus admitted with a sigh. "And I will scarce be missed. If it is no imposition?"

"None at all," she assured him.

"Then I look for a rematch this very night," he promised, and rose and bowed himself out.

Robin gazed at the empty doorway long after he had left. "If he had been, indeed, what you first took him to be," she said slowly, "you would—"

"Hush!" Gwynn said in alarm, with a nod at the door. Robin bit her lip.

"Well, you would have been playing chess over every evening meal, as you now plan to be," the girl said instead of what Gwynn feared she had originally intended. "So it seems that the fates have brought you to that place after all."

Was there a movement in the shadows of the stairs? Gwynn could not tell, nor did she hear a footfall. It could have been an animal, a cat or a dog, or nothing at all. But one never knew who might be listening at doors, especially here, and she felt more than ever that her decision never to be unchaperoned and to keep the door to her solar open except when she and Robin were painting or sleeping was the right one. Had she not warned Robin, her maid might well have said what Gwynn herself was thinking—that had Sir Atremus been her husband instead of Bretagne, she would be a happy woman today.

That would have been a severe misstep, if there was a spy on her. It could be, that for all his apparent indifference, Bretagne was watching her closely. She should have expected that; no matter how little he cared for her, no man wishes to be cuckolded, and Bretagne most of all was the sort to hold greedily to any possession, however despised it was. For all *she* knew, Bretagne was having her door barred from the outside at night, even as she barred it from within. She had her own chamber pot and a garderobe to pour it down, and if the bar was lifted by servants in the morning before she or Robin tried the door, she would never know.

Well, and if he was, he was only doing her a favor. Little though he knew it.

She sent Robin down to the kitchen to make sure that there were no questions or problems; Robin returned with the cook's tale of woe—not that anything this evening was going wrong, but that Bretagne blamed *his* eel pie for what was really a hangover. And Ursula was sulking, and though Robin could not report why, both of them guessed. Ursula had gotten little pleasure out of the baron last night and would probably get none tonight.

In due course, Robin went down a second time and returned, closely followed by Sir Atremus, both of them burdened with the evening meal for three. Gwynn felt suddenly touched and her heart warmed with gratitude. Atremus need not have burdened himself with anything; it was Robin who was the servant, and he could rightly have left her to struggle with the additional weight on her own.

They set up the board beside the fire for the light, with a table beside them laden with the food and drink that Robin had brought. Robin watched, as she had watched their afternoon game, with interest but no understanding, while they played.

This time the knight did not underestimate his opponent and Gwynn had a hard fight on her hands. She kept an ear tuned to the noise in the hall below. She wanted to know when Bretagne left the table—because even if the game was not yet at an end, she would send Atremus away.

But it seemed that Atremus was also listening and had a keener feeling for the rhythm of the goings-on in the hall than she, for at a point, perhaps two hours into the game, he feigned a yawn. She knew it was feigned; it hadn't called up a corresponding yawn from her.

"Ah, my lady, I fear I have not the energy I had when I battled your father," he said with real regret. "I fear I must seek my bed."

"Then we will continue this game tomorrow," she

replied warmly, allowing him to take her hand and kiss it. "Good night to you, and I thank you for a most pleasant contest."

The door had, of course, remained open all during this time, and now Gwynn was certain that something—or someone—slipped down the stairs before Sir Atremus could move toward the door.

So there was a spy, although it was impossible to tell if it was someone set there by Bretagne, by Ursula, or was merely someone hoping to profit by telling one or both of them of her activities.

Fine. She wished them joy of it, sitting in the dark and cold stair, with nothing more amusing to listen to than the idle conversation of two chess players.

Atremus limped out the door. Robin watched him down and around the curve of the stair, then closed and barred it behind him.

"We had a watcher," she said flatly.

"I know," Gwynn replied and laughed. So, finally, did Robin. Gwynn took up some plain sewing and moved back to the fireside, while Robin curled up on the hearth, staring into the fire, until the last of the sounds below died away. Then, after a cautious peek into the stairwell—which proved that at least tonight no one had barred the door from outside—they began the evening's painting.

Chapter 6

The next several days passed with little change from this one, except that her eye and bruises faded and healed. She went about her daily business, seeing Bretagne only in passing as he came and went with his men. Ursula, however, was a constant presence; when she wasn't lounging at one of the fires in the hall, she was in the second seat at the otherwise empty High Table. Gwynn could only imagine that she *thought* she was establishing—or re-establishing—her position as the most important woman of the household, but the only thing she accomplished was to look like a bone-lazy layabout. Perhaps the men-at-arms weren't affected, but every working woman, and a good many of the male servants, began casting looks of resentment at her before too very long.

Ursula was in the process of making herself cordially hated by every underling in the keep, which had the effect of edging more support over to Gwynn's side. *She* was not closing herself up in her solar, playing the fine lady, although she and everyone else in the keep knew that she was perfectly within her rights as Bretagne's wife to do so. No, she was down in the stillroom making medicines, remedies, soaps, rushlights, tallow-dip candles—the many items long needed in the running of the keep, which no one had been making for many years now since Bretagne's mother had died. Or she was in the kitchen, not only supervising but teaching, even preparing food herself, helping the cooks become proper cooks again. Or she was helping to clean, as well as directing the cleaning, or in the tiny dairy—for there was one, after all, though all the milk had to be brought up from the keep farms down below—or…

Well, there were hundreds of tasks to be done, and unless she was recovering from a beating, she was down there doing them. Nor was there any doubt, when she finally appeared after the beatings, of *why* she had merely issued orders rather than appearing herself for a day or two and that she had not been lazing about.

She had been accustomed to being the lady of a much smaller household than this, where every person needed to turn a hand to the work; she saw nothing demeaning in continuing that practice here. And though this might be a *much* larger household than her father's, it had been so long since it was properly run that only the oldest servants truly knew what must be done and how to do it. There would be no sitting for hours at an embroidery frame in the solar for her for a very long time to come.

Not surprisingly, she was dreading the day when she would have to once again present herself to her husband for his—ungentle attentions. If only he could have been summoned to the King for some campaign or other! Her life had been so very peaceful, even pleasant, during the week when her courses kept her from his bed—

She greeted the first morning when they were over with a sigh and a distinct lowering of her spirits. Robin noted, of course, but a few of the more perceptive of the servants noticed, as well, and probably guessed the cause. There was one relief, at least; good, clear weather sent Bretagne out with a hunting party at dawn, so at least the keep would be utterly free of his presence until near sunset.

A great keep such as this one could not store enough to feed all of the people within it, and hunting was necessary to keep everyone fed over the course of the winter. The huntsmen would go out every day for the hares that had been snared, and other small game, but only the nobility could slay the deer and boar—the deer by King's law, and the boar because it took a well-armed hunting party to bring one down. With good fortune, Bretagne and his young knights would return with fresh venison or wild boar to augment the larder.

With *better* fortune, he would return gored to death or with his neck broken—

She winced and set those thoughts aside, attractive as they were. She knew better than to make such a thought into a wish, for there was always the chance it might come to pass, especially for one such as she. If such retribution came upon him, she did not yet have the right to be the engineer of it.

Now, if he came back black-and-blue and aching in every limb, after having been carried by a runaway horse through a thicket of low-hanging branches, then dumped into a thorn bush or a rocky streambed, *that* would be just retribution....

The thought made her smile and brightened her day, just a little, as she bent her attention on the rescue of a kettle of stew that had suffered at the hand of an undercook with no understanding that a "pinch" of salt did not mean a handful.

Then she retired to the stillroom, where she could work quietly and peacefully, with nothing more to worry about than ointment for chilblains, from which nearly everyone in the keep was suffering. Robin assisted her, which was a great help, for it often took four hands when things were at a critical point in the compounding.

She had just finished putting the last of the cooling ointment into a jar when—

"Milady! Milady!"

The frantic—nay, hysterical—call from the back of the keep startled her, but no more so than the knowledge of danger and urgency that sent her running in the direction of the voice, Robin following, hot on her heels. She literally ran into the maidservant who had been calling her, and the young woman clung to her, sobbing in panic and fear.

This was the way of things in a well-run keep; trust as deep as instinct sent underlings running to the lady, sure that no matter what the crisis, she and she alone could solve it. At that moment, Gwynn knew she had come into her own sort of power here.

"The baby…the baby—" it was all the maid could get out around her tears, but she seized Gwynn's hand and dragged her in the direction of the servants' quarters with surprising strength.

"What about the baby? *Which* baby?" Gwynn gasped as the maid hauled her through a part of the keep that she had not yet been to, one that housed most of the lower servants. There were babies enough here, she supposed, but she didn't *see* most of them; they were kept well out of the way of the adults, or at least, the adults of any rank. Some of them supposedly were Bretagne's get—another and more compelling reason to keep them out of Lady Gwynnhwyfar's way, she supposed….

"My baby—oh, milady—" she wailed, and that was all that Gwynn got from her before they reached the site of the trouble, at the back of the keep, in a windowless little room—and then, all she had to do was to point—

Point to a hole in the floor of a tiny little alcove of a room, from which a thin, weak wail arose.

"The well—" the maid sobbed. "He fell down the well!"

It was easy to see how—there was a wooden cover

that was supposed to shut the well up, but either someone had carelessly left it to one side or the child himself had been just old enough and strong enough to drag it off. In either case, it would take very little to send a young and curious child tumbling down into the depths. Gwynn seized a torch from the wall and dropped to her knees, her heart in her mouth, to peer down the rock-carved shaft—

A contorted face looked up at hers, red, tear-streaked, and another wail echoed up to her. Too young—oh, blessed Jesu, far too young to grab and hold to a rope dropped to it, and heartbreakingly out of reach.

The walls of the well shaft must have been hard to cut, for they narrowed abruptly right at the point where the baby had lodged. Unfortunately that was a good four yards down, and even though the baby had both fat little hands stretched up to her, there was no way in which to get hold of its wrists to haul it out.

And there was always the danger, increasing with every moment, that whatever had caught the baby would give way at any moment, dropping it into the water below, where it would surely drown.

But Gwynn was her mother's daughter—

Gwynn spun and faced the maid. "Run!" she snapped, breaking through the maid's hysterical tears. "Find the cook and Sir Atremus. Get more help. Now!"

Without a word, the maid turned and ran.

"What on earth—" Robin stammered as Gwynn fumbled at the laces of her gown.

"Help me get this off—I can't go down there wearing this—I'll get down as far as I can, then you'll have to hold my ankles and lower me as far as you can—"

"And then what?" Robin demanded, even as she obeyed, stripping the heavy woolen gown from her mistress and leaving her standing there in her linen undergown, her skin already prickling with gooseflesh. "You can't reach the baby even with me holding you!" Then, "Oh," she said numbly as she realized what Gwynn meant to do.

"Yes. And I dåren't have any witness," she said flatly, then pulled the undergown over her head and dropped it on the floor. "Now, hold my ankles and lower me over."

Robin made no further objections. Gwynn edged over the side of the well, crawled down the shaft, then felt Robin's powerful hands grasping her ankles. She waited until Robin was well-braced and slipped down into the dark shaft without any support but Robin's hands. Dark, damp, cold and with the child's frantic wails coming up to her, it was like falling into a pit of the damned for just a moment.

But of course, with a whisper, she called up a witch light, a dim, blue orb that was enough to show her the claustrophobic confines of the shaft and the baby below her, but not enough to dazzle her vision.

This would drain her past anything she had ever done before; it didn't matter, not when there was a child's life at stake.

She concentrated on the baby and began to whisper, to chant under her breath; the chant of the magic mill—the rhythm of magic itself, in time with the heartbeat pounding in her ears.

''Air breathe and air blow, make the mill of magic go, work my will and spin my charms, bring the babe safe to my arms—''

She felt the air begin to move around her, spinning up the power of air to answer her need. A good sign; the magic moved freely here, open to her will.

''Fire seethe and fire burn, make the mill of magic turn, work my will and spin my charms, bring the babe safe to my arms—''

Above her, in the keep, all the flames in all the fires would be spinning now, whirling up the chimneys, adding their power to that of air.

''Water freeze and water boil, make the mill of magic toil, work my will and spin my charms, bring the babe safe to my arms—''

There was water enough here and more, in the breath of the well alone, to add that element to the threefold power that she had woven; she sensed it moving below as the well water began a slow spin deosil to match the air in the well shaft.

''Earth without and earth within, make the mill of magic spin, work my will and spin my charms, bring the babe safe to my arms!''

She felt it—felt strength and energy draining out of her—she heard it, heard the little grate, the scraping below her. And she *saw* it, saw the child shake a little, then saw him start to rise, slowly spinning with the air, magic spinning around it, scraping along the wall, his little skirts tearing loose from the rocks that the fabric had caught on—

She continued to whisper the charm, willing the baby closer, closer—until…

With a yell of triumph that started the child into fresh wails, she caught its wrists with her outstretched hands. The magic snapped then, but no matter; she could hold him and the weight pulling her arms was welcome, welcome—

And just in time; she heard the noise of a crowd, shouting and running footsteps rushing up above where Robin still held her. She extinguished the witch light, lest they catch sight of it, and now with the light gone, the baby howled in fear.

"Pull me up! Pull me up!" she shouted to Robin.

But at that moment she felt more hands than Robin's grabbing her; on her ankles and calves, then hauling at the hem of her shift, pulling her and the baby out of the well shaft together in a tumbling of hands and bodies.

Her body, and that of Robin's—and Sir Atremus. His had been the extra hands on her legs that she had felt pulling her up so quickly!

But she still had the baby as she rolled over. She pulled it to her chest, only half hearing the stammering apologies for the "insult" the men around her had done in placing their hands on a lady, and let them get her to her feet again, still clutching the wailing child, looking for its mother in the crowd.

There! She shoved the baby at the maid who had called her, but it was one of the men-at-arms who snatched the howling child up, as Robin swiftly, and with some indignation, bundled her back into her gown. Of course, the servants had seen far too much already, for there wasn't a great deal of concealment available to one who was dangling head-down in a well, dressed only in a shift....

Her head was swimming, but she fought back the need to collapse onto Robin. The man who had taken the child, though—when Gwynn's head emerged from the folds of the gown, she saw with some surprise that it was—

The captain of the set of guards that had come to bring her to Clawcrag in the first place, who she now knew was named Wulfred. He was—great heavens!—he was cuddling and comforting the boy like a nurse-maid, his own face tear-streaked, one large, scar-seamed hand on the child's back, the other arm supporting him as if this was something he was entirely used to doing, while the maidservant clung to both of them and wept in relief.

"Wulfred?" she said incredulously. "Is this *your* lad?"

He looked up at her with eyes, not cold and calculating, but full of—blessed Mary!—something very like worship. "Aye, my lady. God bless you, my lady. God bless—"

But that was the moment when it all caught up with her, for every bit of power she had needed to haul that child into her own arms had come from her, of course. The four elements—the air and the water, primarily—had only been the extension of her will, something like her arms; the strength had come from her. Only magic that had been planned in advance, calculated, scribed into words of power and shaped into glyphs and figures, using wands and talismans, crystals and potions, came "without effort." "Without effort"—hardly that, but the effort was spaced out over days, weeks, months, even years. Hasty magic, the kind she had just performed, came from the heart and the soul—

—and, unfortunately, the body.

So just as Wulfred set his baby into the mother's arms and went down on one knee to her, she felt her eyes roll up into her head, her knees buckle, and she fainted dead away.

Chapter 7

She woke in her own little bed, in her firelit solar, with no idea of how she had gotten there. "Robin?" she faltered.

"I'm right here," came the familiar, friendly voice. "And cook will have my head if you don't eat *this* and drink *this,* right this instant."

As she sat up, taking support from the head of the enclosure around her cupboard bed and the pillows, Robin walked over from the fireside with a bowl and spoon in one hand, a cup in the other and a great smile on her face.

"What are they? Oh, never mind, I'm hungry enough to eat what passed for food our first night here," she replied, and took the cup first and took a sip. "Good heavens! I hadn't known there was mead to be had in this benighted place!"

"Cook's private stock, or so I was told," Robin replied, and handed her the bowl. "You have made an unconscionable number of allies today. I think if you told Wulfred to lead his men over the side of the keep, he'd do it without looking down."

The bowl held another surprising serving of custard, a much better version than the last—but then, cook had the knack of it now, after her careful teaching. It was topped with beaten cream sweetened with honey, and just the thing for someone who had done the equivalent of running up to the top of a mountain this afternoon. Her hands were even trembling with fatigue as she handled the spoon. It had been this sort of instinctive magic that had killed her mother—but then, her mother'd had no warning of Black Anghus's sorcerous attack, and her mother's magic had been needed to accomplish a far greater goal than lifting a child twelve feet up a well shaft.

"Let us hope it never comes to that," she replied soberly. "Please, tell me that no one told Bretagne what happened this afternoon!" She could just imagine her husband's reaction—rage, of course. He would be angry that she had "exposed herself" in the course of the rescue, angry that she had bothered about a lowborn child, and absolutely enraged that she had won the devotion of the men-at-arms, especially his captain.

"Be easy. No one is foolish enough to have breathed a word of this to Baron Bretagne," Robin said tartly, making her heave a sigh of relief. "Nor has Ursula heard aught. His men know him and his tempers better than you, my lady, and as for you—well, all that Bretagne knows is that you are ill. He was told that you swooned for no particular reason, as delicate ladies are often known to do, and both the baron and his leman have been loud in the scorn that you are such a poor stick of a woman. Neither of them, of course, took any thought as to whether his last beating might have caused you some lasting injury."

"Or perhaps they have," Gwynn corrected with a tightening of her lips.

Robin frowned. Gwynn finished both the mead and the custard without further comment. She discovered that she was still fully clothed, though, and decided to assess her own recovery by climbing out of bed. "I hope that you have brought me stronger fare than custard," she continued after a step or two proved that she was strong enough to stand on her own—and anything more would be easily remedied with food and rest. "I still hunger, let me tell you!"

Robin had brought plenty of food, of course, for this was not the first time Gwynn had depleted herself in such a manner, and Robin knew well what Gwynn would need afterward. But as she ate, she realized that she had escaped her husband's attentions for another night. And that seemed reward enough.

At that moment a tapping on the door frame made her look up with dread, fearing that Bretagne had decided to see what ailed his wife himself. But that dread turned to delight when she saw that the visitor was not Bretagne, but Atremus, peering anxiously from the doorway, his face clearing as he saw that she was all right.

He entered the room when she beckoned, and then, unexpectedly bowed low to her.

"How now, Sir Knight!" she said with surprise. "What means this?"

"My lady, were you my esquire, I would have knighted you this day for your valor," he replied, bending to kiss her extended hand. "As it is, I can only offer my acknowledgment, small thing though that be. And—if you will take this as the great compliment that it is—my humble assertion that you truly *are* worthy of your blessed mother's memory."

She felt herself blushing and withdrew her hand slowly from his. "I accept the compliment, with gratitude, though I fear that you rate me overhigh. But I wish that you join me in a chess game, sweet friend," she replied, to which he laughed and agreed.

They spent a pleasant evening there by the fire, though Gwynn was wrapped in a great fur coverlet and would look every bit the invalid if anyone should come spying. As it happened, there was little enough chess played that night and a great deal of conversation. She learned more about Atremus than she ventured he would have guessed....

And the only unfortunate aspect of this was that she was only confirmed in her feeling that if she could have been wedded to this man, rather than the one she was, she could have been a very happy woman.

But that was of no matter. A marriage to Atremus would not have bought her father protection. Only marriage to Bretagne, or someone like him, could have.

It had, evidently, been Atremus who had brought her up here to the solar when she had swooned, despite the handicap of his bad leg, just as it had been Atremus who had been first on the scene when Robin summoned help.

She bade him farewell for the evening feeling sad and wistful, though she took pains not to show it.

But she could not help but wonder, as she retired to her bed after another night of painting, if Atremus knew just what that special compliment about her mother's memory meant—to her.

Then, just before sleep, it suddenly occurred to Gwynn, as a bolt from the blue, if perhaps the question she had asked of the Almighty not long ago was the wrong one. Perhaps she should not have asked "Why do I suffer?" but "Why am I here?"

For there might be a reason for her being here—perhaps beyond the simple one, that she had bought her father's protection with her own sacrifice. Perhaps—

Well, that would lead to a further question, wouldn't it? And it was the question that the faithful heart should have asked in the first place.

"What must I do?"

And in the stillness of the winter night, she heard a single word in the depths of her heart.

Listen.

She knew, *knew,* that this was no echo from her

own mind. This was the "still, small voice" within one's heart, but from the Source outside of oneself.

There it was, the answer to the question. This time, the right question. She must listen, and she would learn what she must do, for there was another purpose to her being here that went beyond the simple bargain she had struck.

As the days of winter dragged on to spring, she sometimes wondered how she could bear her life a moment longer—then something small would happen to prove to her that, if nothing else, she was needed here, if only by the common folk of the keep. She was not the only one to suffer from Bretagne's black moods, but sometimes she could deflect his rage onto herself, or find something that would distract him. Unfortunately there was not much she could do to protect any woman of the keep or village that Bretagne found attractive.

She could only pick up the pieces afterward—but at least, she could do that much. And she could advise anyone likely to catch Bretagne's eye how to avoid it, or how to make themselves look unattractive, at least as long as he was about. Binding generous breasts was the least of her lessons, which included the creative use of dirt and the making of temporary warts and blemishes. She knew that her efforts were bearing fruit when she overheard Bretagne complaining how ugly the women of his lands seemed to have become. "Half of 'em are squint-eyed hags, and the other half are poxy," he growled to one of his knights.

She was needed by Atremus, too, and over the course of the weeks, she learned more and more of the knight's history, not that there was much detail to it. He had taken service with Bretagne's father shortly after the last time that Gwynn had seen him—and she suspected, although he did not say as much, that he had been smitten with the elder Gwynnhwyfar, her mother, and had looked for refuge in service elsewhere. He had served his baron well and truly, and he had pledged his liege on the baron's deathbed that he would serve the son likewise. And so he had, until he had taken an injury in a tournament melee on Bretagne's behalf that had left him crippled, at which point he learned just how seriously Bretagne took his own vows to his liegemen. Which was to say, not at all.

Gwynn got the distinct impression from what Atremus did not say that if Atremus had taken more care of his own safety and less of Bretagne's, Atremus would not have been hurt and Bretagne might not have survived to rule.

Atremus was left to heal or die on his own, and discovered that he had been demoted in importance to the very least of Bretagne's knights. Hence, the subtle insult to *her* when he was selected to meet her at the door.

"He would probably have dismissed me, except that if he did, he knew he could get no other knight to serve him—ever," Atremus told her sadly. "And there are times when I wish he would, but at least I have a roof above my head and food on my trencher, and if

I swallow insult with my beer, at least I have beer to swallow.''

There was nothing whatsoever she could say to that; all she could do was to cover his hand with her own in an attempt to comfort. But the touch on his hand made her face suddenly flush, and she averted her gaze so that he would not see it. But she knew what it was; even Robin knew, though thanks be to God, no one else saw, because no one else saw them together.

''You're in love with him,'' Robin said flatly one night after closing the door behind him.

''And I am not foolish enough to risk his life and mine to say or do anything about it,'' she replied just as flatly. ''Perhaps Isolde and Arthur's queen could not control themselves when the passion was upon them, but I *can,* and will.''

Robin nodded with satisfaction. ''Good. I'm pleased to see you aren't going to lose your head over him—literally! Though it isn't beheading you would fear.''

''No. They drown adulteresses,'' Gwynn replied softly.

Robin wasn't finished, though. ''But in that case, are these chess games wise?''

''They are my only unmixed pleasure,'' she admitted sadly. ''And if I did not have them—''

Robin waved her hands wildly, as if to cut off further explanation. ''Never mind. *I* could not bear to see you drooping about like a broken flower. At least now you are holding your head up and even smiling now and again.''

And that was the end of that conversation, but it

lingered in her thoughts long afterward, along with one other thing. The great diagram and all of the spells and enchantments woven into it, was almost complete. There were two days of the year in which it could be used for the purpose that Gwynn intended, and one of them, May Eve, was fast approaching. She wanted to use it. Robin kept giving her impatient and significant glances, as if wondering when she would.

But she did not, as yet, have a justifiable reason to do so. Nothing had changed between her and Bretagne.

Nor had anything come of that single command—to listen—although listen she most certainly had, every day.

Finally, near the end of April, on a cold and rainy day, in absence of any other guidance, she went into the tiny chapel to pray for guidance.

It was shrouded in darkness, with only the tiny, flickering Presence lamp on the altar providing any light at all. Nevertheless, because she did not want to be disturbed, she took a flat cushion and knelt in the corner, where she could not be seen unless someone was actively searching the chapel for occupants.

She emptied her mind and clasped her hands before her—but what came then was no "still, small voice" in her heart. No indeed.

It was, in fact, a clear, distinct, but far-distant echo of voices from some other place in the keep.

One of the voices was Bretagne's. One was another man, whose voice she did not recognize.

"—Border Lords want me that badly, eh?" Bretagne said with a chuckle. "That's a rich price—but how do I know I'll get it once the King's been driven back and the north is free of him again?"

The words made Gwynn grow cold.

"You don't trust a sworn oath?" the stranger replied.

"You're asking me to break mine," Bretagne pointed out. "Why should I trust yours?"

"Would marriage to Lord Seward's eldest daughter serve to appease your concerns?" countered the stranger.

"I have a wife," Bretagne said.

But the stranger laughed. "A wife who you are known to despise, who is apparently barren, who suffers from fainting fits. A man who cannot find a route to bachelorhood with a wife like that is not as clever as you claim to be."

The words made Gwynn grow colder still.

But the next ones turned her to ice.

"Putting her aside," Bretagne said slowly, "would mean losing the income from her rents and rights, which I will not do. The Devil knows I've *earned* it, looking at the whey-faced bitch in my bed, night after night. I might require some help from outside my household, lest suspicion fall on me."

"A small thing to arrange." The stranger sounded indifferent.

"Then...very well. When you next come to me, you must bring word of these arrangements," Bretagne replied, his voice full of gloating. "And when I am a bachelor again, then I shall be glad to entertain your—friends—and their propositions.''

Listen. Well, she had. And she had certainly heard. *This* was justification; Bretagne planned her murder, and treason, both.

She had often wondered why the chapel was where it was—an out-of-the-way corner, inconvenient, cold in every weather. Now she thought she knew; it was the long-ago listening post of some long-dead baron. She would probably never discover who it was, or why he had built it, but it was enough that it had given her what she had not had before this.

She waited for some time with her head bowed over her hands, but either Bretagne and his visitor had moved away from the place that brought their words down to her, or Bretagne had dismissed him. Finally, when her knees were aching and she was so cold that her nose felt numb, she got to her feet and returned to her solar.

As she had hoped, Robin was there; the girl gave her an odd look, for she was not normally in this room during the middle of the day. ''My scissors—'' she said with a sharp glance at the girl, for the scissors were there, in plain sight, on her chatelaine belt.

''Ah. Why...*here* they are!'' The girl walked toward her, feigning to carry something in her hand. As she bent to ''fasten'' the imaginary scissors to her lady's belt, Gwynn whispered. ''We act. May Eve.''

Robin cast her a startled look that turned to one of satisfaction, and nodded.

Gwynn left, to return to her duties, but it was with

her own head a'whirl. Somehow she would have to get Bretagne up to the solar that night—a man who so despised her that he had just planned her murder. It was the one flaw in her plan and it had to be overcome.

Somehow.

Because if she didn't—she might not be alive to try on All Hallow Even.

Chapter 8

Gwynn would have expected Bretagne to pay as little attention to May Eve and May Day as he did every other holy festival, but he surprised her by declaring a tournament for May Day, and a feast for the evening before.

Then again, May Eve was well known for licentious behavior, what with young men and women staying out all night to go a'maying, gathering the spring blossoms with dew still on them. ''May nights make New Year bellies,'' was a saying among the old women, meaning that there were plenty of babies born January to May Day sweethearts who might have actually wedded only in August. And apparently this was something of a tradition for Clawcrag, at least according to Atremus; a May Day tournament and a Harvest Feast were the two celebrations that Bretagne preferred to hold.

Bretagne even went so far as to suggest that *she* ought to try another local custom, of visiting a certain standing stone on May Eve, one that was reputed to bring fertility. She, suspecting that this might be the setup for an ambush, countered gaily with a plan to make a torchlight procession of it of *all* of the married women of the keep and village, and he quickly lost interest in the idea, which only hardened her suspicions. She had kept vigil in the chapel every day since the fateful one, but had not overheard another such conversation. She had also discovered from Wulfred who Bretagne's visitor had been, and obtained a pledge from him to tell her if the fellow turned up again. Thus far, he had not—but Bretagne could easily have arranged to meet him away from the keep.

If he had—if the suggested trek to the standing stone had been an attempt to place her where she could be done away with—then her days truly were numbered. Sooner or later, either his co-conspirator would find a plan that would work or Bretagne would become impatient and do the job himself....

This was hardly a pleasant frame of mind to be in as she woke on the morning of the last day of April and tried to fix her mind on the preparations for the night's feast. Bretagne had invited guests—none of them known to her, and she wondered how many of them were his prospective allies. At least none were Lord Seward and his eldest daughter. The guests had been installed in every available room in the keep—

and some that were *not* technically available; many of Bretagne's knights and a great many of the servants had been displaced, and were either packed double and triple the usual number to a room, or were in the stables or anywhere else a pallet could be laid. Only the solar had not been invaded, but only because up until this very moment Gwynn had been storing the barrels of wine and beer, the precious spices and the expensive sugar and white flour for the feast there for safekeeping. Now the drink was in the hall, kegs tapped and ready, the food in the kitchen and her solar was empty.

The rest of the keep was in a fever of good humor and anticipation, enhanced by the fact that for the first time in years—thanks to Gwynn's planning and preparation—everything was going smoothly. Bretagne himself was nowhere to be seen in the keep; he was down just outside the village, at the tourney ground, where he and his guests were watching the peasant competitions of wrestling, archery, single-stick, quarter-staff and stone-tossing. Which was perfect, for it left the keep empty of demanding guests and allowed the keep servants to get on with the feast preparations.

As the afternoon burned on, Gwynn felt but one thing preying on her mind—that at some point after Bretagne returned, she had to lure him to the solar. The exact time of the spell did not matter, but it must take place between sunset and midnight, or wait until All Hallow Even. And she still had not managed to think of a way to bring him up there in the midst of the feast.

"My lady?" came a call from the door to the kitchen, interrupting her thoughts. She turned with a frown; the last thing she wanted at this point was an interruption! But the speaker was Sir Atremus, and she knew at once that something was wrong—

Nevertheless, she hurried to his side.

"My lady—" he began to whisper, but with great difficulty. "There is something you must know—about the baron—the King—and you—"

His face had begun to sag on the left side, like melted and softened wax. He appeared unsteady...and as he took a single step into the room—

—he collapsed.

Two of the kitchen maids screamed and Gwynn dropped the bread she'd been holding onto the table as her heart seemed to stop, and ran to his side. His face worked as he tried to speak to her, but he was no longer able to do more than make inarticulate sounds. Neither his left arm nor leg were working at all, and his right hand could not manage more than to paw at her.

"Take him to my solar!" she cried, and miraculously, two of the men obeyed her without a word, picking up the stricken knight and carrying him off. And she ran after them, biting her lip to keep from scolding at them, for they were carrying the knight very gently and with as much care as she could have asked.

Up the stairs they went, with the sunset light pouring in scarlet and gold through the window slits on the stairway. She wanted to weep, and dared not; she *knew* what this was, for the same ailment had struck her father in a lesser form—only her father had not collapsed with half his body completely useless.

This was a brainstorm, and in this strength, it was a death sentence, for there was no cure for this, and Atremus, her only friend here, would surely die within days or weeks. He would not be able to swallow, and would waste away, for how could anyone get food or drink into him? And the cruelest blow of all, he would be perfectly awake and aware the entire time—

She heard horns blowing from the walls and the clatter of hooves in the outer courtyard—Bretagne and the guests were back, which would signal the start of the feast. She heard another horn echo inside the keep—the call to table. She wouldn't be there—

It didn't matter.

The servants had their orders and knew what to do. He would hardly miss her. He would probably put Ursula in her place.

Robin arrived at that moment and took in the situation at a glance. As the maid helped her lady, Gwynn turned to one of the two fellows who had helped carry the knight here. "Tell them what has happened, and that either I will be down in a moment or I will send a further message."

Atremus could never fit into the cupboard bed; as a consequence, she took cushions and blankets and made a pallet for him on the floor. And it was at that very moment, when a chance movement uncovered a bit of the painting on the floor, that it came to her.

She suddenly knew exactly what she was going to

do tonight; there would be a change in plans. It was audacious; it was, possibly, the most foolish thing she could do. But it would give Atremus another chance at life and perhaps—

She would not think of the "perhaps." Only what this meant to Atremus.

She knew the exact placement of every bit of the diagram; she placed the pallet with excruciating care and the men lowered Atremus down into it. Now only his eyes could follow them as his limbs and mouth trembled.

"You can go, and thank you," she told the remaining man, who bowed to her, cast a pitying glance at Atremus and fled. He, too, knew very well what fate awaited the poor knight.

"Blessed Jesu," Robin muttered, looking down at Atremus, her face a mask that concealed her feelings. "My lady, what is to be done? He—"

"Robin, you know what we do tonight," Gwynn replied, standing up and taking the maid's shoulders with both hands. "And I can only think one thing—*he* is to take your place."

Robin stared at her, and if the situation had not been so grave, it would have been comical to see how relief and horror chased each other across her face. "But…my lady! The risk for you! He has not been—he does not know—"

"I am about to tell him," Gwynn replied, her heart pounding in her ears with fear, the taste of fear metallic in her mouth yet not unmixed with hope and excitement. "And as for what will happen when we are done—that is in God's hands. Now, do you clear and prepare the room, while I explain it to him."

Once again, Gwynn knelt at Atremus's side while Robin prepared the room for a Great Work. She cleared away the rushes, lit candles she removed from the secret compartments of the chest and placed them at cardinal points in the diagram, lit incense in a censer, and placed Gwynn's white and black knives in the center of the diagram, awaiting Gwynn's hands.

"My sweet friend," she began, taking his unresponsive hand in hers and swallowing back tears at his state. "What has struck you has no cure, and you will not recover from it. There is nothing that can be done for you, as you are."

His eyes stared into hers and she thought she read in their sad depths the acknowledgment of that truth, the knowledge that he was doomed.

"But I do not intend for you to die." She gulped. "Though what you will think of what I am about to do, I cannot tell. You spoke more truth than you knew when you compared me to my mother. Like her, I am a sorceress. I learned my business at her knee. Like her, I bought my father's safety with my life—in her case, it was to save him from the evil power of the black magician Anghus, and in mine, I purchased his safety against Anghus's mercenaries from the King with my marriage to Bretagne. But it was always a possibility that Bretagne would continue to prove treacherous, and so we prepared for that eventuality, Robin and I, though the King knew it not, and does not know how dearly we hold our liege's safety. And indeed, Bretagne has proved a traitor still. I heard him, with my own ears, plotting the overthrow of the King with the Border Lords—and *his* price for that treachery was *my* death. I think perhaps...you learned something of that today and came to warn me."

A slight dilation of Atremus's pupils and an inarticulate moan was all that showed his shock and dismay, but as he tried to nod, she knew, then, that he had somehow learned of the baron's plans, as well. She patted his hand.

"Nay, listen, for all is not lost. I told you, there was always the chance that he would prove to be a traitor still, or to wish me harm, and Robin and I did plan for that. Now, let God be my witness, I had every intention of being a good and true wife to Bretagne. I did my best, with all my heart—which he spurned. There is justice in what I do!" The last was a cry, a cry to him for understanding.

He simply stared at her. Did he understand or not? She could not tell.

"Good, my friend—oh, my love!" she said, and then sobbed—then got control over herself, though she thought her heart would burst with the force of her emotion. "Atremus, I confess that I love you. I loved you as a child, with a pure and simple child's love—but when I saw you standing at the door of this keep, my heart leaped to you with a woman's feelings! And the more time I spent in your company, the more I came to love you—the man, the spirit within your shell of flesh, a spirit I would love if you were old as Methuselah, foul as a leper, scarred or maimed! And it is out of that love I bear you that I will dare this thing, whatever you may think of me, though you may repudiate me! This night, nay, this very hour, I shall exchange your soul with that of Bretagne—you shall possess his body, and he yours, and he will die in it, as you would have. I told you that Robin and I had planned for this. It is no light sorcery, and I do not do this without much thought. It would have been Robin's spirit not yours, and this will put me in much peril, for he has always been my helpmate.''

She saw a fog of puzzlement in his eyes and laughed sadly. ''Yes, you heard me a'right. Robin is not my half sister, but my bastard brother, for this sorcery can translate only male to male and female to female. A clever actor, is he not?''

She glanced over her shoulder at Robin, who shrugged and grinned wryly. ''And a cursed ugly wench I am, which made me both my lady Gwynnhwyfar's best guard and safest servant,'' Robin said, dropping his voice into his normal tones for the first time in half a year. ''I practiced this ruse for so long it was second nature e'er we rode here.''

Gwynn nodded as Atremus blinked in shock. ''And it was as brother and sister we would have afterward lived. Robin was prepared to take Bretagne's place and would not have betrayed me afterward—you, well, you may well feel that so wretched a sorceress as I must needs be sent to the stake.'' Her voice shook a little, then recovered. ''I care not. I will take that chance. I only ask this—that you remember your oath to your King supersedes that of your oath to Bretagne and his father, and that when you wear his seeming, you will serve him as loyally as we, in our way, have done."

There was no time to say anything else, for by now even Bretagne would be wondering at her absence. She rose to her feet and beckoned to Robin. "Tell Bretagne that—" she thought quickly "—that Atremus is dying and that he has something of great import to tell his liege, and that it concerns his fortune."

That should be more than enough to bring Bretagne, hot-foot, from his own feast. He would hear the word "fortune" and in his greed, would assume that the old knight had a treasure squirreled away somewhere.

Robin nodded and marched out the door without a single word. Gwynn took her place in the middle of the diagram, took up the black knife made of volcanic glass in her left hand, the white one made of bone in her right, crossed her arms over her chest and, with three words of power, activated the first of the spells.

The lines of the diagram flared with sudden incandescence and glowed a fiery red. A wind of both air and magic, carrying tiny motes of energy like sparks from a fire, swirled up and around her, making her skirts dance and tendrils of hair that had escaped from her braids float in the light.

She heard heavy footsteps running up the stairs and smiled. It was as she had thought. Bretagne's greed brought him to the trap.

"Atremus!" the baron shouted as he burst through the door. He was three steps into the room—and right in the middle of the second circle of the diagram, before he realized that all was not as it "should" be.

He stopped dead in his tracks. "What—" he said stupidly.

She shouted three more words of power and froze him where he stood.

Once again the lines of sorcery flared and glowed brighter than before. The wind borne of magic picked up, now swirling her skirts around her, surrounding her in a storm of sparks. Robin edged inside the door, slammed it shut and barred it against intruders. Not that Gwynn expected any. The servants were all fully occupied, and the guests being served the first of many delicious courses of food, with a set of comic tumblers giving them good and noisy entertainment. Even if Bretagne could have bellowed—which he could not, his voice being paralyzed along with the rest of him—no one would have heard him.

No, now was her hour—and she felt, for this moment at least, like a goddess of Justice.

"Bretagne of Clawcrag!" she shouted against the whine of the wind of power, flinging out her left hand, pointing at him with the black-bladed knife. "As God is my witness, I call you murderer, traitor and oathbreaker! Oathbreaker, that you forswear your vows that you made in exchange for my hand and fortune! Traitor, that you betray your liege lord and King to his enemies! Murderer, that you conspire to slay your King and your wife! I call you to justice, Bretagne of Clawcrag! I call you to answer for your crimes, and I summon all the powers of Earth, Air, Fire and Water to aid me! Gabriel, Michael, Raphael and Uriel, witness this work and lend me your power!"

She pointed the white-bladed knife at Atremus. "Atremus, Knight of the Realm, true-sworn liegeman to our King, I make of you the instrument of Justice! Let *him* serve your life, what is left of it, and let *you* take his place to be a true and loyal knight to your King! Gabriel, Michael, Raphael and Uriel, witness this work, and lend me your strength! *As I will, so mote it be!*"

From the tip of each knife, with a crack like lightning, a lance of power shot out and impaled each man. Gwynn was the center through which the power flowed—Bretagne convulsed and shook, his eyes bulging, his mouth open in a silent scream. The chamber was lit as bright as day by the glowing lines of energy, by the bright lances of magic, by thousands of tiny lightning bolts crackling from Gwynn's body and striking randomly about the chamber. The pentagrams she had painted invisibly on the walls were glowing, too, feeding the spell, and she felt, heard, tasted, smelled nothing but the mighty force that held her transfixed, the still center of a whirlwind.

It was—intoxicating, and all-consuming; there was no room in her mind for anything but the words with which she shaped the spell and she held them…held them…held them—

Until, with a sudden *snap,* and a last flare of light, the spell was complete.

The chamber dropped into darkness, lit only by the candles on the floor and the fire in the fireplace, silent and still.

Bretagne swayed and nearly fell. Atremus thrashed—or tried to—and began to howl, a garbled and inarticulate jumble of nothing like words. By that alone she knew that her magic had worked—it was Bretagne's foul spirit that was lodged in Atremus's poor, failing body, and Bretagne was not amused.

Bretagne—or his body, at least—recovered first. He blinked; he looked around. His gaze fell on Gwynn and he took four purposeful strides that carried him across the room to stand beside her, before she had even gotten her wits about her.

"My lady," he said. "I believe we have some business below. The company awaits, and there is much that I must say to them."

And before she could say *anything,* he seized her hand and led her—nearly dragged her—toward the door, then out of it, then down the stairs.

She was tired, so tired—and so numb of spirit, the expected aftermath of great sorcery—that she simply *let* him lead her. She did not know what he intended, but it hardly mattered. Her fate was in God's hands now and if he chose to denounce her in front of the entire company—

Well, if she could not live with the man she now knew she loved with all her heart, she was not sure that life was worth the living.

As he drew her onto the dais behind him, the entire hall fell silent.

Ursula was, as she had expected, in *her* seat, looking smug and self-satisfied. When she saw Bretagne dragging Gwynn by the hand, she looked even more pleased.

Bretagne pulled Gwynn to the side of the High Seat—then suddenly dropped her hand and grabbed Ursula's chair with both strong fists and yanked it out from under her. The strumpet landed on the floor of the dais with a *thud* and a yelp.

"Out!" Bretagne shouted. "*Out!* Gather your goods and go! You may have a single mule and all you can carry, but be gone from my lands by sundown tomorrow, or by sweet Jesu, you'll find yourself in a Magdalene convent before you can blink!"

As Ursula scrambled to her feet, her face holding mingled disbelief and anger, he "helped" her up with a toe to her well-padded backside. "You and you—" he said, pointing to two of his men-at-arms, neither of whom had any love for the wench. "You go with her and see that she doesn't take what she isn't entitled to, then follow her until she passes our Borders!"

Without further ado and with great relish, one yanked Ursula off the dais, and both of them hustled her out of the hall before she could even squeak.

Now Bretagne turned to Gwynn—and with both hands on her waist, he lifted her to stand on the seat of his chair.

"Friends, neighbors—" he said, addressing a company still held silent by shock and surprise. "This sweet lady...this, my good and true wife, has been—much abused. He to whom she should have looked to for protection and honor has been treating her as...as—" He shook his head. "I cannot say how ill he treated her. This wretch, my former self, this vile creature who she consented to wed—did not and does not deserve so good a woman, and the fate and words of Sir Atremus have brought a revelation. I am reborn into a new self and I see what great ill, what terrible dishonor has been done to her, and I hope in time to achieve her forgiveness."

He turned and took both her hands in his, as she stared down at him, hope and joy beginning to dawn in her heart and tears starting in her eyes even as a smile curved her lips.

"So I ask you, my lady, my friend and my love, will you forgive me all that has been heaped upon you these past six months? Will you permit me to be to you the husband of your hand and heart? Will you allow me to lay my life at your feet?"

She tried to answer his eloquence with her own, but tears flooded her eyes and choked her throat, and all that she could do was to answer, "Yes—"

But it was enough. With a mighty roar, the entire hall erupted with the cheers of the assemblage, as Bretagne lifted her down and into his embrace.

A gentle embrace, not the crushing grip that the "old" Bretagne had once used to flatten her into submission. The kind of embrace that she had dreamed of and never dared hope for, as Bretagne turned her tear-streaked face to his and placed his lips on hers in a warm, passionate kiss.

Her knees went weak, she melted into his arms, half delirious with a surge of unexpected desire that fired her loins and wilted her will. It was a very good thing that his arms were supporting her or she might well have collapsed to the floor at that moment.

But he was not finished.

He lifted his mouth from hers long before she was ready and signaled to two manservants. "Go to my lady's solar," he said quietly, "and remove that poor old knight. Place him in Ursula's chamber, and send someone to tend him. We must keep him comfortable until he dies, which, for his sake, I pray will be soon. I would not have him suffer longer." The men nodded sympathetically and hastened to do their lord's bidding.

He looked back to the assemblage. "Let it be known both far and wide," he said, his voice now full of threat as well as promise. "That he who so much as offers insult, much less an injury, to my lady, will feel the full weight of my wrath—and hell itself will not be so deep that it can hide them!"

There was a hidden meaning there, which would be understood only by those who had attempted to conspire with Bretagne to murder Gwynn and to undermine the King. *There will be no bargain.* Whoever they were—and for Atremus to have come to her this afternoon with his own warning, some one or more of those conspirators must have been among the company—they would probably be puzzled, but they would not be unclear about Bretagne's feelings.

Then Bretagne looked about the company again, with Gwynn nestling in his arms. His eyes scanned the crowd below the High Table, and when his gaze found a monk among the crowd, a stranger in the robes of the Poor Friars, he beckoned to the man.

"Father," he said as the man came forward and the cheering eased then stopped so that those watching could hear what was to come next in this evening of surprises. "I have a great favor to ask of you. In light of this, and of my pledge to now be a true and gentle husband to this lady, would you say the words of marriage over us again, and renew our vows?"

The monk gaped at him, but quickly recovered his wits and nodded hasty agreement. His eyes gleamed a little, perhaps anticipating a golden reward, and he raised his hand to make the sign of the cross over them both.

The vows were quickly exchanged, the blessing as quickly said, and the monk got his anticipated reward as Bretagne stripped a ring from one of his heavily laden fingers and pressed it into the fellow's hand.

Then he led Gwynn to the High Seat and placed *her* in it, taking the second chair from which he had so lately evicted the wretched Ursula. From there, throughout the feast, he plied her with selected dainties, pressing upon her the tenderest bits of meat, the crispest bits of crust, the sweetest pastry. Gwynn was in a daze of happiness throughout the meal, hardly able to think, only to look into the eyes of her husband and see her beloved Atremus twinkling back at her. This, some six months late, was the bridal feast that she had hoped for. And she thought she knew very well why Atremus-Bretagne had had the monk wed her and her husband all over again....

And when the last of the meal was done, the last of the entertainment over, he took her by the hand and led her, once again, up the stairs to the room that had seen so much pain.

There he shut the door behind them both and once again took both her hands in both of his.

"My lady—my dearest lady—" He faltered. "I cannot ever thank you enough, nor repay you for this gift of life that you have given me. And if it is your will that we should live, as you had planned with your sibling, as brother and sister—"

"No!" she all but shouted, then moderated her tone. "No, my good lord," she said more softly, gazing up at him through her lashes, feeling her cheeks warm with blushes. "I told you that I have always loved you, your spirit—how can I love you the less now? It is still *you*—" Now it was her turn to falter. "Unless it is that you have...no feelings for me—"

He laughed—not the loud and crude roar of Bretagne, but the hearty peal of laughter that she remembered from the days when her father had bested Atremus at chess. "No feelings? Oh, my heart, I have loved you from the moment I saw what a woman you had blossomed into! Why do you think I asked that monk to resanctify the vows? I wished to make certain that we were bound in body *and* spirit in the eyes of God!" He clasped her to his chest and once again she melted into his embrace. "My love, my very love—" Then he stopped and pushed her a little away. "But...what are we to do with Robin?"

She laughed. "We send my maid back to my father, where Robin-the-maid will vanish and bonny Robin-the-lad will reappear! My father will legitimize the boy and make him his heir, and a true reward that will be for all his labor and love! He loves Robin as I do, and surely that is a meet recompense for all he has done on my part!"

Once again Bretagne laughed, a true and free sound of joy. "Then I am content, my only love. Now shall we—" His eyes moved to the waiting bed.

Which no longer held any fears for her. She smiled up into his face. "My lord and love," she said softly, "with all the will in the world."

And she knew that she did not need to count crows this time to know what the future held for her.

High up under the eaves of the lady tower of Clawcrag castle, a crow roused out of sleep at the sound of human laughter. He peered down at the glowing window slit beneath the nest he and his mate of a month had built in a niche where the stone offered shelter. Strange. He'd never heard laughter of that sort coming from that place before—strong, hearty laughter, both deep and male and light and silvery female.

Well, let the silly humans carry on all night. He and his mate had more important matters to tend to, the welfare of their two eggs warming in the nest beneath her breast feathers, the second of which had just been laid today.

One for sorrow, two for mirth, three for a wedding, four for a birth....

* * * * *

DRUSILLA'S DREAM

Rachel Lee

Dear Reader,

As sometimes happens, "Drusilla's Dream" isn't exactly the story I set out to write. Oh, it fits the bones of the proposal I submitted. But the characters...

They had minds of their own. From page one they refused to be twisted into my initial vision for the story. Instead, they charged ahead, doing things their own way, and sweet and gentle turned into funny and outrageous.

I'm not sure why they decided to kick up their heels. Maybe it had something to do with being confined to a cube farm. Maybe it had something to do with the fact that Miles and Drusilla are both dreamers who are fish out of water in their jobs, serving time until their dreams come true.

Funny as it may get, "Drusilla's Dream" is all about dreams. The dreams all of us have.

Enjoy!

Rachel Lee

Chapter 1

Drusilla Morgan walked wearily into the GalaxyCom building, facing her night shift with a sense of dread. Another eight mindless, endless hours at a keyboard, entering data. This was not her idea of a career.

No, her idea was to paint. But her paintings weren't selling for much more than they cost in materials, and she still needed to eat, and needed a roof over her head. Someday, she promised herself, things would change. She wouldn't need to work the graveyard shift so she could paint by day in natural light. In fact, she wouldn't have to do anything at all except paint.

Someday.

Someday looked a long way away right now. Her ordinarily irrepressible high spirits were seriously repressed tonight.

In the lobby, just ahead of her in the line to pass

security, she saw that tech geek from the eighth floor. The cute one. He didn't look like most of the moles who did his kind of work, holed up for most of their lives in a climate-controlled room without windows, talking to computers through keyboards as if they were living beings.

No, he looked as if he spent his days outside doing something athletic. Not geekish at all. He was maybe... what? Twenty-eight? Thirty?

Dark hair, dark eyes, neatly dressed in an environment that tolerated anything, including cutoffs and T-shirts with beer slogans.

And powerful. She'd heard he was the head honcho upstairs on the supercomputers, a man who, if she made the wrong keystrokes, could have her fired for slowing down the system or causing a problem. She always felt a little apprehensive when she saw him, knowing he was for all intents and purposes the czar of the graveyard shift.

On the other hand, just looking at him gave her a little thrill, as if the mere sight of him satisfied some deep, unrecognized yearning in her.

He passed through security and vanished toward the elevator. He had enough status to use the elevator that needed a key. The rest of them had to crowd on the regular elevators.

Drusilla passed security and squeezed into an elevator with the other cube-farm slaves. It was, she sometimes fancied, like working in the mines of Moria. Endless labor in the dark, a computer watchdog keeping track of every keystroke, timing her input to make sure she wasn't slacking off, waiting to pounce on any out-of-normal entry.

But, she reminded herself, it was the price she paid for her art. Besides, since it didn't challenge her mentally, she had plenty of time to daydream.

She got off the elevator with the others, and they scattered to their various cubicles, passing one another with smiles and nods but little verve. Tonight it was as if they all shared her reluctance to be here.

The coffee urns were full and fresh as usual, and she waited briefly in line to fill her mug.

Then it was back to her cube, a place that would have been utterly sterile except for her highly prized Boris Vallejo calendar from 1974 and the little pewter dragons holding variously colored crystal balls that she took out of her purse every night and set beside her monitor.

It wasn't even her *personal* cube. She was merely one of three shifts that worked at this same desk. Apparently her predecessor had left early. A coffee splash on the desk was all that marked his passing.

Sighing, Drusilla sat down, reached for the stack of papers in the In box and logged into the system. At precisely 11:00, she began to make entries.

At precisely 11:05, her fingers warmed up now, she allowed her mind to drift into a fantasy far, far away from the unwinking screen before her and the watching security cameras all around.

On the floor directly above her, Miles Kennedy sat at his gray desk, the supercomputers all quietly humming around him. Well, their fans were humming. Computers themselves really made very little noise, compared to the old days.

He ran a quick system check and found that everything was as it should be. The earlier shift had noted a performance discrepancy that had disappeared on its own.

A lot of things could cause that, most of them actually minor. On the other hand…

He leaned back in his chair and scanned the Behemoths—as he thought of his computers—that surrounded him. Coffee? Nah, he decided. Not yet. He was still feeling invigorated from his nightly five-mile run, a run that woke him up enough to do this benighted job.

He wondered if tonight would be one of those nights when all hell broke loose, a night when he worked his butt off, matching wits with microchips, processors and infinitesimal transistors, not to mention cranky programs that had somehow dropped a few bits. Would it be a night when he'd have to call for reinforcements?

Or would it be a night when he could safely doze with one eye open? A night when he could follow his own pursuits on the Behemoths that right now were barely stretching, let alone using, all their muscle.

He waited awhile, but nothing changed. Nobody downstairs messed up. No program dropped a bit. No transistor failed.

So he turned to the system monitors in front of him and tapped in his secret code, opening a private file only he knew existed. A file that would be invisible to even the most experienced prying eyes.

Then he began to type.

In Drusilla's dream, she was a princess. Not one of those flighty girls in satins and silks who needed to be rescued by a hot-lipped prince, but a warrior princess. The kind of princess who could rule a realm and bring a powerful man to his knees.

The only silks and satins she wore were underwear to protect her royal skin from the roughness of her uniform. She carried a shield and a sword, wore a crested helmet and rode a horse better than any man.

But there was a problem in Drusilla's realm. The Key of Morgania was missing, the key to the ancient secrets of the wizards, secrets desperately needed to save her people from the onslaught of approaching hordes.

And her father, the King, despaired of finding it after these many years of searching.

King Cedrick was elderly, and Drusilla was his only child. She had been born late in his life, when he'd taken time away from other matters to marry and start a family. His wife, however, hadn't survived Drusilla's birth.

Once she no longer required a wet nurse, Drusilla had spent her time hanging around the stables and guards' barracks. At first they'd treated her warily, knowing that any mistake they made would reach her father's ears. Slowly they'd realized she wasn't going to stay away and begun to teach her the basic skills she needed to be safe around horses, weapons and strangers. Eventually they'd accepted her as one of their own and taught her the finer points of riding and fencing. And, when they were sure her father wouldn't hear of it, the finer points of gambling, drinking and singing bawdy ballads of lust and adventure.

Now she was as mighty a warrior as any of them, and the only hope of Morgania, her father's kingdom. It was time to put her skills to use.

But Cedrick was reluctant to send his only child on such a quest, a quest he himself had failed at repeatedly.

"You're needed here, my dear," he told her. "My health is failing and no one but you can replace me."

"It won't do any good to replace you if Morgania is overrun by invaders," she argued. "We need the key. Without it, we're all doomed."

"I searched thirty years for that key," he reminded her.

"I know."

"So what makes you think you can find it?"

Cedrick had never been short on ego, but Drusilla wasn't short on chutzpah, at least in her daydreams. "Well, I have a leg up on the problem, Dad," she pointed out. "I don't need to look anywhere you did."

He laughed, a coughing, wheezing sound, then said, "Go ahead, Druse. But you better be back before the snow falls. I'm not going to make it through another winter, and it will be up to you to keep Lord Hedgehog in line. He has his eyes on the throne and he won't surrender it once he's had a chance to sit here. You can't let him have it. Ever."

"Want a cup of coffee, Drusilla?"

Startled out of her thoughts, Drusilla felt her fingers skitter on the keys. A warning flashed on her screen.

"Jeez, I'm sorry," said Cal Osten, the occupant of the next cube. "Didn't mean to scare you. Coffee?"

"Sure." She passed him her mug, wishing him to the devil as she stared at the blinking warning and tried to figure out how to fix it. And why couldn't Cal get it through his head that she wasn't interested in him? It wasn't that there was anything wrong with him, but he just wasn't interested in most of the same things she was. A Boris Vallejo calendar did not a lifelong relationship make.

Upstairs, Miles stirred out of his preoccupation as a warning flashed red on a neighboring screen. It was one he was familiar with. The Behemoth was hiccuping because someone had hit the F1 key and the U key at the same time.

With a few quick keystrokes he corrected the problem, then returned to his other activities.

Downstairs, Drusilla heaved a sigh of relief as the warning flash disappeared and the screen once again indicated that the computer was ready to receive data. She waited, however, until Cal returned with her coffee. When he seemed disposed to linger, she said,

"Cal, I'm sorry, but I've lost time because of the error. I've got to catch up."

"Sure," he said, looking disappointed. "Maybe at meal break?"

"I'm not taking one. I need to leave early."

"Oh, okay." He drifted away.

Then her fingers, and her mind, began to fly.

Darkness filled the Forest of Nurn. She had been on her quest for some days now, tracking an old rumor that the key had been snatched by a beast everyone called Behemoth. But no one knew if Behemoth really existed or, if he did, where he might be. Or why he would have wanted the key. Or anything else useful.

In fact, she realized as she rode her horse slowly through the dark forest, two soldiers behind her, if she were reading this in a book, she would be bored. Well, it was *her* dream, dammit. She ought to be able to make something exciting happen.

But for some reason, nothing did. It was as if her daydream had slipped somehow from her control. The forest remained dark, the only sounds the quiet thud of the horses' hooves on thick carpets of pine needles and the dripping of water left by a recent rain.

The air felt damp and chill to her skin, and with each passing minute the forest grew darker and more oppressive.

Her artist's eye picked out a hundred deep shades of green and brown, and envisioned the brush- and knife-strokes she would need to capture the images she was slowly moving through. But a painting would need a focal point. Herself and her guardsmen?

"M'lady?"

She recognized the voice of Zeke, sergeant of her personal guard, one of the two she had trusted enough and respected enough to bring with her.

She reined in her mount lightly and waited for Zeke to catch up. "What is it?"

"M'lady...we've passed this spot before."

She turned her head sharply toward him. "I know it all looks the same."

He shook his head. "M'lady, I recognize that sapling yonder. I remember the strange way it's forked. And then I looked down..."

She looked down, too, and saw what he meant. The marks of horse's hooves were ahead of them now, as well as behind them.

The back of her neck prickled. "We're going in circles."

"So it seems." Zeke looked around them. "It's growing darker, but the day can't be that far along."

"We need to find a stream."

"But it's hard to hear running water with all the trees dripping."

"Just don't tell me you've seen stick figures and piles of rock like in that movie."

"M'lady?"

Of course, he wouldn't have seen that movie. There were no movies in this world of hers. "Never mind. There must be a wizard around somewhere."

"My thought exactly."

"So the question becomes whether this is merely a spell for the wizard's protection or whether it's directed at us specifically."

Zeke nodded again. "But how do we determine that, m'lady?"

"Well, we travel at a right angle to our present course." At least it sounded like a good idea. "We'll either get out of range of the spell or run into a wizard." She didn't mention the possibility that they might still run in circles. Nor did she want to think about the fact that she'd never been magically gifted.

Oh, she'd had mages try to teach her; after all, she would someday be the ruler of Morgania. But she'd been a hapless student, more likely to blow things up than to counter spells, much less cast spells of her own.

But hadn't there been something about seeing *through* a spell?

Chin tucked to her chest, she led the way to the right and tried to remember. Magic hadn't seemed very important to her back then, because she'd been more interested in learning the art of war. Now she wished she'd paid better attention, however inept she'd been.

Wrapped in a wizard's web. That was what they were. Caught like flies. The back of her neck prickled again and she had to fight the urge to look around. After all, there were two excellent soldiers guarding her back.

Just as she was about to conclude that she had chosen the wrong direction and that the spell was lessening not at all, she suddenly remembered something a magus had told her when she was very young.

Beware the Forest of Nurn, my lady. It will turn you around.

She drew to a sharp halt and the two guards came up on either side of her.

"What's wrong, m'lady?" Zeke and Tertio asked the question at the same instant.

"It's not a wizard. It's the forest."

"The forest?" Zeke looked as if he'd been made to swallow something utterly unpalatable.

"The forest," she repeated. "It's the old magic."

Zeke scanned the area uneasily. "I recall hearing that at one time the forest was alive."

"It's still alive." And meanwhile, part of her brain was wondering why she couldn't do any better than this. She seemed to be stuck in clichés tonight for some reason. Of course, the whole search for the key was a cliché, so what the hell…

"Well," she said, considering the problem since it appeared that it wasn't going to go away. But as she sat there thinking, her steed quiet beneath her, she heard something else. A steady, quiet thudding.

"Someone's coming," Zeke said, stating the obvious. Why had she never before noticed how often he stated the obvious?

"Yes."

She drew her sword, pulling it silently from its leather scabbard. Her two guards followed suit, arranging themselves to back her up.

The steady thud-thud drew closer, even as the forest

seemed to grow misty, transforming slowly into another world.

Then horse and rider emerged from the mist, a tall white stallion mounted by a well-built, handsome man she recognized.

"Hi," he said, looking rather startled at the sight of their swords. "I'm Miles, the Behemoth Tamer. Are you lost, too?"

Chapter 2

They cleared away the pine needles and dug a pit, in which Zeke and Tertio built a warm fire to hold the chilly mist at bay. Then the two men took up guard, while Miles and Drusilla sat by the fire and made a pot of hazelnut coffee.

"I never would have thought of bringing hazelnut coffee," Miles said.

"Why not?" she asked. "It's my world."

"That's a good point." He laughed then, an expression that surprised her with its warmth and also its array of even white teeth.

"I'm looking for the Behemoth," she told him.

"Why?"

"I think he has the Key of Morgania."

He frowned. "What's that?"

"It's..." She sought a way to describe it. "It's a

book, actually. A wizard's book. Full of knowledge of how to protect Morgania."

"Magical knowledge?"

She nodded.

"Sounds important."

"So if you're the Behemoth Tamer," she said logically, "you must know where he is?"

His hazel eyes met and held hers. "You're very pretty, Princess."

In spite of herself, she flushed. "Stop it. We have important things to discuss."

He shrugged and laughed. "I feel like I've seen you somewhere before."

"Lots of people have seen me before," she said with mild irritation. "I'm the princess. I make a lot of public appearances. So where's the Behemoth?"

"In a cave."

"Ooookay," she said, her tone indicating impatience. "Which cave?"

"I don't know."

She gaped, then frowned at him. "Then what good are you?"

He shrugged, a twinkle in his eyes. "None right now. But if I ever find him, I can tame him."

She sighed and poked at the coals under the coffeepot. The delicious aroma rising in the steam from the spout told her the coffee was just about ready. "So that's what you're doing? Looking for him?"

"Isn't that what life is all about? A quest?"

She glanced his way again and felt their eyes lock,

felt something pass between them, something at once electrifying and terrifying.

Quickly she dragged her gaze away. "It's not funny. My people will be overrun by the southern hordes if I don't find the key. It's the only way to save them."

"Hmm." He nodded. "Is that coffee ready?"

She considered beaning him with the pot, then reminded herself that a Behemoth Tamer could eventually be useful. Instead, she filled the two tin cups waiting beside the fire. "So there really is a Behemoth?"

"Yes, there really is a Behemoth."

She could almost hear the word *Virginia* tagging along at the end of his sentence. "You've seen him?"

"Her. Yes. She's huge, gray and scaly. With an unpredictable temperament."

"So what happened?"

"She vanished one night." He lifted his cup and sipped the coffee, sighing with satisfaction. "Delicious, Princess. Thank you."

"You let her go?"

He eyed her. "Princess, I'm telling you, Behemoths are unpredictable. Sometimes, even with the best taming in the world, they still run away. I've been looking for her ever since."

"I thought she was only a myth."

"That's because she doesn't usually hurt anyone. She just goes off and does her own thing somewhere. But if she's in a foul mood she might, um, cut my career short. Or someone else's."

Drusilla nodded, absorbing this information. "So she's dangerous."

"She can be, yes."

She looked straight at him. "Can we join forces?"

He thought for a moment. "I don't see why not. But our first problem is getting out of these woods."

"Uh...yeah." She sipped her own coffee and called to Zeke and Tertio, telling them to come get some. They emerged from the mist like wraiths, and moments later disappeared back to their posts.

"Your bodyguards?" Miles asked.

"You could say that. Or you could just say they're my fellow soldiers."

"Yeah, I saw how you pulled that sword. A feisty princess, huh?"

She scowled at him. "I'll have you know I'm one of the best warriors in Morgania."

"Good. Maybe you can protect me." Then he laughed, and she wanted to smack him.

She gave him her best royal frown. "I'm not kidding."

He stopped laughing, but his smile remained. "I didn't think you were. I've always been attracted to Amazons."

"Will you get serious?" She didn't like the way her heart fluttered, especially since she knew nothing about this man.

"I'm perfectly serious. But if I'm disturbing you, I'll stop. Anyway, before we can find any Behemoths *or* any keys, we've got to get out of these woods."

"You said that already."

"I know." Again that hazel twinkle. "I'm just moving us to comparatively safer ground."

Drusilla wasn't used to men who made such bold references, not in her fantasies or in her real life. In fact, in both, she avoided men who were like that. Where had this one come from? He wasn't the kind of character she usually dreamed up.

For an instant the fantasy shimmered and she could almost see her computer and the keyboard and the lists of numbers she was entering so industriously.

She had a choice. She could focus on her work. Or she could put up with this presumptuous, unpredictable character who had emerged from some strange corridor of her unconscious.

She would put up with the Behemoth Tamer, she decided. At least he was interesting, however irritating. Anything was better than endless streams of digits.

The shimmering stopped and the daydream fell firmly into place again.

But as it fell into place, she realized things had changed. Miles was standing, his back to the fire, a short sword in his hand. Where had that come from? She didn't remember him being armed.

"What's wrong?" she asked, immediately springing to her feet.

"Didn't you hear it?"

"Hear what?"

He glanced at her. "Something's out there."

"Zeke and Tertio?"

"Shh."

She didn't like being hushed, never had, but this time she simply clamped her jaws together and listened. All she could hear, though, was the endless dripping of water from the trees, sounding magnified in the thick mist.

Then, as if from a distance, came a low moaning. It sounded like nothing Drusilla had ever heard before, a strange ululation almost beneath audible range.

"What is that?" she whispered, feeling her neck prickle atavistically.

"I don't know." Miles looked at her. "I've never heard the like."

"Me neither." Instinctively she moved closer to him and drew her own sword, though she suspected it would be useless against whatever was making that sound.

"Zeke?" she called. "Tertio?"

"Shh," said Miles again. "Do you want it to know where we are?"

But there was no response from either of her guards, and Drusilla's stomach sank. "I think it already knows."

Their eyes locked. The moaning came again, this time from somewhere closer.

Drusilla drew a sharp breath.

"Want some Skittles?"

If murder hadn't been a crime, Cal would have died right then. He was peering over the cubicle wall at her, holding out the colorful bag of candy.

Ordinarily she would struggle to be polite and say,

"No, thank you." But her hair was still standing on end, her heart was hammering, and the echo of that moan was still loud in her ears.

So she glared at Cal, her fingers frozen over her keyboard. "Cal, I'm concentrating."

He smiled sheepishly. "You're typing so hard and fast, you're going to burn up the keyboard."

"I told you, I have to leave early."

"Yeah, but you don't have to make the rest of us look bad by getting so much done."

The warrior princess would have climbed over that fragile wall and put Cal in his place: butt firmly planted in chair, face pointed toward his monitor. But Drusilla of the real world couldn't do that. Here, she was an ordinary mortal, bound by the laws of the land and the rules of her company.

"Cal, please," she said. "Please don't interrupt me. I've got to get through this stack before I can leave."

"Okay." His face fell. "Sorry, Druse."

"Sure. No problem."

She turned back to her keyboard, settled her fingers over the data entry pad and fixed her eyes on the endless rows of numbers she needed to record for GalaxyCom's many subsidiaries. Sometimes she thought it was a duplication of effort, but it had been explained to her, and the rest of the clerks here, that written reports were required from each subsidiary, so they could be matched up to the data entered automatically in the system. To catch problems. In short, to catch embezzlers and the careless.

Now where was she?

But she couldn't remember. She'd been running on automatic and had no idea what she'd already entered and what she hadn't.

Oh, God. Now she *was* going to kill Cal.

Reaching for her mouse, she scrolled upward, hoping to find her place. Yes, there it was.

Relieved, she began to type again and hoped she could recover her daydream. It had been so real. So amazingly real. And the anxiety she was feeling right now about the princess's situation was not in the least imagined.

Where had she been?

The moan. From somewhere nearby...

Miles put a finger to his lips and gestured to her. She followed him out of the circle of light cast by the campfire and into the dark, misty woods. When they were deep within the shadows, the firelight dimmed by the perpetual fog, they hunkered down at the base of a huge, ancient tree.

"I need to look for Zeke and Tertio," she whispered.

"Later. If they have any sense, they're hiding, too."

"But what if...?"

He laid a finger over her lips, silencing her. The touch was warm, gentle. "Don't think about that. Right now we've got to figure out what we're up against."

Reluctantly she agreed. Both Zeke and Tertio were among the best of the guard, and they would know what to do. It disturbed her, though, that they hadn't come to check on her. Warrior though she was, capable though she was, she was still the princess of the realm, and they were supposed to keep an eye on her. She feared something terrible had happened to them.

A chattering caught Drusilla's attention, followed by a burst of recognition. The chattering came from the teeth of her two guards. And the distant, growing howl they'd been hearing was the north wind of Trayen.

"We have to cover up," she said to Miles. "Now."

Chapter 3

"We can't be that far north," Miles said, even as he slipped his blanket roll off his shoulder and carefully opened it. "We'd be leagues off course."

The wind soon proved them wrong, sweeping through the woods with a bone-numbing chill. Drusilla found herself sharing the blanket with Miles, and not entirely sure how she felt about that. On the one hand, she was at least warm, physically. On the other hand, there was another warmth building, a pleasant heaviness in her loins. On the third hand—she made a note to add a three-handed creature to the story—she had not come on this adventure to get laid. There were bigger fish to fry.

"Shh," Drusilla said. "Did you hear that?"

There was a sound. In the distance. Faint but audible

above the wind, a *thump-squish-creak-plop-swish,* repeating again and again.

Miles's face darkened. "Oh, no."

Zeke and Tertio materialized at the edge of the clearing, Zeke's eyes wide despite his attempt at courage. "What was that?"

Drusilla glanced over at Miles, catching the briefest of nods. "Somehow, we're way off course. We're almost to the River Mopenwachs."

Tertio shuddered. "That's not good, is it?"

"No," Miles said. "For one thing, it means we're too far north."

"And the other thing?" Zeke asked.

"Is Krusti Olfard," Drusilla said. From the look on Zeke's face, he wasn't familiar with local mythology. "The keeper of the river. Legend has it that he can make the river itself move."

"Mean as a snake," Miles said. "And he has powerful magic. The Wand of El Pomposo. The merest wave of it, even at a distance, can make your stomach roll over. At closer ranges, it causes light-headedness and retching."

Drusilla gathered up her coffeepot and bedroll. "We have to get away from the river. There aren't enough of us to confront Olfard."

But even as she said it, the sounds of the river were coming closer. And they hadn't moved.

"He really can make the river change course," Miles said. "I thought you said it was only a legend."

Drusilla was already fitting her coffeepot into her saddlebag. "Legends have a way of proving to be true.

So let's think about this. The river runs through the woods. If we keep the sound of the river to our left, we should come out on the east side of the forest."

"Right," Miles said.

Drusilla arched a brow. "No. If we keep the river to our right, we'll come out on the west side. We need to get to the east side."

Miles held up a hand. "I meant, right as in correct. We need the river to the left."

"Right," she answered with the barest flicker of a wink. Zeke and Tertio exchanged confused glances. Drusilla mounted her horse. "Let's get moving."

They mounted their horses awkwardly, still wrapped in their blankets, and once again tried to negotiate the twisting paths of the forest. Even with the sound of the river as a guide, navigation was not easy. The trails all seemed to turn in the wrong direction at the wrong time. Worse, the sound of the river was beginning to overshadow that of the wind. Miles seemed to read her concern.

"I know," he said. "It seems like the river keeps getting closer."

"Rivers bend," she said, trying to be brave.

"Sure they do. But this seems more...focused."

"Like Olfard is working his way toward us?" she asked, trying to ignore the faint but growing scent.

"Exactly," Miles said.

A little while later, Drusilla reined in her steed and sat listening for a few moments. "It's definitely coming nearer, and I really don't want to get dunked by the Mopenwachs. Does anyone have any idea what time it is?"

But of course she'd forgotten to provide watches in this world of hers. "Okay, okay. Maybe it's not past darkfall. I'm going to climb a tree and see if I can get a sense of which way to go."

Miles startled her by reaching over and touching her gloved hand. "I'll climb the tree, Druse. It's something I have to do all the time when the Behemoth is around. Standing out on limbs is something I'm good at."

She hated to let anyone else do anything heroic that she could do herself, but it was so very cold right now that her fingers were feeling stiff. She pulled her cloak around herself, trying to create a tighter cocoon, and nodded royally in Miles's direction.

He slipped off his horse easily and picked the nearest tree that both looked stout and had limbs low enough to reach. He grabbed one of those limbs and, with a movement that would have done an Olympic gymnast proud, swung himself up. Lickety-split, he disappeared upward into the concealing branches, like Jack on his beanstalk.

The horses were snorting steam now in the cold air and moving skittishly, as if they feared holding still. Only Miles's mount seemed oblivious to the threat, nosing around in the shrubs for something edible. He was, thought Druse, probably inured to terror, having seen the Behemoth in real life.

Her own horse was not so lucky. Or unlucky, as the case might be.

Up above, a limb cracked loudly. The three on the ground exchanged glances, but no body came tumbling down at them. Drusilla tilted her head back, looking upward, and realized the treetops had vanished into the mist.

Moisture was now raining down steadily from overhead, dampening their blankets. It smelled strongly of pine, which she thought odd, considering the forest was filled with oaks.

The River Mopenwachs? Was this the spray from it?

Tree limbs began to rustle wildly, then all of a sudden Miles appeared on the lower branches. He whistled and his mount came over to him, allowing him to climb into the saddle from the limb he stood on.

Neat trick, Drusilla thought. She needed to learn that one.

"Well?" she asked.

"The river is surrounding us."

The frigid, damp air suddenly cut through her cloak like a knife. "All the way?"

"We need to get to high ground," Miles said. "Fast."

"Where is that?"

He pointed with a jerk of his chin. "Let's go."

"You know," Zeke said, muttering from right behind her, "this wizardry thing is all good and well, but moving rivers is beyond the pale. And how can he turn a whole damn river into a circle anyway? Where's all the water go?"

"I think," said Miles, "that he's just closing a portion of it around us, like an oxbow."

"Well why in the name of Pampeus would he want to do that?" Zeke demanded. "We haven't done anything to him."

Drusilla answered him. "We got too close." That was the only excuse needed, she thought bitterly. After all, look at the threat against Morgania. Had Morgania done anything to the southern tribes? No. Not a thing. Yet they were about to be overrun. "Some people are just that way."

"All too sadly true," Miles agreed.

And Krusti Olfard had a real reputation that way. An ornery, just-keep-clear-or-else kind of guy.

"Well," said Miles, "he can only move the river. I've never heard that he can move a hill, and there's a hill thataway."

They started in that direction, but one thing concerned Drusilla. "He may only be able to move the river, but he could keep us trapped on that hill for a long time. I don't have a lot of time."

"Who does?" Miles asked philosophically. "Life is short under the best of circumstances. You have to seize the day, as it were."

She frowned at him. "Don't pontificate. I've got a kingdom to save."

"As true as that may be, Princess, a gal can only do what a gal can do."

"I'm not a gal, I'm a woman!"

"Patently."

A few rather bloodthirsty images came to mind, but

Drusilla wasn't a bloodthirsty person by nature, and Miles was, after all, a Behemoth Tamer. She would get even with him later. When there was plenty of time to plot her revenge.

Almost as if he were reading her mind, he laughed. "I *could* just let the Behemoth eat you."

Zeke didn't take kindly to that and moved forward, inserting himself between Miles and Drusilla. "Take care how you talk to m'lady here."

"I'm taking care," Miles said unrepentantly. "I'm just reminding her that she needs to take care, too. After all, she's going to need me. If we find the Behemoth."

"When," Drusilla said pointedly. "Not if. Not even Behemoths can hide forever. They are, after all, big. Or else they wouldn't be Behemoths. It's hard to hide when you're big."

Oh God, had she really looked at his trousers when she'd said that? Had he seen it? This was spinning entirely out of control.

She cleared her throat. "Let's get moving."

"Druse? *Druse!*"

She turned from the screen. Cal was once again hanging over the cubicle wall.

"Do you have a death wish?" she heard herself ask.

Cal blanched. "Jeez, Druse, what's with you tonight? The mouse that roars?"

She wasn't about to answer that question. She wasn't sure she knew the right answer, and wasn't sure she liked the answer that came to mind. "What do you want this time?"

"You have a phone call. I've tried transferring it to you three times, and you won't pick up."

Only now did she hear the faint *bing-bong* of the muted ringer and see the light flashing.

"Sorry," she said, reaching for the phone. "I'm caught up in my work."

"I guess," he said, dipping below the wall before she could launch another verbal broadside.

She brought the phone to her ear. "Hello?"

"Drusie!"

"Dad."

"How's my princess tonight?"

"I'm busy, Dad."

"Are we still on for breakfast?"

Damn. She'd forgotten. "Yes, sure. Casey's at eight, right?"

"That's the plan," he said. He paused for a moment. "Drusie...I saw the doctor today. He said it looks to be in remission. All the blood counts were good."

She let out a long, slow breath. "Thank God."

"I did that tonight. Several times. My energy's back up, too. If I'm feeling this good tomorrow, I may hit some golf balls after breakfast. Wanna join me?"

"I can't, Dad. I need to paint in the morning light. I'm sorry, but I can't."

"You're just afraid I'll beat you again," he said, mirth in his voice.

"Dad," she said with a chuckle, "you haven't beaten me since I was in college."

"You should've gone pro," he said.

"Maybe so."

She'd had the skills. She'd learned the game hanging around the course when he was the greenskeeper. The club pro had taken a shine to her and given her free lessons whenever she was there. But golf was fun, and painting was in her blood. If she'd joined the tour, she would have lost a hobby *and* a dream, all at once. Her future lay with a paintbrush, not a seven iron. Still, she missed the breath of the breeze on her face, the sun in her eyes, the smell of fresh-cut grass. It had been too long.

"Dad?"

"Yes, Princess?"

"If you're up to it, I'll hit some balls with you tomorrow."

She could hear his smile. "I'd love that, Drusie. I'll see you at Casey's."

"At eight. Get some sleep, Dad."

"Now you sound like your mother used to."

She laughed. "Somebody has to do it."

"Nobody better," he said. "Night, Drusie."

"Night, Dad."

It was time for a jolt of caffeine and sugar, Miles thought. The night was deadly dull, except for the one glitch from downstairs. Worse, he'd sat looking at a blinking cursor for the past ten minutes, not sure where to take his story next. With an affectionate pat of the computer and an admonition for it not to blow up in the next ten minutes, he walked down to the break room.

She was there. The pageboy blonde from data entry, the one with the deep blue eyes that always seemed focused on something far away inside her own head. A bit bloodshot tonight. The strain of looking at a monitor for hour upon hour? Or had she been crying?

He slid a dollar bill into the machine and punched a button, listening as the can clomped and banged its way to the slot at the bottom. He glanced over his shoulder as he popped the cap and got the beginnings of his energy fix. Her back was to him, and he watched her draw long, slow breaths.

"You okay?" he asked.

She started. "Huh? Oh. Yes. Fine."

Was that the flicker of recognition in her eyes. He held out a hand. "Miles Kennedy. Graveyard sysop."

She nodded and shook it briefly. "I know. I'm Drusilla Morgan. Data entry."

She'd said the last with an almost apologetic shrug. He met it with a smile. "We get a lot like you."

"Oh?" she asked.

"Sure. People who are obviously too bright to be working down there. University students. Or people who want to do something else and can't yet."

"Well, I'm not a student," she said.

He looked toward the chair opposite hers, a brow arched. "May I? I need to be away from my desk for a few minutes. And I'd rather not read yesterday's newspaper."

She held up the back section. 'Yeah. Someone already did the crossword and the cryptogram. And I hate chess."

"The day shift gets all the fun," he said.

She returned a faint smile, then looked down at the bag of cheese crackers between her hands. Smudges of green and blue at the knuckle of her index finger. A fleck of orange on the outside of one thumb.

"You paint?" he asked.

She looked up. "How did you know?"

He pointed. "Your hands."

"Oh. Yes." She scraped at her knuckle with a thumbnail. "It's hard to get oils off, sometimes."

"I could never paint. I can't draw stick figures."

She nodded. "It's fun. I've done it all my life."

Her responses were a half degree out of sync. Her mind was elsewhere. And that elsewhere didn't seem to be a happy place.

"You sure you're okay?"

The mask descended. Walls went up. "Yeah. I'm okay. Aftershocks of a problem that went away."

"Good that it went away," he said.

"Very good." She rose. "I need to get back to work."

He picked up his can. "Me, too. Have a nice night, Drusilla."

The same small smile. "I'll try. You, too."

"I thought you weren't taking any breaks?" Cal asked as she returned to her desk. He was nothing if not persistent.

"I lied," she said.

"You mean you changed your mind," he said. The subtext was in his eyes: *if you'll change your mind about one thing, maybe you'll change your mind about me.*

Not likely.

"Cal..."

He put his hands up. "I know. You need to work. Nose to the grindstone and all that."

"Something like that," she said, settling into her chair and returning to the endless columns of data. And a world she could control.

Chapter 4

"But enough about me," Miles said. "Let's go find the Behemoth."

Drusilla blanched yet again. So much for fantasy worlds being under control.

"There's still the problem of the river," she replied. "It seems to have wrapped itself completely around us."

"Yeah." They'd reached the top of the hill, which was bald of everything except brush and a few graceful trees, and from their vantage could clearly see that they were surrounded by water.

"Well," he said after a moment, "I guess we wait."

Drusilla looked at him. "Wait? That's hardly a heroic response." Or a heroic adventure. What was going wrong tonight? Why couldn't she slay dragons, defeat wizards and just generally star in her own video game?

"Maybe not," he said, patting his mount on the neck. "But the truth of the matter is, Drusie, Olfard can't keep this up forever. He's an old man. He'll get tired, and the spell will wane, and next thing you know, we'll be crossing dry land."

She scowled at him. "My hero."

He laughed. "Brains beat brawn any day. Well, any day you're dealing with a cantankerous old wizard."

She wanted to argue with him but had trouble coming up with a good reason to. Then it struck her. "My dad is seriously ill, you know. I don't have a lot of time to waste."

Something in his face changed, surprising her. He was not the typical hero at all. Typical heroes didn't get a soft look in their blue eyes, or a gentle curve to their mouths. "I'm sorry, Druse. I really am. How bad is it?"

"He's doing okay at the moment. But I don't know how long it will last. And I have to find this key before...before..."

She was going to cry. But tough warrior princesses didn't cry, so she looked away and swung down from her saddle. With a quick gesture, she signaled Zeke and Tertio to take up watch a distance away. Far enough away that they wouldn't see the glistening of her eyes. She wished she could send Miles even farther away. For some strange reason, she did *not* want him to see her weakness.

Too late. He was already beside her, placing a hand on her shoulder.

"I'm sorry, Princess," he said quietly. "I'm really sorry. If you want to cry..."

"No!" She barked the word and dashed her hand across her eyes. Princesses were tough. She'd been tough all her life, learning to be a fighter rather than a simpering clotheshorse, learning to deal without having a mother. Learning to be a woman in a man's world because someday she was going to be alone on the throne of Morgania.

"You're strong, Drusie," Miles said, stepping back. "Tears aren't weakness."

"Maybe not in your world."

"Anyway," he continued, letting the subject drop, "Olfard has gotta run out of steam soon. Do you have *any* idea how much energy it takes to wield that damn staff of his?"

She looked at him from the corner of her eye. "No. Do you?"

"I tried it once. While I was going to Behemoth taming school, I took a part-time job working for a wizard. Had to wield one of those damn staffs up and down and all around, and when you're doing the water thing, it weighs a ton. I vastly prefer charming Behemoths."

"Do you have any other kind of magic?"

He smiled. "Could be. Maybe you'll find out."

She wasn't sure what to make of that glint in his eye. Deciding it was safest to ignore it, she tethered her horse to a tree near some tasty grass and sat cross-legged on the ground, watching the river that ran all around the base of the hill.

A minute later Miles joined her, sitting near enough to be present, but not near enough to make her uneasy.

"Why," she asked him, "do you think he did this?"

"Krusti Olfard? Who knows. The guy's cranky. We're too close. What other excuse does he need?"

"Well, if we were too close, why didn't he just use the river to drive us south? Why did he encircle us?"

Miles rubbed his chin; she could hear the rasping of the stubble on his cheeks. "Good question," he said presently. "But there's no explaining Krusti."

"You know him?"

"I've met him. Briefly. He doesn't encourage gabfests. In fact, he's single-minded, if you ask me. When he gets to waving that staff of his, you'd better get out of his way."

"Well, I don't care what his problem is. I haven't got forever to get that key."

"Sorry, Princess, but it doesn't matter whether you care. In case you haven't noticed, we're trapped." He pointed toward the water. "And it's getting closer."

A wet splash on her wrist was all the confirmation she needed.

Drusilla jerked back from her keyboard, looking at the water drops on her wrist. A moment later, something heavy and wet snaked around her ankle.

Cal was leaning over the cubicle top, laughing at

her. "Boy, you sure are out of it tonight. Olsen here has been telling you to move."

She swung her chair around and looked into the face of the night janitor, who was swinging a string mop around her cubicle as if she wasn't even there.

"You got me wet," she said.

He looked up at her, his face annoyed. "Not my problem. Next time, don't get in my way."

Cal laughed again. Frustrated, Drusilla refused to leave her cubicle. Instead, she turned around and resumed typing data. This night couldn't end soon enough. Even her sanity-saving daydream wasn't going her way.

"The water will ebb in a minute," she told Miles, once again firmly planted on the hilltop with him, the horses, and Zeke and Tertio.

"How do you know?" Miles asked.

"Because something got into my world that shouldn't have. It'll go away."

He looked at her, brows lifted. "Like this is *your* world? Only *yours?* Isn't that just a bit egotistical?"

She scowled at him.

"Oh, yeah, a *real* princess," he said sarcastically. "Like this isn't my world, too."

With a sigh, she gave up. Clearly things weren't going to go her way. None of them. For whatever reason, events were taking on a life of their own.

"I mean," he said, leaning toward her, "I'm here, too, Princess, oh high-and-mighty one."

"Will you cut it out?"

"Why should I? Just because you happened to be born in a palace doesn't make the rest of us mere ciphers. And surprise, surprise, we don't always do what you think we should."

Instead of feeling stung, she merely felt sad. Very sad. When she looked at him, she could feel her eyes burning. "Life almost never does what I want. Nor do the people in it."

His mouth was open, as if he were about to continue his tirade, but the words never came. His expression changed, annoyance slipping away, gentleness moving in.

"It seems that way sometimes, doesn't it?"

"Most of the time, if you want the truth. I just figured my big adventure ought to go my way just a little."

"It will," he promised, suddenly all heroic and firm. "We'll find that key of yours."

"It's not your problem, you know."

"Of course it is. I made it my problem. Besides, I have a Behemoth to tame." He smiled. "We'll do this together."

"Why?"

"Just cuz."

Then, without so much as a by-your-leave, he scooted over beside her and put his arm around her shoulders.

"You're a pretty good princess," he said bracingly. "I realize I haven't known you that long, but it's obvious, anyway. I mean, you're willing to put your life on the line for Morgania."

She didn't know how to reply to that.

"You could just have chosen to stay home and marry a prince."

"Gag me with a spoon," she said.

He laughed. "Not a homebody?"

"Not me. It's not that I object to the idea of a prince someday, but I'm not gonna hang around the castle and supervise the maids."

"Exactly. You'll be an active ruler. A partner in Morgania. You'll take care of your people."

She looked up at him, wondering why he was saying these things. "It's my job," she said finally.

He nodded solemnly. "The really good people in the world never make sacrifices."

Startled, she almost pulled away. "What does that mean?"

He touched her chin with his finger, a warm, gentle touch that made her want to fling herself into his arms. "What that means," he said, "is that the good people do what's needed and never see it as a sacrifice...even when others would."

"Oh." She still didn't know how to take that. But she didn't have time to think about it, anyway. Because his head was lowering and his face was swimming closer, and she realized that she was about to be kissed by a man.

A real man. Not the childish gropings of her boyfriends from school, but the knowledgeable, knowing kiss of a man.

Her heart quivered and something deep in her belly

quivered, and her quest and the river suddenly seemed far, far away.

In fact, it *was* receding a bit. She looked furtively around and realized that Zeke and Tertio were nowhere in sight. Which meant they couldn't save her. Then she looked at Miles again.

"I don't usually move so fast," he said.

"Move?" Her heart began hammering like a wild thing.

"Um..." He seemed to realize that was a mistake, but it was already too late as far as Drusilla was concerned.

She scooted away from him. "Move? *Move?* Is that what you're doing? Making a move?"

He winced. "I didn't mean it like that."

"You're just like all the rest. Moves and scores, like a woman is nothing but a goal post."

His eyes widened, then a snicker escaped him.

"What's so funny?"

"I didn't mean it that way at all. But now that you mention it, it *does* sound funny."

She glared at him and considered chopping his head off with her sword, but the fact was, she wasn't really as bloodthirsty as that, and besides, she needed him to tame the Behemoth...if they ever found it.

"You're disgusting," she said.

"No, I'm not. I was simply apologizing."

Her jaw dropped. "Do you think I'm stupid?"

"Not at all, Princess."

"Yeah, right." She folded her arms and looked at

the river. It was subsiding, but not fast enough to please her.

"Really." His voice was a purr, and it was coming from way too close. She hunched her shoulders, trying to hold him at bay.

"Princess," he said, "I wasn't making a move on you. I was trying to say that...well...I was getting carried away. I usually wait until I've dated someone to decide whether to kiss her. I...just wanted you to know that I don't kiss every woman I meet the first time I set eyes on her."

She pursed her lips, not wanting to believe him. And also wanting to. Mixed up, in short.

"Really," he said again. "I'm sorry I offended you. I just wanted to kiss you so bad...."

If there was a woman on the planet, this one or the real one, who could resist that, it wasn't Drusilla. Reluctantly, almost shyly, she looked at him from the corner of her eye. Not many men had wanted to kiss her in her life, and most of those had had their eye on the goal post.

"No scores," she said.

"Hell no. What do you think? That I notch my bedpost? I just wanted to kiss you. Really, really wanted to kiss you. Although at this point, I'm beginning to wonder why."

That stung. She turned her head, looking at him fully. And once again his face softened.

He touched her hair ever so lightly, sending a quiver through her. "You haven't been treated very well, have you."

It didn't sound like a question, so she was relieved not to have to answer it.

"I'm sorry." His voice was suddenly low, husky, his breath a warm caress on her cheek. "I guess, being a princess, people want you for all the wrong reasons. That's terrible. But...I just want a kiss. Just a little one, if that's okay?"

Before she could answer, he took matters into his own hands. His warm lips touched hers, light as a butterfly's wings, the merest brush.

But the effect on her was as huge as if he'd set off a bomb in her center. She quivered. She thrilled. She ached.

And she wanted more.

It was impossible to know who moved, but all of a sudden their lips were melding, pressing, caressing. Everything inside her turned soft, compliant, yielding.

And when his arms locked around her, she felt she was in the safest place on earth.

They broke apart, just an inch or two. He looked as startled as she felt. Then they came together again, the kiss deepening, a promise of greater things to come.

Drusilla's fingers dug into his back, clinging to leather and cloth, wanting to get as close as she could. Needing to be closer still. Aching for things she could barely imagine.

All thoughts of her quest vanished, all thoughts of the river, Krusti Olfard, her dad, everything just flew from her head. This moment, this very now, was all that existed.

"Ahem."

They jolted apart and looked around. No one was there.

"Did you hear that?" she asked.

He nodded.

"*Ahem.*"

"Miss Morgan," said a stern voice, "you're not typing."

Drusilla jumped and looked around to discover that the shift supervisor was standing at the entry to her cubicle.

He was a thin man with a long funereal face.

"I'm sorry?" she said, confused.

"Miss Morgan, I've been alerted to the fact that you haven't entered data in the last five minutes."

Damn that computer upstairs. Damn the keeper of that computer.

"I'm sorry, Mr. Wise. I'm...having a cramp."

"In your hand?"

"Uh, no."

The excuse had the desired effect. His face reddened, and he began to back up. "Do you need to go home?"

"No, sir. I, uh, took something for it."

He nodded quickly. "Very well. Very well. Do what you can...."

He fled.

Drusilla would have laughed, except that he might hear her. Except that she was really annoyed he had disturbed her daydream.

On the other hand, getting so involved in a daydream that she forgot to do her work wasn't a good thing. She didn't want to lose her job.

Sternly telling herself to pay attention to the numbers and skip the fantasy for the rest of the night, she put her fingers to the keys again, located her place and began typing.

The fantasy, however, would not be banished....

"Time to move," Miles said briskly. "The river's down. And I don't like hearing things that aren't there. Some wizard has his sights on us for sure."

Reluctantly, Drusilla got to her feet. "But why? We haven't done anything yet."

"I'm beginning to wonder if word hasn't gone out that you're looking for the key."

Their gazes met, and at once she felt a thrill and a chill. "But no one should know. I only told my dad, Zeke and Tertio, and you."

That last suddenly seemed powerfully significant. All the good feelings his kiss had given her began to drain away.

He looked indignant. "Who the hell would I have told? I haven't been away from you for a minute since we met."

"True." She sighed and looked at the ground beneath her feet. "This isn't going at all the way I thought it would."

"Nothing ever does." He sighed. "But somebody else is paying attention to what we're doing. This is one coincidence too many. Voices in the air. Sheesh."

Zeke and Tertio returned then, marching steadily

over the brow of the hill. "The river's passable, Princess," Zeke said. "We can go now."

"It'd be better if I knew where to go," she said, feeling inexplicably sad, as if something had been lost.

"Well," said Miles, "there's a rumor of a Behemoth over on Mount Ayth."

"Really?"

He nodded. "I was headed in that general direction. It'd be a good starting place. I know there are caves big enough on Ayth."

So that was the way they set out, wading through the almost dry River Mopenwachs and through the dark wood beyond.

Chapter 5

The forest gave way into a narrow, twisting canyon. Its walls seemed to lean in on them, as if the earth itself were looking for an opportunity to swallow them. Zeke and Tertio halted their mounts.

"Is this safe, Princess?" Tertio asked. His face clearly said, *I don't think so.*

"People travel this canyon all the time," Miles said. "It's the only way to Mount Ayth."

Tertio didn't look convinced and nudged Zeke. "I hate canyons. I'm bathophobic."

Zeke sniffed. "I can tell."

Tertio punched his arm. "No, dummy. Bathophobia is a fear of depths. Canyons, wells, things like that give me extreme anxiety attacks."

"So do bathtubs, apparently," Zeke muttered, rubbing his arm.

"How extreme?" Drusilla asked, seeing the sheen of sweat that had already broken out on Tertio's face. He was supposed to be among the bravest soldiers in her father's army. Like everything else in this fantasy, this was not working the way she'd planned.

Tertio looked down, humbled. "Um, nausea, shortness of breath. One of the palace wizards gave me spells for it, but I've run out."

Drusilla thought for a long moment. She'd hoped for protection, but it would be a cruel abuse of power to force him to go on. She would hate herself if something happened to him. Finally she drew a deep breath.

"Zeke, please accompany Tertio back to the castle. You know your way back through the forest, right?"

Zeke nodded, looking a bit dismayed, as if he didn't want to return to the workaday world of castle guarding. Then his eyes twinkled. "Yes, Princess, I do. Maybe I can even get him to wash off in the river along the way."

"It's not about baths!" Tertio said, punching his arm again. "It's about depths."

"So take a shallow bath," Zeke said. "Soon."

To Tertio's apparent relief, the two turned their mounts and headed back for home.

"Tell my father I'm okay!" Drusilla called to them.

And then she and Miles were alone....

From ahead came a low, thudding rumble.

...or not.

"I brought you a soda," Cal said. "You look like you need serious caffeine."

Drusilla turned to face him. What *was* his problem tonight? "Cal..."

"Drusilla...you're not right tonight. You're not yourself."

"I'm tired and busy," she said simply.

"Maybe. But you're almost dozing off at your desk. And the shift supervisor keeps looking over here. So...what's wrong?"

The shame of it was, he cared. But she didn't. Not that way. And she knew his type...express even mild friendship and he would read it as an invitation to more. She let out a quiet sigh.

"Cal, please?"

"I'm just trying to help," he said, looking like a lost puppy that had been caught in the rain.

"I know you are. But it's really better for both of us if you don't. You'd get nothing but hurt, and I'd rather not do that."

He nodded. "Will you at least accept the soda?"

"What was that?" Drusilla whispered.

"Unless I miss my guess," Miles said, "it's the Kolakul."

"Tell me you're joking."

He shook his head. He'd heard that sound far too many times to mistake it. A welcoming glow to seduce passersby, then the rumbling, interrupted thudding as it stole one coin after another. In theory, the Kolakul would discharge a shiny, metallic egg when a passerby offered it coins. In practice, it simply took the coins, answering the pleas for eggs with its deep, interrupted laugh. The laugh they'd just heard. And they needed the nourishment of its eggs, without which it would be all but impossible to climb Mount Ayth and capture the Behemoth.

"What do we do?" she asked.

"We hope it's in a nice mood today."

The canyon echoed with its occasional derisive laughter, sometimes punctuated by muttered oaths, as they rode along. Their mounts seemed to edge closer to each other, sensing comfort in proximity, which raised an entirely new discomfort for Miles.

He liked this princess. He'd always wanted to be a brave hero, accompanying an adventurous princess on a dangerous quest. But like so much in his life, he'd doubted that would ever happen. Now it *was* happening, and he wasn't quite sure what to do about it. Truth was, despite his confident demeanor, he really didn't consider himself brave-hero material. There was fantasy, and then there was reality. And history...

"What's wrong?" the princess asked him.

He wasn't ready for this conversation. Not with her. Not with anyone. Not ever. Or so he told himself.

"Nothing," he said quietly. "I'm just thinking about how to coax a couple of eggs out of the Kolakul."

Their calves were almost brushing—their mounts were that close—and Drusilla reached over to touch the back of his hand.

"That's not true," she said. "I've seen your eyes when you were trying to solve a riddle. This wasn't the same look."

Just what he needed. To be a not-so-brave hero with an all-too-perceptive princess. "I'll be fine."

She simply nodded and rode on silently. Dammit, she was supposed to pry. She was supposed to draw the truth out of him, that he was a man who spent his life in the company of Behemoths because he had a genius for them. A genius that had set him apart from his classmates. A genius that his parents had never failed to cite as evidence that an "A" grade wasn't good enough when an "A+" was available. A genius that had hung around his neck like a millstone, damning him to those awful words, "But you have so much *potential!*"

In a world of his choosing, he would put Behemoths behind him and spend his days hammering out and polishing his dream, the great Morganian novel, a story that would lift hearts, elicit tears, keep readers turning pages into the wee hours of the morning and leave them begging for more. He would be comfortably wealthy, take long breaks between books to research, think, plan and crystallize each one into a perfect whole. He would travel, not to tame Behemoths but to experience more of the beauties the world had to offer, to learn about new cultures, to meet new people and enrich his writing.

And he would do all of that with the love and support of a woman who understood what it meant to have a dream and to chase that dream day after day, when it seemed so distant and unreachable, until finally they could claim it together as their own.

Instead, in a world not of his choosing, he tamed

Behemoths, and his dreams were crammed into the fringes of his life. He tapped away at his story when the Behemoths were sleeping, scrawled notes as he rode in search of the next Behemoth, and fought sleep to get down just one more scene before exhaustion claimed him. And all of it in secret, for to fritter away his time on his dream was to betray his genius, his millstone, his *potential.*

The princess should have coaxed this out of him, word by aching word, until she took him in her arms and told him he should forget his *potential* and fulfill his dreams. But she hadn't. She'd simply nodded and turned to the trail that lay ahead.

Anger surged within him, followed immediately by a mental kick to the seat of his pants. This princess was not a character in one of his stories. She couldn't read his mind and shouldn't be expected to perform to a script that only he knew. He was, he realized, being a fool.

He sighed.

"What is it?" she asked.

"I'm sorry."

"For what?"

Confession was good for the soul and lousy for the reputation. Oh, well. "I got angry because I wanted you to pry. And I realized that was foolish and unfair."

She smiled. Not a patronizing smile, but a smile rich with warmth. "No. We never know how much to reveal when we meet people. We don't want to seem narcissistic or maudlin, so we follow social convention and wait for them to ask.''

Now she touched his hand again. ''But I don't like social convention, and I think people reveal things when they're ready and for their own reasons. So I'm willing to wait.''

He nodded and fought the rolling lurch in his chest. She was gracious, honest and apparently patient. An endearing combination. And all the more frightening for that. His hand tightened on the saddle horn.

''Thank you,'' he said.

She apparently felt the tension in his hand, for her fingertips began to gently push between his fingers, as if willing him to let go.

''I was raised to be a princess,'' she said quietly. ''I learned how to use a sword because I hung around the guard barracks. For a while, I considered entering tournaments. But the thought of losing, and disgracing my father, held me back. And I guess somewhere inside I knew that wasn't really what I wanted to do, anyway.''

''You wanted to be a princess?'' he asked.

She let out a short laugh. ''Well, no, not really. But I don't get any choice in that. My father is the king, and that makes me the princess by default. What I'd like to do is paint.''

He arched a brow. ''Paint?''

''I know, I know,'' she said, smiling. ''Fierce, strong, independent warrior princess who'd rather be smearing oil on canvas. Doesn't fit, does it?''

''Actually, it does.''

"Oh?"

"Sure," he said. "First, while you're certainly strong and independent, you're not fierce. A fierce princess would have ordered Tertio to go on, despite his fears. You're compassionate."

She seemed to consider the thought for a moment, then nodded. "And second?"

"Strength and independence aren't inconsistent with being an artist. I'd say they're essential, in fact."

"Perhaps."

"No, think about it, Drusilla. As an artist, you don't have a boss. You have to discipline yourself to sit down and do it, knowing that someone else may look at it and see nothing but meaningless smears of paint. If that doesn't call for strength and independence, I don't know what does."

"It's hardly Behemoth taming," she said.

Now it was his turn to laugh. "Behemoth taming isn't all it's cracked up to be. Believe me. Yes, there's a lot of skill involved, but often as not, one Behemoth has pretty much the same anxieties as the next. It's not what I want to do for the rest of my life."

"Oh?"

And damn if she hadn't coaxed it out of him anyway! She was good at this conversation stuff, far better than he was. She'd probably had to learn it hanging around court, watching her father deal with emissaries and ministers of state. What was it he'd once read? Diplomacy is the art of letting the other person have it your way.

"I like to write," he said simply. "If I could do whatever I wanted, that's what I'd do."

Her fingers wove in between his. "What do you like to write? Behemoth-taming adventures?"

He withdrew his hand. "No."

"I'm sorry, Miles. I didn't mean it like that."

He nodded. "It's okay."

"No, it isn't. I'm sorry for assuming. What *do* you like to write?"

He looked away, studying the canyon walls. That was the rub, wasn't it?

"Miles?" she asked, her voice gentle and reassuring.

When he turned to face her, her eyes offered comfort. She nodded quietly. He drew a breath.

"I like to write love stories."

Oh, now this just wouldn't do, Drusilla thought, jerking herself out of the daydream. She was pleased to discover that her fingers had been busy tapping the keys. At least the shift supervisor wouldn't be looking over her shoulder. She sipped her soda.

Love stories?

Was it some law of the universe that *nothing* could go according to plan? Not even her daydreams? She was supposed to be hacking her way through hordes of monsters en route to slaying a dragon, with a brave, handsome hero beside her, looking for the treasured key that would save her kingdom. Winning eternal fame and her people's everlasting gratitude. Becoming the stuff of legend.

Love stories?

Love was for other people. Soft, simpering women who fell into men's arms, murmuring vacuous words while giving in to their pulsing desires as their bodices ripped and their heaving bosoms burst forth. Then came the happily-ever-after of waking up to dishes in the sink, dirty socks on the floor, kids wailing for breakfast and a skin-raking stubble-flecked peck on the cheek before he went out to work while she tried to bring order to domestic chaos.

Or worse, sinking into his warm embrace, finding two hearts that beat as one, watching the sun rise in his eyes, seeking out soft, tender kisses, working through the trials and joys of life together, hand in hand, heart in heart...until the morning when she woke up and he didn't. Then came the aching, ripping, clawing, cavernous, insatiable emptiness of eternal absence.

She'd watched her parents live out that scenario, two people whose lives and souls seemed so perfectly enmeshed that it was difficult to tell where one began and the other ended. Until the day her mother simply hadn't awakened. Despite her father's kisses, passionate and then desperate, and his plaintive pleas. Heart attack, the doctor had said. She'd gone painlessly.

And he had survived. Painfully.

He'd never been the same since. It had been three years, and her clothes still hung in the closet. Love had gone, and disease had taken its place. For months after he'd learned he was sick, he'd done little or nothing about it. It didn't matter, he'd said. We all have to go sometime, and he would be with her mom again. The downward spiral had continued until finally she'd gone over and screamed in anger and pain and frustration that yes, Mother was gone, but he was still here and she still needed him. Then the tears and the hugs and the resolutions, and the months of chemo and putting her painting on hold to sit with him while he fought nausea and finally began to regain his strength.

That was love.

It bound you to endure someone else's pain, to bear someone else's burden, to cherish someone else's hopes and needs and dreams above your own, until death wrenched them away and left you empty and grieving.

Love stories? No thank you.

She'd seen the best and the worst that love had to offer, and she couldn't face the prospect of having to endure what her father had gone through these past three years. Better to have her own soul, even alone, than to have half of it ripped away by a scattered electrical discharge across the surface of a muscle that lay in the chest of the one you loved and left that muscle and that person limp and lifeless.

"Drusilla?"

She turned, ready to lash out at Cal for his constant interruptions, but it wasn't Cal. It was Miles from upstairs. The real Miles, not her dream Miles. She wiped a hand over the corner of her eye.

"Yes?"

If he'd seen the glistening in her eyes, he had the

courtesy not to let on. "The mainframe says there's a glitch in your terminal."

"It's probably me," she said. "I haven't...I probably hit the wrong key."

He smiled. It was a reassuring smile. "Maybe, but that's not the problem. It's reporting a system error. I need to check your hard drive."

"Okay."

He stood there for a moment, still smiling. Not a geeky, goofy grin. Just a patient, reassuring upward turn of the lips, matched with a softness in his eyes. It was a face she could get used to all too easily.

"May I?" he asked.

"Oh! I'm sorry." He'd been waiting for her to move, so he could do his job. "I guess I'm kind of in space tonight."

"We all have nights like that," he said, offering a hand.

It was a chivalrous gesture offered without a hint of self-consciousness. She normally cared little for urbane courtesies, but his was offered with such casual ease that she couldn't resist taking his hand as she rose from the chair. It was a soft but strong hand, steady. She could get used to that hand in hers.

Stop it! she told herself, remembering her thoughts from only moments before. No. *No!*

She released his hand and he sat, his fingers flying over the keyboard, her data screen giving way to a blur of arcane scripts, seemingly indecipherable codes and file trees. Yet he seemed to know exactly what he was doing, homing in like a guided missile until he finally leaned back.

"Do you go on the Internet here?" he asked.

It wasn't an accusation, although that was strictly forbidden by company policy. It was simply a question.

"No," she answered.

"Then someone on the day shift does." He tapped another couple of keys. "Yeah, it was downloaded this afternoon. Dumb."

"What is it?" she asked.

"Oh, the day shift person downloaded a game. I guess things were slow, or he was just lazy. What he didn't know is that he also downloaded a virus."

"Yikes."

"Relax," he said. "It hadn't detonated yet. It had only just propagated to the mainframe. Just give me a moment and I'll have the little bugger gone."

"Of course."

He tapped a few more keys, and the computer made a self-satisfied beep. He turned in the chair. "All done."

"Thank you."

He smiled. That smile again. Dammit. "No problem. That's why they pay me to be here. And don't worry, I'll make sure the report says it was the day shift guy who did it. You won't get in any trouble."

She nodded. That smile was cruel, tearing the scar tissue she'd wrapped around her heart. No. *No!*

"Oh, your chair," he said, a quiet laugh escaping. "Now it's me who's out in space."

He rose and edged around her in the cubicle as they traded places and she sat. He paused for just another moment at the entrance to her cubicle; then the smile fell. "Well, back to the salt mines for me."

"Me, too," she said. "Thanks again."

"My pleasure," he said before walking away.

Moments later Cal's head poked over the cubicle wall, a conspiratorial smile on his face.

"Don't even *think* it!" she said.

"Consider it not thought," he said. "At least now I know how to get you to take a break, just send you a virus."

"Cal..."

He raised his hands. "Okay, okay. But he was cute."

Her brows arched. "Huh?"

He chuckled, then stopped. "Oh, my. You didn't know. You thought..."

"Well, if you're...why are you always fawning over me and pestering me?"

He patted the top of the cubicle. "Because there's more to life than this. And you're missing too much of it. I figured you needed a friend."

A distant part of her said she ought to scrape her jaw off the floor. Instead she simply nodded.

"Back to your salt mines?" he asked.

"Yes."

"Okay."

Something in his voice wavered. She realized he'd just taken a risk, and though she was turning away for her own reasons, he could read that as something else.

There were days when life was just too damn complicated.

"Cal?"

His eyes and nose poked back above the wall, like the World War Two-era Kilroy drawings. "Yes?"

"Thanks."

The eyes smiled. "No problem. Now let me get back to work, will ya?"

She laughed. "Yes. The salt must be mined."

And a love story had to be avoided at all costs.

Chapter 6

"So you write straining loins and centers of her desire, huh?" Drusilla said.

"That would be it, yes," Miles replied. "Molten, quivering nubs and passionate gasps as fireworks explode in night skies."

Something in his voice told her that while he'd played along, he wasn't thrilled with the joke. Her laugh died in midstream. "I'm sorry."

He waved a hand. "Everyone does it. I'm used to it."

"No. I insulted your work."

"Nah. It's just a hobby."

"It's your dream," she said. "Dreams matter."

"Yes. I suppose they do. But for now, we have to find a way to beat that Kolakul and climb Mount Ayth, so we can capture that Behemoth and save your father's kingdom. There'll be plenty of time to think about dreams later.''

He had closed a door, she realized. He'd opened a part of himself that he rarely revealed, and she'd replied in exactly the wrong way. The door was now closed, and he was pure business. She wanted to apologize. She ached to reach out to him and say how much she admired his dream, to listen to him talk about it. But she'd blown that chance.

''Yes,'' she said. ''Let's go battle the Kolakul.''

The canyon snaked around in a large loop, and the growls grew louder with every passing step. Drusilla couldn't resist a slight shiver. Battling monsters was all fine and good in theory. The fast-approaching reality might be something else altogether. Her hand moved to the hilt of her sword.

''You won't need that,'' Miles said. ''The Kolakul rarely responds to force.''

''What does it respond to?''

He shrugged. ''That, Princess, is one of the great mysteries of life. Wizards through the ages have studied that question and never reached an answer.''

''Okay. So what's the plan, then?''

''We feed it coins and pray for divine intervention.''

''Some plan,'' she said.

''I tame Behemoths, not Kolakuls.''

Although their horses were nearly touching, they might as well have been miles apart. They rode on in silence, listening to the Kolakul's derisive laughter echoing off the canyon walls.

Finally they rounded another corner and the beast

stood before them in all its terrifying fury. Taller than a man, broad as a horse, it emitted a siren's call, a glow from an inner light, as if to say *I dare you.* Drusilla studied it for a long moment, then reached into her bag.

"I have two large silvers and one small silver. The rest is all in the king's scrip."

"It sometimes takes scrip," he said. "We can try, at least."

She peeled out a piece of paper that bore the king's picture and slid it into the Kolakul's mouth. The Kolakul spat it back as if it were day-old gruel.

"Try smoothing it out," Miles suggested.

Drusilla carefully smoothed out the paper and tried again. Once again, the Kolakul spat it back.

"Maybe if I turn it over," she said.

Same answer.

"Another page of scrip?" he suggested.

She went through each of the five pieces of paper in her bag. Same response. She stuffed the paper back in the bag. "I guess it's in a mood."

"I guess so. You said you had two large silvers and one small?"

"Yup." She held out the coins in her palm.

He nodded and dug into a pocket. "I have two smalls and a bunch of coppers, but it hates copper. Hates it."

"Well, between the two of us, we have enough silver."

"True."

He handed her the coins, and she was just about to

feed them to the monster when it seemed to blink out to her mind with a psychic message.

Exact change only.

Oh, now this is absurd, Drusilla thought, fighting the urge to break out laughing at her desk. Was this the *best* she could come up with? She took a sip of her soda and plunged back into her work.

One by one, she fed the coins into the monster's mouth. It swallowed each coin with a quiet, thunking gulp. Now came the moment of truth, when she beseeched it to lay one of its eggs. She reached out and gently touched one of its eyes.

Nothing.

"Damn," she said.

"Maybe another kind of egg," Miles said, touching another of its eyes.

Nothing.

They took turns pressing its other eyes, with ever-increasing force.

Nothing.

Finally, Drusilla stabbed the bottom eye. It wasn't the egg she would have preferred, but it would have to do.

The Kolakul made another of its low, rumbling laughs...but didn't lay the egg.

"Well, hell," he said. "Maybe force will be required, after all."

He grabbed the monster and gave it a hard shake.

Nothing.

He kicked.

Nothing.

He cursed.

Of course, nothing.

Slap.

Nothing.

Lean.

Nothing.

"We're getting nowhere," Drusilla said. "Maybe it's sick. Do Kolakuls get sick?"

"This one sure isn't well," he said.

He was just preparing to give it a good, hard kick when an overpowering stench filled the area. They turned to see Krusti Olfard, standing there with his stink wand, a pitying, patronizing smile on his face.

"It's broke," Krusti said.

"Well, duh!" Drusilla answered. "It would've been nice to know that before I gave up all my silver."

"All of *our* silver," Miles interjected.

"You and everyone else," Krusti said without a hint of sympathy. "You're all so damn smart you can't read."

With that, he stuck his stink wand in his mouth, emitting another cloud of noxious fumes, and pointed to the hand-lettered sign taped to the top of the Kolakul.

Out Of Order.

Drusilla wanted to cry. There was no way they could reach the top of Mount Ayth without an egg. Krusti looked her over. The look began as a leer but softened when he saw her eyes.

"What is it?" he said.

The story tumbled out. "We have to climb Mount Ayth, tame the Behemoth, find the Key of Morgania and save my father's kingdom."

"And we have to do it before the day comes," Miles added. "And we really need a Kolakul egg."

"Well, everybody needs something," Krusti said. "Ain't that the way of life?"

Drusilla drew up to her full, regal height and stared the wizard straight in the gray hair that spilled out the neck of his robe. "Has anyone ever told you that you're a cantankerous, vile—"

"—smelly," Miles cut in.

"Crusty old fart?" the wizard concluded. He blew another foul plume from the stink wand. "Hell, yeah. Every day. But then again, I'm not out a bunch of silver to a sick monster."

He had a point. Wizards usually did.

"Can you help us?" she asked, batting her princess eyes. "It's very important."

"Ain't important to me," he said.

"I can pay," she said.

The wizard laughed. It was a gap-toothed laugh. "Now you're talking my language."

She handed him two pieces of scrip. He merely blew on his stink wand. She handed over another, choking. He blew again. She gasped, gagged and handed him the last two. He seemed to check her bag before finally nodding and pulling out a huge ring of magical keys, one of which fit neatly into the Kolakul's belly button.

The Kolakul seemed to split open and half a dozen half-delivered eggs tumbled out onto the floor. Miles reached for one and Krusti let out a snort.

"Don't even think about it," he said. "The Mopenwachs has already flowed through here tonight, and I'm not gonna turn it back around just because you people are too dumb to know what happens with shaken Kolakul eggs."

He reached into the monster and pulled out an egg, handing it to Drusilla. "There. Satisfied?"

"Most expensive egg I've ever had," she said, her fingertip dancing an irritated staccato on the top of the egg. "You're no different from a highwayman."

Krusti shrugged. "What can I say? Wizarding the River Mopenwachs around doesn't pay a whole lot, and I owe my bookie. Consider it your good deed for the day."

She reached for her sword, but Miles put a hand on her arm. "He's not worth it. Let's take the egg and go."

"My father will have words with you," she said, fire in her voice. "You just wait."

Krusti blew on the stink wand again. "Better your dad than my bookie. Have a good trip."

"Two more hours," Cal said. "What a dull night."

"Yeah, it pretty much has been," Drusilla replied, tossing the empty soda can in the trash bin beneath her desk. "Not at all what I'd hoped for."

"Well, you could always download a virus so the cute systems guy will come back."

"Puh-leeze," she said. "That's the last thing I need."

"Maybe. Maybe not."

"Cal..."

He raised his hands in surrender. "I'll say no more. But if it were me and I'd been grinding away all night with hardly a moment's break, I'd consider taking a walk. Maybe climb some stairs. To refresh myself for the last push. But that's just me."

"Yeah," she said. "That's just you."

But he did have a point, she thought. Her back was awfully sore, as it always was after endless hours in this chair. A walk wouldn't be the worst idea ever. Just to shake out the kinks. That was all. Really.

Refreshed, they were ready to begin the slow climb up Mouth Ayth. The way was steep and narrow, twisting around and back on itself again and again. They had to lead the horses, who couldn't have managed such a climb carrying riders. By a third of the way up, Drusilla's calves were starting to burn.

"Long climb," she said.

"You get used to it," Miles replied.

"You do this a lot?"

He nodded. "The teleport chamber is usually full, or busy, or delayed. And I need the exercise."

"You've been to the top of Mouth Ayth?"

"Didn't I tell you?" he said, smiling. "I live up there. Alone, on the top of a mountain."

"Don't you get...lonely?" she asked.

"Sometimes. But it also gives me time to write."

She smiled. "Well, that's a good thing, isn't it?"

"Mostly. Call me the Behemoth-taming introvert."

Drusilla laughed. "I could just use the acronym—BTI—but that sounds like a government agency or a trash pickup company." She paused. "I mean, if we had government agencies or trash pickup companies in this world. So...tell me more about what you're writing?"

He looked down. "You really don't want to know. It's...silly."

"Try me."

"Well, um, it's a story about a guy and a girl who work in the same building, but he can't muster up the courage to talk to her face-to-face, so they get to know each other by telling a story on interoffice chat."

No! Drusilla thought. That was *not* what was happening here. First, she wasn't chatting. She was working—well, she was taking a stretch break at the moment, but she had been working—and daydreaming. And even if she were chatting, she wouldn't be carrying on a silly office romance. And furthermore, she wasn't interested in anyone. Most especially not the sysop from the eighth floor, who certainly didn't lack for courage, since he'd spoken to her twice tonight already. This daydream was getting way out of control.

Climbing stairs reminded her of another good reason to go golfing with her dad when she got off work. She'd been too sedentary. Her legs weren't used to this. And she'd worn the wrong shoes.

* * *

"Are you okay?" Miles asked, studying her features. It was evident that she was not. With every step, she let out a tiny twinge.

"These boots are great for riding," she said. "Not so good for climbing mountains. But let's go on."

"We should rest a minute anyway," he said. "I need it, even if you don't." Which wasn't true. He could have climbed to the top of the mountain without pause. He did it often. But she would feel less self-conscious about stopping if he said it was for his benefit.

They sat on a ledge and looked out over the world spread beneath them while she sipped from the Kolakul egg to refresh herself.

"All of that will be yours?" he asked.

"I guess. I mean, it's my father's. So I guess it would be mine. But...I don't want it."

"Don't want it?" he asked. "Or simply don't want to lose him?"

He knew the answer, saw it in her eyes. But she kept silent, and for a time they looked out at the deep, shadowy umber of the canyon, the wandering silver sliver of the river, the lush green carpet of the forest and the city of Morgania in the far distance.

"I've never been to Morgania," he said. "It looks beautiful."

"You've *never* been there?"

"Like I said, I live at the top of a mountain."

Her eyes brightened a bit. "It's a beautiful city. My father designed it, you know. He even did some of the work himself. Streets of beautiful slate tile. Full of art and tapestries and the smells of cooking all around. I love it there. So what's the summit like?"

"Well, I can see everything all around," he said. "But it's all very small and at a distance. You might say I can see the forest but not the trees. And certainly not the birds in the trees."

"So you live on imagination?"

"By and large. I get out some...go around taming Behemoths. But yes, mostly I live in my head."

She flexed her boot and grimaced again.

"Let's see that foot," he said. "You might have a blister."

"What's wrong?"

Drusilla turned on the landing to see Miles coming down the stairs. Oh, great.

"Just getting some gum off the sole of my shoe."

He glanced at the shoe. "I don't see any gum."

"I got it off already."

"Your heel looks pretty red."

It did. New flats were not ideal for climbing stairs. She would have a nasty blister by the time she got home. So much for playing golf with her dad.

"Hold on," he said. "I have a first-aid kit upstairs. I'll be right back."

"Let me see what I have in my pack," Miles said, looking at the open sore on her foot. "I ought to have some healing herbs that will take care of that."

"I didn't know you were a healer," she said.

"I'm not, but Behemoth taming can be dangerous sometimes. So I know a little."

Minutes later Miles returned with a white plastic box in his hands. He extracted a bottle of purple fluid. "It's an astringent, to draw the moisture out of the skin. It may sting a bit."

Drusilla winced as he dabbed the fluid on. It stung, but not badly. His hands were tender as he applied two Band-Aids, then covered her left heel with a layer of white adhesive tape.

"That should keep the friction off the skin until you can get home and change shoes."

"Thank you," Drusilla said, looking down.

Just what she needed on a night like this. To be rescued by a knight in shining armor who would probably think it meant he had a right to whatever else he wanted. But that wasn't fair, she realized.

"No problem," he said. "I often ride my bike to work, so I keep this in my office for miscellaneous scrapes and such. Glad I could help."

She could only nod.

"Where were you going?" he asked.

"I don't know. Just taking a break. Figured I'd walk around and stretch."

He nodded. "I do that sometimes, too. It gets kinda boring some nights."

She suspected "boring" translated to "lonely," but she didn't want to go there. He didn't seem like a morose person. Not like she could be when she started thinking too much. No reason to drag him down.

"Say," he said, "do you have a couple of minutes?"

"I guess so, why?"

He almost blushed.

"What?" the princess asked as she tugged her boot back on. "What is it?"

"I just... Nah. You wouldn't want to."

"What?" Drusilla asked as she slipped her foot back into her flat.

"Well," Miles said, "I write, and I'm stuck on where to go in this scene. I was wondering if you could read it over and tell me what you think?"

Drusilla gaped at him. They'd passed hardly two dozen words for the first time tonight, yet he was asking her to look at his art. She couldn't believe he was so brave.

Then she realized her hesitation was giving him the wrong idea. She could see the tentative hope on his face closing down.

"I'd love to see your writing," Drusilla said.

"It's not very good," he warned. Why was he doing this? She was going to hate it, and promptly hate him. She'd already made fun of love stories. Why did he think his work would be special? "You don't have to."

"I'd be honored," the princess said, touching his hand. This time, an electric thrill ran through her as her fingertips grazed his skin. Oh, no, she didn't need this, not in fantasy, not in real life.

But the fantasy was dragging her along, and her feet began to climb again as Miles led the way.

"It's up on the mountain," he said. "You can read it if we have a minute before we find the Behemoth."

"A minute? You haven't written very much?"

"Well…I thought you wouldn't want to see anything except the last little part where I'm having trouble."

"Oh." She didn't know whether to feel relieved or hurt. "How can I give you any ideas if I don't know what's come before?"

He sighed. "Well, that *is* a problem. But there isn't time."

"Time," she agreed. It was running out.

Her heel felt better, though, thanks to his ministration. But as they climbed Mount Ayth, she noted he was growing more and more cautious. She looked around at the trees that grew on the craggy mountainside and wondered what was making him nervous.

"What's wrong?" she asked when his hand strayed to his sword hilt.

He didn't answer immediately. Behind them, following with equal caution, came their horses, stepping carefully over loose talus.

"There's always a chance," he said finally, "that we could run into a guardian."

Drusilla stopped suddenly. "Guardian? What guardian?"

He stopped, too, and turned to face her. "The mountain has guardians. Protectors. Sometimes they let me pass, sometimes they hassle me."

She bit her lower lip. "How much hassle?"

"Once they kept me prisoner until I fought my way free."

She sighed and looked up toward the mountaintop, realizing that it was no longer visible. At least not from where they were perched. She had no idea how much farther they might have to climb, or how long it would take even if they met with no impediments.

"Look," she said. "My father's ill."

"I know, Drusie."

"He's okay for the moment, but I don't know when...I mean...he can't be *cured.*"

He reached out, clearly on instinct, and took her hand. "I'm sorry, Princess."

"So I don't have much time...." Suddenly feeling desolate, she perched on a boulder. Her mount took the opportunity to graze on the thin growth at their feet.

Miles sat on the rock beside her. "Time for what?"

"Time to...time to succeed."

"Ah." He nodded, and deep in his blue eyes she was certain she saw understanding. "That's hard. Very hard." He slipped his arm around her shoulder, a comforting hug that was somehow far more than comforting. She had to fight the most unwarrior-like urge to turn her face into his shoulder and bawl her eyes out.

Stiff upper lip, she reminded herself. Her dad would expect no less. "I guess it's silly," she said, her voice cracking. "I can always succeed...later. All that matters is that sooner or later I save Morgania. But..."

"But you'd like him to be here when you succeed."

She nodded, feeling her eyes burn, and looked at him, thinking he was amazingly understanding for a Behemoth dweeb. "It's crazy."

"I don't think it's crazy at all."

"No?"

He shook his head. "No. Our victories in life have a whole lot more meaning when we can share them with people we love, people who love us."

"Do you have someone to share yours?"

He shrugged, his mouth tightening. "A Behemoth."

"Oh, that's not enough!"

"Right now it's all I've got, and it's missing. Although I'm pretty sure it's hiding out in the cave up there. It goes into a funk every so often, you know. Wants to be reassured that I'm still around and still care enough to come straighten it out."

"Pouty?"

He half smiled. "That's a good word for it. Maybe I'll name him Pouty."

"What happens if you can't straighten him out?"

"I'll be replaced. Behemoths are totally useless without tamers." He sighed. "But enough about me. I'm worried about you."

"Me?" She shook her head. "I'm tough. I'll be fine."

"Sure you will. But it's easier to be fine when you're not alone."

Was he saying something? She searched his face

but couldn't be sure. His mouth opened a little, then closed, and his gaze seemed to become fixed on her mouth.

"You have a pretty mouth," he said.

Somehow that remark didn't seem to come out of the blue. "Thank you."

With apparent effort, he looked away, but he didn't take his arm from her shoulders. "We'll get that key of yours, Princess," he promised. "And we'll get it soon. But I bet your father is proud of you anyway."

"He is." Her throat tightened. "All he's ever wanted is for me to be happy. I could have sat around the castle and spent all my time reading and eating bonbons, and he'd still be proud of me."

He nodded. "That's beautiful."

"What about you? Your parents are proud of you, right?"

"I don't know."

Her jaw dropped. "You don't know?"

"I haven't seen either one of them since I was fourteen."

She waited for him to go on, but he didn't. "I'm sorry," she said finally.

"I'm not. Life got a lot easier after that." He turned to look at her again, a wry smile on his lips. "There's a plan in everything, you know. It's just hard to see it sometimes."

"Now you sound like my dad."

He laughed. "Sweetie, I'm *not* your dad."

It was as if those simple words changed the entire

atmosphere of the mountain around them. His laugh stopped short; their gazes locked.

And all of a sudden Drusilla was finding it hard to breathe. Her heart began to pound heavily, and no matter how deep the breaths she drew, there wasn't enough oxygen in the air to sustain her. Her eyelids suddenly felt heavy, and between her legs a weight settled, a heaviness that cried out for a touch. Helplessly, she shifted on the rock, trying to ease the growing ache.

Miles kissed her. Without so much as a by-your-leave, something every princess deserved, he took her mouth with his, reminding her that he was a tamer, not a courtier, by nature.

No artful flattery, no gifts, no songs or poems written for her. None of the things she had always imagined would be her due.

Just a kiss. A soul-deep, searing, wrenching kiss that took her entire world and turned it upside down and then welded her to him with a need so strong it struck with all the force of an earthquake.

Then, all too soon, he wrenched his mouth from hers, leaving her feeling dazed.

"Not here," he said, as if it were a foregone conclusion. "Not here. The guardian..."

He grabbed the horses' reins and her hand, and drew them all deeper into the forest, so deep that it seemed almost night. He tied the horses to a tree, then faced her.

She could have fled. She should have fled. But with one kiss he had conquered her in a way that no one ever had before. The whisper of the wind in the pines overhead seemed to echo the flow of heat through her veins and the softness that filled her entire being.

"My princess," he said huskily, and drew her into his embrace, an embrace that seemed to block the rest of the world from her senses and mind.

Miles was all that existed. *All.* And she wanted to share things with him that she had never before wanted to share.

His mouth took hers again, a deep promise of things to come. She'd had many kisses in her life, but none like this one, which seemed to weld her to him, to make her part and parcel of him.

His chest was hard against the softness of her breasts, a softness she had tried to ignore most of her life because she had to be tough, had to succeed, had to be ready to replace her father.

The softness seemed right for the first time in her life, right and ripe both, as if her breasts had just been waiting for the right time, the right person. When Miles's hand slipped down her back and tucked her hips against his, she felt his hardness against her softness with a thrill that made her moan.

Even her quest faded into the distance, borne away by the force of the storm rising within her.

Chapter 7

The bed of pine needles was soft beneath the cloak he had spread for her. Overhead, visible through the trees, the moon had risen, and around it the sky was fading into darkness. They could travel no farther to-night.

But travel was the last thing on her mind. She lay on her back on a bed that seemed softer than any she had lain on, while he propped himself on one elbow beside her and leaned over her.

His head blocked the moon, a dark shadow; then his lips found hers again, this time with a velvety touch. She strained up toward him, wanting a deeper pressure, but he pulled back a little, just enough to keep on teasing her with a gentleness that to her no longer seemed necessary.

"No hurry," he whispered. "We can't travel any farther...."

She wanted to agree with him. She knew he was right. But inside her was a pressure of things that needed doing, of things that could go wrong if she didn't keep going.

"I'll take care of it all, Princess," he murmured, as if he could read her mind. "All of it. These moments belong to *us*."

Which was exactly what she wanted. With a deep sigh, she gave herself up to the moment, putting away all the burdens of her life and stealing just this little bit of time for herself.

That meant trusting him, trusting him to take care of the Behemoth for her and to help her get the key back safely to Morgania. And surprisingly enough, she found it easy to trust that he would. Easy to trust that he would take care of everything.

It was a heady feeling to no longer be alone with her burdens, and even headier to feel free to let go of them if only for a short time.

When his lips returned to hers, they remained tender, but now his hand stroked along her side, as if gentling a mare. The touches, light as they were, made her feel as if she were melting inside, softening.

Yielding. Never in her life had she yielded anything to anyone. She had been a scrapper from birth. Now some transformation was happening deep within her, and she was finding she liked it.

Reaching up, she placed her hands on his shoulders,

opening herself even more, needing something to cling to as reality spun away.

It was as if Miles picked up the reins of her existence with his touches, moving her past thought and will. When chilly air touched bare skin, it felt right. When his warm fingers followed, it felt even more right.

There was magic in his touch, a wizard's knowledge of spells, and the spell he cast over her like a gentle net lifted her so completely out of herself that she felt she had moved to a higher plane.

As if to protect her from the chill and the reality that would come with it, he opened her clothes only in a few places. The ties on her tunic came undone, but he parted them only enough to slip his hand inside and to cup her breast as if he held a priceless jewel.

The touch, so fresh and new in her experience, caused her to gasp and arch toward him as spiraling thrills ran through her to the very center of her existence.

With that touch, like the mage he was, he enslaved her, making her wholly his. When his hand began to gently knead her flesh, she was utterly lost in sensation and need.

It was as if he held all the answers she would ever need. As if he held the keys of her existence. She gasped again, and writhed, wanting even more.

"Shh...." His breath was hot on her lips; then he seized her mouth in a deep kiss that plundered her very soul. His fingers found her hardened nipple and pinched, just enough to send the most exquisite pain-pleasure sensations racing through her. Between her legs a strong throbbing began, a heaviness that demanded a response.

But still he held back, teasing her mouth, plundering her warm wet depths, then sliding downward until he took her breast into his mouth.

His suckling caused new waves of pleasure to fill her, and she clutched his head, holding him close and closer still. Overhead, the dark shadows of trees sheltered them, the moonlit sky outlining them in silver. The air grew chillier even as her body grew warmer.

She wanted to share with him some of what she was feeling, but his spell held. He would not let her move except to respond with groans and shivers to his knowing touches.

She throbbed all over now, and felt like a torch aflame with need for him.

And finally, finally, he undid the ties at her waist and tugged. Cold air hit her belly and the apex between her thighs, a stimulating contrast that seemed to tighten her need even more. Then her pants were gone, as were her boots, tugged swiftly away.

But before the cold could penetrate his spell, he covered her with his body, warm and heavy, his clothing opened only that little bit that was needed.

She felt his hardness pressed against her, a promise he didn't yet exercise. Instead he found her other breast with his mouth and suckled until low moans issued from her, until her hips rocked against him, offering and pleading. Seeking fulfillment.

There was a moment of sharp pain as he breached

a barrier never before breached. She cried out, and he stilled, holding her tightly, dropping a rain of kisses on her face and chest.

"Shh," he whispered. "I didn't know..."

She didn't care. She was past caring about anything so paltry. "Please...please..."

He obliged, moving at first slowly, tentatively, within her. The pain slipped away with the rest of reality, and the pressure built within her anew, the need, the hunger.

It was as if a vise tightened inside her, a vise of pleasure that approached pain in its strength. Harder and harder it felt within her as he moved, each stroke winding it tighter.

And then...the heavens exploded and she surmounted the highest of peaks with a cry. Moments later, before her own throbbing had even slowed, she felt him shudder and groan, then collapse against her.

This was a place she never wanted to leave.

Drusilla looked at Miles, realizing they were almost to the eighth floor. And realizing what she had been thinking. Color stained her cheeks with painful heat, and she turned around, starting down the stairs.

"Drusilla?"

"I've got to get back to work," she said. "They'll fire me." What the hell had she been thinking?

He said something else, but she was too embarrassed to hear. A minute later she was back at her desk, her cheeks still hot, hunting for her place in the data. At least her boss was leaving her alone because she had claimed female problems. But this was awful!

What if Miles ever guessed what she had been dreaming? She would die of embarrassment. Gosh, she hardly knew him. Five words of conversation....

It was ten or fifteen minutes before she was once again completely calm, safe in the sanctity of her own mind. Then she drifted away again....

Miles rested atop her for a long time, holding her to earth when she might have flown away, keeping her warm when the night would have chilled her. His weight comforted her deeply.

Then, gently, he moved again to her side and drew his cloak around them both.

"In the morning," he said, "we'll reach the top of the mountain."

In Drusilla's mind, they already had.

The first streamers of dusty rose were lightening the sky when Miles awoke her. "Good morning," he said, a smile deep in his blue eyes.

She blushed and tried to look away, but he touched her chin and drew her face back around so that she had to look at him. Then he kissed her, a touch that was at once a thank-you and a promise.

"Time to climb," he said. "Breakfast first?"

"I'm not hungry."

"Later, then," he agreed. "It won't be long now. If that Behemoth has the key, we'll have it soon."

* * *

Drusilla was glad that the Miles of the real world couldn't read her mind, because she wouldn't have been able to face him right now.

But the Miles of her dream was a different matter. What they'd done in the night, they had done together, fictional though it was.

She glanced at her watch and saw there wasn't much time left on her shift. Good.

Then she continued to climb Mount Ayth with Miles the Behemoth Tamer.

The climb was arduous, but not too difficult. They paused frequently to catch their breath, and sometimes they had to be especially careful around talus, but they made steady progress. As long as they didn't run into a guardian, everything would be fine, right?

But of course they ran into a guardian, an officious pain in the neck with a sword strapped on his waist, who wanted to see their permission to climb Mount Ayth.

And he looked ready to fight about it.

His first words were, "Get back...get back...."

Huh?

Drusilla paused, looked up from her screen, and wondered at the strange noise, which might have been singing, or might have been the mating call of the North American river otter. Now it was her turn to poke her head over the cubicle wall.

Cal was oblivious to her or anyone else, headphones from his portable CD player over his ears, singing along to the Beatles. Or mating along to them. She was tempted to tap his shoulder and suggest that he not quit his day job, then remembered that he worked nights. Which raised a terrible specter: what if singing *was* his day job? Suppressing a giggle and trusting to the mercies of a loving God, she sat back down and returned to her own private world.

"I'm going to where I belong," Miles said with chilly defiance in his voice. "I live up there."

"She doesn't," the guardian said. "So either she turns back or you both do."

There was nothing more frustrating than a petty tyrant. The guardian was the kind of man who, having only a tiny amount of authority, was determined to exercise it at every opportunity. There were two ways to deal with such people.

Tack one. "Look, we're on an important mission. The princess needs to see the Behemoth, and I'm her guide and bodyguard. And we don't have a lot of time to argue."

The guardian wasn't buying it. "Yeah, yeah, everybody has a story. But I'm the law around here, and I don't buy excuses. So turn yourselves around."

Which left Tack two.

"You're not the law. But you are a very important cog in the security machine on this mountain."

The guardian looked up a bit. His chest seemed to swell an inch or two before collapsing into its previous sullen stoop. "Flattery will get you nowhere."

"I'm not flattering you. I'm telling the truth." Miles

stepped forward, laying a hand on the guardian's shoulder. "I don't know where we'd be without people like you. The Behemoth would have been slain long ago."

The guardian's head perked a bit. "Yeah? You're just saying that."

"I'm serious. I know they don't treat you like you matter. Hell, they don't treat any of us like we matter."

Drusilla wondered who *they* were, then decided it was wisest to keep her mouth shut.

"No they don't," the guardian admitted with a scowl.

"That's right," Miles went on. "They treat us all like we can be replaced with the flip of a wrist. But that's not true."

"No?"

"No." Miles's voice was firm. "They don't know how much trouble there would be without good guardians like you. What if you weren't here and the gremlins got up the mountain?"

Now the guardian *did* puff his chest. "That's right. They never think of that, do they?"

"Never. They hire you, then forget all about you as long as you keep working. You become invisible."

"I'm tired of being invisible," the man admitted.

"Of course you are. We *all* are. But you do a damn fine job, Guardian, and I'm glad you're protecting *my* Behemoth."

The guardian nodded, standing straighter still. "This one's your Behemoth, is he?"

"She," Miles corrected gently. "Yeah, she's mine. And I need to get back to her before she gets a bad case of hiccups. If she does, the whole mountain will start shaking. It might even come down."

The guardian nodded. "Okay. Sorry I stopped you. But..." He eyed Drusilla uncertainly.

"She's okay," Miles assured him. "She's a Behemoth feeder. I'll vouch for her."

"Well, okay."

Miles smiled. "Thanks, buddy. I know I can count on you to keep the gremlins at bay."

"Yeah." The guardian scowled and patted his sword hilt. "And *them,* too. They got no business up here."

"You got that right. Thanks for doing such a good job."

The guardian actually smiled and waved them on their way, looking like a much prouder man.

"You're shameless," Drusilla said when they were out of earshot.

"Who, me? No way, Princess. I just told the truth."

Which was true, Drusilla decided as she hiked upward behind him. The guardian was an important man, however officious.

"We're all important," Miles said over his shoulder. "Each and every one of us, no matter how much we feel like invisible cogs. No matter how much we get treated like interchangeable parts in a machine."

"That's true."

He paused to smile at her. "We've all had a taste of that from time to time, haven't we?"

"Even princesses," she admitted.

"It's like the world forgets we're people and sees only what we can do or who we are. Sad. Very sad."

Drusilla nodded and tried to keep up with his long legs. It *was* sad, she decided. Because every person mattered, no matter who he was or what he did. Knowing that Miles felt that way made her feel very close to him. Very warm toward him. He was a special man.

Miles paused, giving her a chance to catch up. "Sorry, I don't mean to walk so fast."

"It's not a problem," Drusilla said, then startled them both by leaning forward to kiss him.

His lips were so warm and soft that she wanted to melt into them forever.

A cheerful whistle dragged Drusilla back to the present. She turned around in her chair to see the nighttime security guard striding down the hallway between the cubicles, matching his steps to the theme from *The Bridge Over the River Kwai.*

When he saw her, he winked and gave her a casual salute. "Nice evening, Princess," he said as he passed.

Which raised a set of strange and somewhat frightening possibilities. Could her fantasy be spilling out into the real world, affecting the people around her? Or was she somehow tapping into what was happening around her, even things she couldn't see, and pulling them into the story? Neither possibility was comfortable. For if it were true, that would mean Miles was somehow involved, as well. The real Miles. The Miles who might rock her comfortable if unfulfilling existence in the real world. This was not good at all.

It was time to take the Behemoth—*and* the Behemoth Tamer—by the horns.

Chapter 8

For a few moments there, Drusilla had forgotten her quest. And the ache that filled her now was almost such that she didn't want to continue. She had to force herself to square her shoulders and back out of Miles's arms. The future of Morgania lay in the balance.

The flicker of sadness across his face tugged at her heart, but she had to be strong. This could lead nowhere good.

"I'm sorry, Miles. We need to find the Behemoth, get the key and save my father's kingdom. And not let ourselves get distracted by…other things."

He nodded. "Sure. Okay. Let's go, then."

The last bit of the climb seemed steeper, although Drusilla wasn't sure if that was the terrain, her tired legs, or the weight of what she'd just done. He deserved better than to be labeled a distraction. After all, she had wanted it as much as he had. But still, she had her life in order—for all its good and bad points—and she couldn't afford to rattle that order. Not right now.

At the summit of Mount Ayth, a cavern yawned open. Distant, disinterested hums emerged from within. The kind of hum that said, *I'm not interested in the petty doings of the likes of you.*

"Is that...?"

Miles nodded. "That's the Behemoth."

"It sounds busy."

"It usually is."

"So what now?" she asked.

"Now we get really, really careful."

He stepped into the cave with cautious confidence. She followed with a good deal less certainty in her stride, peeking over his shoulder.

And there it was.

It wasn't what she'd expected. Come to think of it, she didn't know what she'd expected. Something large and hairy, with glowing eyes, gleaming teeth, sharp claws and a bad attitude. Instead, it was...well...rather drab. It looked like a big, boxy earthworm, with a segmented body ten or twelve feet long and about waist high. If it had eyes, it kept them well hidden. It must have had eyes, though, for this was without doubt the cleanest cave she'd ever set foot into. Apparently it had a neatness fetish. It also seemed to like cold. She shivered.

"So that's it?" she whispered.

Miles nodded. "That's it. It seems content enough. This might be easier than we'd hoped."

"Famous last words," she replied.

As if on cue, the Behemoth let out a series of sputtering belches. Iridescent scales twinkled angrily and the belches turned to repetitive yips.

Eeep-eeep-eeep-eeep-eeep!

"Oops," Drusilla whispered.

"Oops," Miles agreed.

"Now what?"

"Now I earn my keep."

It seemed like an odd comment. His company had hardly been an imposition on this journey. And he'd certainly pulled his share of the weight all along. So why did he feel a need to earn his keep? Maybe he simply enjoyed the opportunity to show off his Behemoth-taming skills. Maybe it was simply a verbal tic. Maybe she was trying to parse too much from every word, every action, wondering if he felt the same things she was feeling, and if he was as afraid of them as she was. Maybe she should stop thinking about maybes. Maybe she should stop thinking, period.

He approached the Behemoth with a surprising calm, walking down one side, then around to the other, studying it, as if divining its intentions from the pattern of its yelps and flashing scales.

"Be careful," she whispered.

"That was the plan."

"Will it breathe fire?"

He shook his head. "That only happens in stories.

Behemoths are actually rather sedate, unless you try to poke around inside them without putting them to sleep first. And I've rarely had to go there. But they're still dangerous."

She was ridiculously disappointed. What was a fantasy without a fire-breathing Behemoth to defeat? "What do they do?"

"Well," he said, taking a closer look at some of its scales, "if it gets really angry, it'll cast a spell of forgetfulness."

"That doesn't sound good."

"It's not. It's diabolical. It will find everything you most need to remember and make it forgotten. Poof. As if it hadn't even happened."

Maybe this was more dangerous than fire-breathing after all. She stiffened her spine, ready for a fight. "Definitely not good. So how do you stop it?"

"Carefully," he answered. "Very carefully."

If there was any meaning to the Behemoth's squeals, burps and flashes, she couldn't see it. But apparently he could. He seemed to stalk the problem like a heron eyeing a fish. Long moments of stillness. A careful step. More study. More stillness. Waiting for the right opportunity. Waiting to strike.

It was surprisingly mesmerizing. She'd thought he would use a sword, or powerful magic, or at least a whip and a chair. Then again, she'd thought the Behemoth would be large, hairy, toothy, clawy and attitudey. Life had a way of not giving you what you expected. And yet giving you exactly what you'd hoped for.

Finally he stopped circling it and looked up. "I think it's ill. Seems to have caught a cold."

Her entire mental image of Behemoths—what little had survived the initial sighting—collapsed. This was no vile monster. Instead, she found herself thinking of chicken soup, hot chamomile tea, lots of rest under a warm blanket and a heaping-double-extra-helping of womanly TLC.

"How can I help?"

"I'm not sure," he said. "It's pretty technical."

"It's not technical. The poor beast is sick."

"Yes, but it can get very cranky."

She waved the warning away. "Pish, tosh. Women are used to dealing with beasts that get cranky when they're sick. We call them 'husbands.'"

"I don't get cranky when I'm sick," he protested.

"And you're not a husband, either, are you?"

He smiled mischievously. "Not yet."

Her heart slammed in her chest. She was suddenly more afraid of him than she'd ever been of the Behemoth.

The Behemoth let out another series of sputtering squeals. His face shifted in a heartbeat. "This is bad. We need to get to work. There's a stack of crackers over there. Hand them to me, please?"

"Of course." She walked over to where he'd been pointing but saw nothing that looked even remotely edible, or at least not for a human. "What do they look like?"

"They're round and shiny, with a hole in the middle."

"Oh...these?" she asked, holding them up. "These are crackers?"

"Behemoths have strange tastes," he replied.

She handed him the stack, and he began to sort through it, apparently looking for the right flavor. After what she'd seen on this quest, the notion that a Behemoth might be cured of a cold by the right flavor of cracker was no longer a stretch. The world was far weirder than she had ever imagined. And yet, also far more beautiful.

"Let's hope this works," he said, tickling the Behemoth's mouth. He saw the quizzical look on her face. "I'm trying to get it to stick its tongue out."

She merely nodded and watched as he gently touched and tickled. Finally, seemingly convinced that he meant no harm, the Behemoth's tongue slid out of a tiny slit of a mouth. A creature this big had a mouth that small? Chalk up another one to unrealistic expectations.

Miles put the cracker on the creature's tongue and tickled again. The Behemoth seemed to consume it warily, drawing the cracker into its mouth and pausing for a long moment before letting out a tiny shudder. Drusilla hoped it was a shudder of relief. It wasn't.

The Behemoth regurgitated the cracker, uneaten.

"Not good," Miles said. "It must have the flu. Or some virus worse than a common cold."

"Can you take care of it?" she asked.

"I can, I think. But at this point, the treatment gets pretty radical. You might not want to watch. It could get ugly."

She smiled. "You shouldn't have to do this alone."

"Don't say you weren't warned." He drew a breath. "I'm going to have to give it an artificial brain for a little while, until I can find the infection in its real brain. And it's nauseous, so the timing is critical. I have to get it to eat a very particular kind of cracker, then knock it out before it can spit it back up. When it wakes up, it'll swallow it. I hope."

"And the cracker has the artificial brain?"

"Exactly."

"And if it doesn't swallow it when it wakes up?"

His face paled at the mere thought. "Let's just say I hope you'll remember me, Princess. But first things first. Let's find that cracker. It should be in a box marked *Boot.*"

She paused, looking at him with a cocked brow. "You keep artificial brains in a box marked 'shoes'?"

"Not shoes. *Boot.* A very big difference."

"Yeah. One has a high top."

He frowned at her, but she could see the twinkle in his eyes. "Boot. Look for Boot."

"This doesn't make any sense at all."

"It doesn't have to. It's a tamer's code word."

"Oh." She was beginning to think Behemoth tamers were a little...odd. Odder than most folk, which probably wasn't saying much, now that she thought about it.

Considering that the Behemoth's cave was neater than a guard barracks before a royal inspection, finding the boot crackers should have been easy. But many of the boxes seem to have been labeled by a drunken chicken during a rainstorm. She could go blind trying to decipher the smeary scrawls. Miles, on the other hand, found the scrawls suspiciously transparent.

"You wrote these?" she asked.

He flushed the tiniest bit. "Penmanship was never my forte."

"I guess not."

Now that she knew whom to ask for decoding help, however, the search went faster. Finally she found a hand-labeled box that looked vaguely like it might be the one. She held it out to him. "This says boo, or something like that. I'm guessing that's 'Boot'?"

His eyes brightened as he took the box. "You're learning to read my writing. That's scary."

She chuckled. "Don't let it go to your head. My father may be the king, but there's a reason he has scribes to do his writing for him. His signature looks like the death throes of an ink-covered beetle."

He nodded, but she could tell he wasn't really listening. He'd already opened the box and was digging through the crackers. "Ah, here it is. The freshest boot-flavored cracker."

"I can't believe that creature eats boots."

"Behemoths have strange tastes," he said. "Now comes the tricky part. See that fluorescent scale over there?"

"Which one?"

"The green one."

"Which green one?"

He walked over and pointed. "That green one."

She couldn't resist the opportunity and leaned up to kiss him. "Gotcha."

"Princesses." He shook his head. "Okay, that's the one. Push on that scale when I tell you."

"Yes, sir."

"Puh-leeze."

He carried the cracker back over to the Behemoth's mouth and began tickling its lips again. After a bit of coaxing, the beast tentatively offered its tongue. He put the cracker on its tongue and tickled it into the mouth.

"Now."

Hoping the beast didn't do something terrible to Miles, Drusilla pressed the scale into its boxy body with the very tip of her finger. In an instant, the beast shuddered and went deadly still. The fluorescence of its scales faded to black.

"Oh, no," she said, a sinking feeling in her stomach. "I messed up. I'm sorry. I killed it."

"No." His voice was reassuring. "It's just in a deep sleep for a moment."

"You mean...?"

"Yes, Princess. You just tamed a Behemoth. Now let's see if we can wake it up. Push that scale again."

"Are you sure?"

He simply smiled. She pressed on the scale again. The Behemoth let out a series of belches, buzzes and grunts. Miles's eyes were fixed on its mouth. The cracker stayed down. After a minute or two, its scales began to twinkle happily.

"Is it all better?" she asked.

"Not yet. It's using the artificial brain now. But that means I can fix its real brain."

With practiced ease, he stroked and massaged the Behemoth's scales. It responded with satisfied blinks and grunts, obviously trusting him. After a few minutes he stepped back. "Nasty bug. But I think we caught it before there was any permanent damage."

"You're sure?"

He touched her hand. "Princess, with a Behemoth, you're never sure until it works. We'll know after we put it to sleep and wake it again."

He pressed a scale, and the Behemoth obediently, almost cheerfully, stuck out its tongue. The boot-flavored cracker was still there.

"It didn't eat?" she asked.

"Oh, it did. It's Behemoth magic."

"Ah."

This, of course, made perfect sense. Behemoths truly were strange creatures. Miles put the cracker back in the box, let the Behemoth withdraw its tongue and nodded to her.

"Press that green scale again."

"Which one?" she asked with a mischievous wink.

"You just want another kiss."

"You're right."

He came to her and their lips met, softly at first, grazing, almost tickling, until she opened her mouth the tiniest bit and let the tip of her tongue touch his. He let out a low groan.

She pressed the scale and sent the Behemoth into sleep again, then woke it with another press. All the while, her lips and tongue never left his lips. The Behemoth let out a happy sigh.

He smiled. "You sure know how to push the right buttons."

She suddenly felt giddy. "Call me the Behemoth-Tamer Tamer. Now let's find that key."

Chapter 9

Drusilla felt like a fool. Her shift was over. She was supposed to meet her father in half an hour. Then they were going to breakfast together, followed by the driving range to hit some golf balls. Then, if all went well, she could paint a bit before hitting the bed. And in fourteen hours, she would be waking, getting ready to come back here again. On any normal morning, she would be leading the pack in the dash for the parking lot. Instead, she was standing in a corridor on the eighth floor, getting ready to tap on Miles's door.

This was stupid. This was not the Miles of her fantasy world. This Miles was real. And she was about to let this Miles screw up her world.

She rationalized that she was simply fulfilling a promise to read over his work. But it had been a promise made in passing, and she doubted he would remember it, much less care whether she kept it. On the other hand, as an artist, it was exactly the sort of promise she would have wanted someone to keep. So she would keep it. Even if it did screw up her world.

She tapped at the door.

"Hey," he said, glancing up from his keyboard, then down at his watch, then up again. He let out a sigh. "My relief is late, as always."

She nodded. "You asked if I wanted to read your work. I said I would."

A dozen emotions flickered through his eyes in an instant, most of them damnably inscrutable. Had he forgotten? Had she just made an utter fool of herself?

"Yes, I remember."

The pause grew pregnant. She shifted her weight from her left foot to her right, to avoid the still painful blister. He seemed to see the faint grimace in her eyes.

He rose from his chair. "I'm sorry. Your blister must be sore. Please, have a seat."

"Thank you."

She settled into the chair and looked around. His office was neater than her cubicle, although the modular bookshelves on the walls were crammed with software manuals, three-ring binders, gem cases with CD-ROMs, all of which bore obscure labels. Even more impressive were rows upon rows of large tape spools. This was, she found herself thinking, the mother of all computers.

Behind a glass partition, in a brightly lighted room, lay the mainframe computer, a double row of waist-high gunmetal-gray boxes. Miles kept the lights off in his office, apparently content to work by the spillover from the computer room.

She shifted her feet beneath his desk and bumped a green nylon bag. He leaned over to retrieve it. She closed her eyes for a moment and allowed herself to enjoy the brush of his shoulder against her hip.

"My cycling clothes," he offered in explanation, scrambling back to a safe distance. "I'll toss them over here, out of your way."

"Your writing?" she asked.

"Right." He turned and pulled a half-inch-thick stack of paper from a shelf. "I...printed it out for you. Easier on the eyes than staring at a screen. Especially when you've been doing that for eight hours already."

So he had remembered.

"It's rough," he said. "A lot of it is still first draft. And of course I need to flesh it out more for a full novel. I guess it's more a very long synopsis."

Anxiety was apparent in his voice, and even more so in his eyes. He held the stack of pages as if it were a freshly decorated wedding cake.

Drusilla tried to offer a reassuring smile. "May I read it? I promise not to say anything bad."

He drew the pages back to himself. "No, don't say that. If it sucks, just say so. I want your honest opinion."

If most artists she'd known were any guide, that translated to, *I want you to honestly tell me you love it.* But maybe he was different.

"Of course," she said, hoping her answer wasn't too obviously ambiguous.

He handed her the pages. "I'll go get another soda while you read. Do you want anything?"

She shook her head. "I'm fine, thanks. If I drink any more, I'll float away."

He nodded. "Okay, then. I'll be back."

He slid out of the room as if trying to avoid a rattlesnake. She remembered having the same feelings the first time she'd let a boyfriend see her paintings. It would be a long time before she made that mistake again. She resolved not to leave Miles with a similar memory, no matter what she thought of his writing.

As she began to read, she realized this was not the entire manuscript. She had jumped into an adventure in the middle, if not near the end. It took a few pages to get a handle on what was happening in the story. When she did, her heart caught in her throat.

> The dragon's golden-scaled lids drooped over moist, emerald eyes. "Thank you," it whispered.
>
> "You're welcome." He reached out to touch its face, the tiny scales silky-smooth under his touch. "I'm sorry I couldn't get here sooner."
>
> The dragon turned to look at the infant nuzzled beneath its wing. "You saved my baby."
>
> "But you..." he said.
>
> "My fate was written in the Elder Stone a thousand years ago," the dragon said, its voice barely a whisper. "You could not have changed that."
>
> Milan's eyes stung. "No, I suppose not."

Behind him, a low moan stirred the near darkness.

"Tend to her now," the dragon said, its nose pressing him back. "I must rest."

With a mighty effort, it drew itself nearly into a ball, its nostrils within an inch of the infant's. The baby's eyes opened slightly at the disturbance. Then it let out a plaintive sigh, as if understanding by instinct what it could not yet know. A tender, tiny, pink-golden paw reached up to its mother's lips, and it drifted back into sleep.

"She's dying," the princess said.

"Yes," Milan answered. "The wound was too deep. And with the stress of childbirth…"

Drusia held out a pale hand. "I'm sorry."

"It wasn't your fault."

"Yes, it was," she said. "If I had been stronger, I could have healed her."

He looked at the wound on her chest. Just a few minutes ago, it had stretched from shoulder to breastbone. Now it was only a small cut above her left breast. She would recover. But it had been a near thing.

"Drusia, if you had taken her entire wound, you would have died."

"And she would have lived," the princess said, unable to meet his eyes. "Now my father's kingdom is doomed. Doomed by my fear."

He placed a hand beneath her chin and lifted her face until their eyes met. "You risked your life for her. That wasn't fear. That was courage.

As she said, her fate was written on the Elder Stone."

"And my father's fate?"

He shook his head. "That prophecy was not cast in the Elder Stone."

"It was no less foretold," the princess insisted. "'And she must give life to save life.' I should have given my life to her."

"No," the dragon whispered, an emerald eye turned to her. "I was not the one."

"Who is?" Drusia asked. "Must I do this all again, and again, and yet again, while my father falls into darkness?"

"You have given life, Princess." The dragon nuzzled her infant. "She shall be called Drusilla, the light of she who gave life. You gave her life. I give her to you."

The dragon drew a slow breath, its emerald eye fixed on Drusia. Then, a quiet smile on its lips, its flank settled for the last time.

"I guess we have a daughter," Milan said, tears brimming in his eyes.

"We?"

He nodded, eyes lowered. "I have loved you from the moment we met, Drusia Morgantide. Let me bear this burden with you. Else I cannot bear her death alone."

His heart beat once, twice, thundering with a fear like none he had ever known. Now it was her turn to lift his face.

"I love you, Milan."

Drusilla laid the last page in her lap astounded by how closely his story paralleled her imaginings. Astounded by what she had discovered there. Her hands were shaking.

He was standing in the doorway. Apparently he had been for some time. She bit her lip, but the words seemed borne by an inner wind which would not be denied.

"I never knew."

He gave the briefest anxious nod. "From the very first day you came to work here."

"I never knew."

"Now you do."

He stepped closer to take the pages from her lap. Their fingers touched. Lingered. She shifted in the chair. This was…what? A dream come true? Did that really happen?

"How did…?" Her voice quivered. "How did we share a dream?"

"Maybe there's a place where it wasn't a dream at all, but a reality."

"You knew."

"I guessed. Didn't you?"

She had, she admitted to herself. Throughout the night she had wondered if she weren't dreaming alone, if her fantasy was merely part of reality. His hand squeezed hers, drawing her gaze back to his.

"Where do we go now?" he asked quietly.

And there it lay. The question she could no longer avoid. Was that the key, that she must give life to save life? Would he? Could she?

Her heart knew the answers that her mind could not. Her hand closed around his.

"How about breakfast?" she asked.

"Breakfast?"

She smiled. "I thought you'd like to meet my dad."

MOONGLOW

Catherine Asaro

* * *

To Mary Jo Putney, with gratitude,
for welcoming me to this genre

Dear Reader,

I've always loved fantasy worlds and romances. When I combined that with my appreciation for the beauty of tesselated mosaics, the land of Aronsdale came to exist. Through the magic of shapes and colors, the mages of Aronsdale, mostly women, are able to bring light and healing into the lives of their people.

The kings of Aronsdale have always married the most powerful mages. I found myself wondering what would happen if a young woman didn't realize that custom would include her—and if her groom is the long-lost heir, a tormented prince who needs a healing greater than anything she could have imagined. She feels her love growing, if only she can reach through his barriers.

I've enjoyed the company of Iris and Jarid on their journeys of self-discovery and romance. I hope you enjoy their story also. I would love to hear from you at my e-mail asaro@sff.net. Or you can visit my Web site at www.sff.net/people/asaro.

Best regards,

Catherine Asaro

P.S. If you enjoyed the story of Iris and Jarid, be sure to pick up Muller and Chime's story, *The Charmed Sphere,* one of the first books in LUNA, available in February 2004.

Prologue

Jarid jolted awake when his mother cried out. Their carriage was lurching through the night much too fast. His mother held him close, shielding him with her embrace. In his six years of life, he had never felt such fear from her. It terrified him. Across the carriage, in the darkness, his father—Prince Aron—was half out of his seat, a dagger clenched in his hand as he yanked aside the curtains on the small window.

Yells erupted outside, chilling and wild. Jarid buried his head against his mother's side and squeezed his eyes shut. The carriage suddenly reared as if it were an enraged beast. Perhaps it *was* angry; made as a perfect sphere, the enchanted carriage focused the mage power of Jarid's mother.

"Mama!" He gripped her arm. "*Papa!*"

His mother thrust a large glass orb into his hands.

She spoke urgently, but he couldn't hear over all the noise. The carriage jerked again, and then they were tumbling, over and over, slamming from side to side in the darkness.

A horse screamed, its frenzied cry splitting the air. Jarid gasped as he was thrown across the carriage. His head hit a hard surface and he groaned, clutching the glass ball in his arms. His mother caught him, holding him so tightly he could barely breathe. With his cheek pressed against her shoulder, he heard her speaking an orb-spell. She curled her body and her spell around him, cocooning him in a protective sphere of life.

With a roar, the world exploded. Jarid hurtled through the air with his mother and they landed hard, slamming the air out of his lungs. Debris rained everywhere, splintering and furious. A shower of pebbles clattered from the sky, and a rock rolled against Jarid's leg.

Then everything became still.

Jarid huddled against his mother. "Mama?" he whispered. "Papa?" He clenched his small hands around the glass ball. "C-can we go home now?"

No answer.

Shaking, he lifted his head and peered into the night. Wreckage lay everywhere, scattered at the bottom of a cliff as if a great hand had flung it there. A chill wind blew his hair, making him shake.

Somehow, incredibly, his mother still held him. Only she didn't move or speak. She didn't even seem to breathe, but surely that had to be wrong. It *had* to be wrong.

His voice caught. "Mama?"

Words carried to him through the night. Jarid froze, desperate for help but afraid of who might be coming. Even the stars had deserted him, hidden behind clouds.

The voices came nearer, resolving into an argument. Two men on horses made black silhouettes against a charcoal-gray sky.

"Damn it all, it wasn't supposed to crash." That came from the man on the larger horse. "You swore we wouldn't hurt anyone."

A deep voice answered. "This makes our job easier."

"Easier?" The first man let out an explosive breath. "Gods, Murk, I never agreed to murder anyone."

"The highway doesn't come with guarantees." The other man, Murk apparently, stopped his horse near the wreckage. "You know the risks you take."

"*You* take them." The first man swung off his horse. "I won't be doing this again."

Murk jumped down beside him. "I never knew you for a coward."

The first man ignored him, the way stone paid no heed to insults. Jarid immediately thought of him as Stone. While Stone approached the ruined carriage, Jarid huddled by his mother, hiding in the shadows, clutching the glass ball. He didn't understand much of what the men said, but one thing was obvious: they believed they had killed his parents. He wasn't sure what it meant to die, but when it had happened to Grandmother, she had gone to sleep and never woken up. Tears welled in his eyes. Surely Mother and Father hadn't done the same.

Stone suddenly swore. "It was an orb-carriage."

"Who cares about its shape?" Murk muttered. "Don't start on me with that blather about spells. Shape-mages are fakes, lording their supposed powers over the rest of us."

"The two soldiers we knocked out must have been their honor guard."

Murk stayed by his horse. "If people in this carriage were mages, why did they have such a small honor guard?"

"I've no idea."

Jarid could have told them; their carriage and the two guards had been cut off from the rest when an old bridge collapsed back at the river. So the driver had been taking them on to the next bridge. Father had said it would be no trouble.

For the first time in his life, Jarid understood that his father could be wrong.

Stone knelt by the body of Prince Aron. "Maybe he was the mage."

"None of them were mages." Murk crossed his arms. "Mages don't exist."

Stone looked around. "How many bodies do you see?"

Still refusing to come closer, Murk motioned at the rubble. "Two over there and the driver beyond."

Holding his breath, Jarid tried to vanish. He wasn't certain how he had survived the crash, but he remembered what his mother had taught him about shape-mages: *Your power is as strong as a life. One life, no more.* The power of a life. It couldn't be. His mother couldn't have used all her power to protect him. Surely she could have saved herself and his father. She *couldn't* be dead. He wanted to cry, but he bit the inside of his mouth to stop himself.

Stone looked up, frowning. Then he rose and came over to where Jarid huddled. When the highwayman went down on one knee, Jarid cringed against his mother.

"Saints almighty," Stone said. "It's a little boy."

"What?" Murk finally came forward, stepping carefully through the wreckage. For all that he denied mages existed, his apprehension rolled over Jarid like clammy fog. Murk's bravado disguised a soul-parching envy and fear of shape-mages that Jarid barely understood.

Jarid thrust out his chin, trying to be strong. "Go away!"

Stone laid his hand on Jarid's arm. "It's all right."

"Tell the brat to shut up," Murk said. Unease oozed from his mind.

"Let him be." Stone gently freed Jarid from his mother's lifeless grip, which remained strong even now.

"Leave me alone!" Jarid wrapped his arms around his glass ball. "My grandfather is coming!"

"Your grandfather," Murk snorted. "Sure, and don't old men scare me."

Jarid wanted to shout that Grandfather was strong and fierce, that he had many shape-soldiers, that he was king in this land. But no words came. Instead, tears ran down his face.

"Hai," Stone murmured. "I am so very sorry."

"Don't bother," Murk said. "He's going to join his parents soon." Crouching down, he poked in the rubble until he dug up Prince Aron's gem-encrusted dagger, which he thrust into the sack he carried. "Take care of the boy. Fast. We have to get out of here."

Stone jerked up his head. "Are you crazy? I'm not going to kill a child."

I will run, Jarid thought, though he could barely move, he hurt so much from the crash.

Then Murk rolled over the body of Jarid's father and began ripping jewels off his tunic.

"Stop!" Jarid cried, trying to scramble to his feet. He made it to his knees before his legs crumpled and he collapsed. He was gripping the glass ball so hard, his arms ached.

Stone lifted Jarid into his arms and stood up, cradling him with unexpected tenderness. "It's all right. I won't hurt you." He touched a place on Jarid's neck that felt wet. "We can stitch this up."

"No!" Jarid fought hard, holding his ball with one arm while he flailed at Stone with a small fist.

Stone caught his hand. "I'll take you to a safe place."

Murk looked up from his looting. "We can't let him live. He's seen us."

Jarid froze, finally understanding. He could tell people what they had done, and he could describe them.

They would kill him because he could see, hear and talk.

"No." Tears ran down Jarid's face. "Please."

"Shhhh," Stone said. "Don't listen to him. We won't hurt you."

"Damn it." Murk jumped to his feet. "We have to get rid of him."

Stone tightened his hold on Jarid. "I won't do it."

Jarid pressed against Stone's chest, trying to hide. "I won't tell anything," he promised Murk, his voice shaking. "I'll never, never tell. I *promise.*"

"Murk, listen," Stone said. "I'll keep him with me. You know where I live. Way out there, up in the mountains, he'll never see anyone, never have a chance to tell what happened. Hell, I've gone for years at a time without visitors." Under his breath, he added, "I should have stayed up there."

Murk scowled, fierce as he came over to them. "We have to get rid of him and get out of here before those guards wake up." He grasped the ball Jarid carried.

"No!" Jarid jerked back. "It's mine!"

Murk's fury sparked, so sharp that Jarid *saw* it in the air. "I'll take care of you myself, you little swamp wart." He wrested the ball away from Jarid.

"Don't hurt it, please." More tears ran down Jarid's face. Mage power saturated the night, straining to change Murk's cruelty, straining so hard that the spell distorted and the sphere began to glow.

"What the *hell?*" Murk hurled the ball away and it sailed through the night in an arc of violet light. Jarid felt power *reaching,* focusing through the perfect shape, the power of a shape-mage, of a sphere-mage, the highest form, *the power of a life.* Even now, the spell sought to help him, as if it knew his terror that Murk would kill him, all because Jarid could tell what he had seen and heard tonight.

As the ball hit the ground with a terrible crash, its distorted spell made one last attempt to save Jarid. Violet light flared—and when it died, it took with it Jarid's sight, his hearing and his voice.

Chapter 1

The Hollow

Iris Larkspur walked down the grassy hill, savoring the warm day. The sky arched above, as blue as glazed china. In a valley to the west, the village of Crofts Vale and its surrounding farmlands slumbered in the morning sun. Even after having been at Castle Suncroft for a year, since her eighteenth birthday, she marveled at this mild climate. Spring came earlier here than in the rugged mountains of her home. These hills had already turned green and were bursting with new life.

Yet all this serenity couldn't heal her loneliness.

"Iris!" The sharp call came from behind her.

Startled, she spun around. Far up the hill, Della No-Cozen, the Shape-Mage Mistress of Suncroft, stood with her hands on her ample hips, her gray curls fluttering in the breeze. Even from this far away, her frown was obvious.

"Aye, well, I'm in trouble again," Iris muttered, aware of the lilting accent that marked her as a stranger in this land, a commoner from the north. She hurried up the hill. In the distance, cresting a taller hill, Castle Suncroft glimmered in the sunlight, gold and bright, its crenellated towers topped by spires.

Seeing her wayward student returning, Della returned to the cottage behind her on the hill. Iris sighed. A pretty cottage it was, but she felt suffocated inside. She missed her home, a tiny village in the Tallwalk Mountains. She had little to go back to, though. Her foster family had been relieved when she left; it meant they no longer had to feed or to house her. Her mother had abandoned Iris with them just days after Iris's birth, an unpromising start for what, until last year, had been an unpromising life. Although her foster parents hadn't ill-treated her, neither had they given any affection. They tolerated her.

Della had discovered Iris during the mistress's travels through Aronsdale. Each year Della went on a tour in search of village girls with mage talent. But Iris had never really felt accepted here, either, and Prince Muller had no reason to continue providing her room and board at the cottage if Iris never progressed in her mage studies with Della.

Pah. As if Muller would care. Although his behavior was impeccable, she knew he loathed his duties. Regardless, he had to become king of Aronsdale; the true heir, Prince Aron, had died fourteen years ago in a carriage accident, along with his wife and son Jarid. Prince Aron's father, King Daron, had grieved for years. Iris thought it heartbreaking; a parent shouldn't outlive his children. Yet Daron had survived them by fourteen years. Now the old king had passed away and Muller, his nephew, would soon wear the crown.

As Iris neared the cottage, she saw a young woman in its doorway. Iris inwardly groaned. Well then, and here it was her bad luck to study today with Chime Headwind. Iris supposed she should be honored. Sure it was true, Chime would marry Prince Muller and be queen. By law, Chime had to marry him; she was the most powerful shape-mage among her generation in Aronsdale. Iris thanked the fates it was Chime and not her. She had no wish for the weight of such responsibilities, and the prospect of marrying Muller would have sent her fleeing to the hills.

Chime and Muller had a lot in common, both of them overly aware of their importance. Yet Iris wondered if their pride served as bravado to disguise their fears about becoming king and queen. Away from the royal court, they were an amiable couple. Given a choice, she thought they probably would have settled in the country as farmers. Many people might covet royal titles, but Muller and Chime weren't among them.

Right now, Chime was standing in the doorway, fixing her hair, carefully arranging the glossy locks. Her appraising gaze made Iris flush. She would never measure up to Chime's impossible ideals. The future queen seemed to care only about appearance. Iris told herself she didn't mind, that it only mattered what a person had inside, but it was hard to remember that when the rest of the world so greatly prized Chime's beauty. Iris's wild mane of chestnut curls would never tame into the sleek fall of Chime's golden hair; her full, curvy figure would never have Chime's willowy elegance; her face would never approach Chime's angelic perfection.

As Iris reached the door, Chime gave her a cool smile. "You look lively today."

Iris blinked. "Lively?"

"Wind-blown." Chime hesitated. "Your hair is a mess."

"I don't mind." Iris enjoyed the breezes.

Chime entered the cottage with her. Iris left her boots at the door, feeling as if she had lost the freedom of the outdoors. She didn't know why the cottage stifled her; it was lovely inside. Sunlight filtered through colored windows of many shapes: triangles, diamonds, hexagons, beveled squares, and others. They made graceful patterns around larger round windows with clear panes. Sunshine slanted through the glass, warming the well-worn tables and chairs, and vases full of colorful shape-blossoms brightened the room even more.

Della No-Cozen bustled in from the kitchen and waved her hands at the girls. "Sit yourselves down, you two. What is all this playing about, eh? We have lessons."

Iris settled at a table beside a yellow window and

tried to look contrite. She doubted she succeeded, judging by the way Della frowned at her.

"Well then," the mage mistress said tartly. "Don't you look healthy today."

A flush spread in Iris's face. "Thank you, ma'am."

"Very healthy," Della grumbled. "What with all the fresh air you get, out who-knows-where instead of studying."

"Aye, ma'am," Iris said, mortified.

"Aye, ma'am?" Della crossed her arms. "I would rather hear, 'Aye, Mistress No-Cozen, I will be on time from now on.'"

"Aye, ma'am. I mean, I willna be late, Mage Mistress." Iris winced, knowing her voice lilted even more when she was nervous.

Della said *humph* and bustled off, probably to retrieve their class materials from her office.

Sitting at the table, Chime brushed an invisible speck of dirt off her sleeve. Then she smiled sweetly at Iris. "Yes, let us proceed, now that everyone is here."

"I didna come that late," Iris grumbled.

"Did I say that?" Chime asked, all innocence.

"Well then, is'n that what you meant?"

"Perhaps we have a language difficulty."

"Nay, Chime, I donna have a language difficulty." Iris felt her face heat as her accent thickened.

"I'm sure you can't help it," Chime murmured.

Iris poked her finger into the petals of a green box-blossom in the vase. "An' I'm sure you canna help but notice, aye?"

"Language, like appearance, is an art form," Chime explained. "Some people have the gift for its graceful expression. Others don't. It isn't their fault."

Exasperated, Iris resisted the urge to snap the box-blossom. Chime, she decided, had been sorely misnamed. "I swear, I do truly think sometimes you clang."

Chime blinked. "Clang?"

"You know the word?"

"Of course." Chime hesitated. "Don't bells clang?"

"Aye, they do certainly."

Chime looked bewildered. "But I'm not a bell."

Iris held back her sigh. It was difficult to make a witty comeback with someone who couldn't figure out what the comeback meant. "It is'n important."

"Your speech is so quaint," Chime said.

Patience, Iris thought. *Be serene.* She felt more like pouring the shape-blossoms out of the vase onto Chime's head. But she shouldn't think such thoughts about the future queen. Really.

"Why are you smiling like that?" Chime asked.

"Smiling?" *Hai!* She had to stop this. Antagonizing Chime would only lead to repercussions from Muller. Iris made a valiant effort to be polite. "I was thinking you look radiant this morning." That was certainly true. Chime was maddeningly beautiful even just after she woke up.

"Oh, well, in that case." Chime smiled. "Of course."

"And humble," Iris added under her breath.

"What did you say?" Chime asked, friendly now.

"Uh...bumble." Iris tried to think of a way out of the insult she had almost given. "Bumblebees."

Chime looked bewildered. "Bees?"

"They are, uh, sunny and bright. Like you."

"Oh." Chime gave her a confused smile. "Thank you."

Della came back before Iris could cram her foot any further down her own throat. The teacher opened a scroll on the table before them. "Here."

The scroll delighted Iris. Inked in bright colors, with finely drawn vines curling around the edges, it showed the shapes that mages used to focus spells. For all that Iris had yet to succeed with even a simple spell, she felt the power in those beautiful forms.

"We will start with the basics." Della lowered her plump self into a chair. "Iris, how do we use the shapes?"

The easy question relieved Iris. "They focus our gifts. The more powerful the shape, the better it concentrates a mage's power." She paused, but the answer felt incomplete. "If a mage tries to focus through a shape too powerful for her ability, her spell will dissipate."

"Good." Della turned to Chime. "And what determines the power of a shape?"

Chime hesitated. "The, uh...number of its sides?"

Ach, everyone knows that, Iris thought. Then she reminded herself she was being serene toward Chime.

Della, however, scowled. "And?"

Chime blinked. "Ma'am?"

"How do the number of sides give a mage power?"

"The more sides a shape has, the greater its power?"

"The shape itself has no power," Della reminded her.

"Oh. Well, yes. The mage has the power."

"Go on."

"The shapes focus her power?"

"All right. How?"

After a moment Chime said, "I don't know."

Della sighed. "Try, Chime. Take your time."

Iris knew Della wanted Chime to describe what a mage could do with her power. Although Chime should have known, Iris sympathized with her confusion. If they could already use shapes to focus their power, they wouldn't need to be here.

Iris touched a glimmering silver triangle on the scroll. She traced her finger over the shapes in order of increasing power: squares, diamonds, pentagons, hexagons and more, the number of sides increasing until the shape resembled a circle. With an infinite number of sides, it *became* a circle, the most perfect flat shape. But those weren't the forms that captivated Iris. She loved three-dimensional shapes: pyramids, boxes, octahedrons and so on, their forms becoming rounder as their number of sides increased, until they resembled faceted balls. With an infinite number of sides, a shape became the most perfect form of all: a sphere. Only the most powerful of all mages could focus through such a shape.

Della was watching Iris now. "Tell me what you see in the shapes."

Frustration welled within her. "To what purpose? I canna use them for even the simplest spell."

"You will," Della said. "You have the talent."

Iris couldn't fathom why Della believed such a thing. Iris had never managed to focus power through *any* shape, not even flat triangles made from red sticks.

Excitement sparked in Chime's voice. "Della, I used a ten-sided shape in my exercises this morning, a blocky ball like my little brother plays with."

Della's expression softened. "I'm not surprised. I'm sure you can go even higher, maybe to twenty sides."

Chime's gaze widened. "That would be almost a sphere."

Iris smiled, caught by Chime's excitement despite herself. "Well then, and sure it is." She tapped a picture on the scroll, a faceted sphere with many faces. "This is your mage shape, Chime." The other girl beamed at her.

"Let's try." Della went to a cabinet by the wall, one with shape-blossom vines engraved on its doors. She opened it to reveal shelves of solid objects. From one shelf, she took a polished jade ball with faceted sides; from another, she took a pearly disk, a lower level shape than the ball, but highest among the two-dimensional forms. Returning to the table, she set the ball in front of Chime and the disk in front of Iris. Then she settled in her chair.

"So." Della tapped the faceted ball. "Chime, try a ruby spell."

Chime squinted at the ball, as if it could reveal the spell she should have memorized. Iris wished she could help. It seemed unfair Chime had so much trouble learning, given the effort she put into her studies. Iris had to respect her for that; Iris could barely make herself stay indoors, let alone study. She often *thought* about doing her studies, but no matter how earnest her intentions, she usually ended up wandering in the woods instead.

The universe had no justice. Chime had great mage gifts and the will to study, but she struggled to learn the simplest uses of her power. Iris learned easily, but she had neither the power to perform the spells nor the will to apply herself. If she and Chime could have combined their strengths, together they might have become the student Della wished.

Even if Iris couldn't do spells, though, they fascinated her. They were a rainbow: red spells created light, orange soothed physical pain, yellow eased sorrow, green revealed the emotions of others, blue healed physical injuries and indigo healed emotional injuries. A mage worked spells at her color and below. Most could do red and orange. It was more difficult to soothe emotional rather than physical pain, and it took a strong mage to do yellow spells. Green mages were rare; feeling emotions was harder than easing them, because a mage could soothe the pain of another person without actually experiencing it. Blue mages were almost unheard of; only the strongest could heal injuries, treating the source of the pain rather than just the symptoms.

No indigo mages existed. How did you cure grief, anguish or misery? Only time could truly heal such wounds. Legend claimed the royal line of Aronsdale, the House of Dawnfield, had once produced indigos, but the historians had never found reliable records of any such mages.

In all Aronsdale, Iris knew of only two mages who had the strength to call on three-dimensional forms—Chime and Della. Right now Chime was squinting at her blocky globe. When she murmured, rosy light flickered in the ball.

"You can do better," Della prodded.

A flush stained Chime's delicate cheeks. As her forehead furrowed, the light within the sphere flared and turned green. A sense of well-being spread through Iris, and she no longer felt so painfully homesick. Her crushing loneliness eased for the first time since she had come to Suncroft.

Chime smiled angelically at Della. "You're frustrated with Iris. You worry she will never achieve her potential."

Iris's good mood crashed down. Only Chime would show her ability to do green spells by speaking Della's disappointment in another student.

"Well then." Iris's voice caught. Dismayed to have her failure made so obvious, she rose to her feet. "And it be a pity for us all."

Then she escaped from the cottage.

Iris ran through the woods. She hadn't stopped to put on her boots, but it made no difference if someone saw her tearing about in stockings and disapproved. She wouldn't be at Suncroft much longer. Chime had only spoken what they all knew: Della had erred. The talent she believed she had seen in Iris was no more than a ghost that didn't really exist, like drifting mist that, for a moment, seemed to take form but then dissipated.

She came out on a bluff above a valley. To her right, Castle Suncroft stood on its hill, golden in the sunlight. The nearby village of Crofts Vale nestled in the valley, pretty houses with thatched roofs. Vines bloomed everywhere, with rosy pyramid blossoms, green and blue box-buds, orange ring-flowers and violet orbs. They climbed trees, spilled down trellises and brightened gardens.

Iris knelt in the grass and bowed her head. A tear ran down her face.

"What is this?" a voice said. "We've hardly started the lesson and already you are leaving."

Iris looked around. Della stood a few paces away, her hands on her hips and a scowl on her face.

"Hai, Della, admit the truth." Iris rose wearily to her feet. "I donna have it in me to be a mage."

Della came over to her. "Is that so?"

"Aye, that be so."

"So now you think you can take my place?"

"Well, sure as the sun shines, I would never be thinking such a thing."

"No?"

"No, ma'am."

Della glowered. "I am the one who decides if you have what it takes to study with me, young woman."

"But I canna—"

"Pah." Della motioned around them, taking in the sky and the distant hazy mountains. "You see all this?"

"Aye, ma'am."

"What is it?"

"Aronsdale."

"Aronsdale, Hairs-in-Dale, that isn't what I meant."

Iris gazed over the enchanting panorama and breathed in the crisp, pure air. "It is a place of beauty and serenity."

"Serenity, pah. Aronsdale is a mess."

"It is?"

"It will be, after Prince Muller's coronation."

"Della!"

"Well, it's true."

"You shouldna speak of His Highness so."

Della exhaled tiredly. "Then who will? He doesn't want the throne."

Knowing Della loved the prince as if he were her own nephew, Iris understood what it took for her to make such an admission. "He is the heir."

Della's voice quieted. "I speak to you privately, Iris, as one of the king's advisors. We have delayed the coronation because if we push Muller, he may refuse the crown."

"But then who will be king?"

"We don't know. Probably another of his advisors, perhaps Brant Firestoke."

Iris didn't doubt Lord Firestoke would make a good ruler. But Aronsdale needed the royal family; the House of Dawnfield was the symbolic heart of the country. Their loss would devastate the people. "Canna Chime reassure Muller? She is well an' sure a green mage, Della. I felt it this afternoon."

"She does have great gifts." Della hesitated. "But one must also know how to use such gifts."

"It is only that the spells are new. She will learn."

Della sighed. "You are kind, especially given how she speaks to you."

Iris hadn't realized Della saw the tension between her two young charges. "I think it frustrates her to learn the spells so slow. When her words bite, it is only her fear speaking. She has a good spirit."

"Now you sound like a green mage."

"It is only common sense, no feeling of emotions."

"You think so? I see the power in you."

Iris answered dourly. "You are the only one who does."

"Well, of course." Della actually smiled. "Why do you think I am mage mistress here? It is one of my best skills, to see gifts in others." Her smile faded. "I saw it even in Prince Jarid, the boy who died in the carriage crash."

"A boy mage? Nay, it is impossible."

"Improbable, but not impossible. History tells of a few. In the Dawnfield line, they seem to skip every other generation. And Jarid's mother, Lady Sky, was one of the strongest shape-mages Aronsdale has known.'' Della's mood turned pensive. ''She and Prince Jarid had so much promise.''

Iris sensed her grief. ''Their deaths were a great sorrow.''

''Aye, all of them.'' Della took a moment before she continued. ''After King Daron lost his son, Prince Aron, his advisors urged him to remarry and sire another heir. But he had never stopped mourning his first wife, who had died many years before. And he refused to see the truth about Muller, his nephew, that the boy had neither the interest nor aptitude for the title.'' She sighed. ''If Daron had a fault, it was that he loved his family too much to acknowledge their flaws.''

Even now, three turnings of the moon since Daron had died, Iris found it hard to accept he was no longer with them. ''He was a good king.''

''He was.'' Della spoke quietly. ''Aronsdale is a small realm. We don't have much else to live on besides farming. The land can offer a good life, yes, but during drought or famine, we have few resources to fall back on.''

Iris's mood dimmed. ''I often saw such in my village.''

''We need a strong king who can guide Aronsdale.'' She paused. ''We have Muller.''

''Aye.'' Iris thought it best to say no more.

''He needs capable advisors, people with intelligence, compassion and foresight.'' Her gaze didn't waver. ''Someday you could be one of those advisors.

You have both the strength of character and the mage power." Softly she said, "Don't give up now."

Iris felt as if she were breaking inside. "I canna pretend to gifts I donna have."

"The power is there." Della made a frustrated noise. "I just don't know how to help you find it."

Iris indicated the woods that spilled down the hills around them. "This is the magic—trees, sky, flowers."

Della's expression turned thoughtful. "The harder I push to make you study, the more you want to come out here."

"I donna mean disrespect, ma'am."

"I know, Iris." Della considered her. "It's as if your studies *drive* you to seek the outdoors."

"It does feel that way," Iris admitted.

"Do you have a special place here, one that makes you feel even closer to the land?"

Iris hesitated to reveal her secrets. But in her own gruff way, Della had mothered her this past year, trying to ease Iris's loneliness, to provide her with a home in the cottage, more than just a place to live. Iris felt she had given back so little, no hint of the gifts Della strove to awaken.

"I have a place where I go to be alone," Iris offered.

"Will you take me there?"

Softly Iris said, "Aye."

Trees and ferns enclosed the glade, curving around on all sides and overhead, hiding this secret hollow from the rest of the woods. A stream flowed off a stone ledge and fell sparkling into a pool. Shape-vines threaded the trees and draped the falls.

Iris sunk into the soft grass by the water. "I come here whenever I can."

Della turned in a circle. "It is lovely."

"It soothes."

"Don't you see what it is?"

"What do you mean?"

Della's voice gentled. "Look at the shape."

For the first time, Iris took in the form of the hollow rather than its beauty. "Hai! I'll be a frog in a fig. It's a sphere!"

Della chuckled. "In a fig, eh?" She settled next to Iris. "I have been through these woods many times and never seen this place."

"It's always been here."

"I recognize the waterfall and some trees. But a sphere? It wasn't like this before. You have changed it."

"Nay, Della. How could I?"

"Perhaps the plants respond to your mage power."

Iris didn't see how such could happen. And yet...each time she visited this hollow, it soothed her more than the last, giving her peace that eluded her elsewhere. Could she have somehow been changing the shape? "It seems impossible."

Della's eyes lit up. "Iris!"

"Aye?"

"Make a spell here."

"Why?"

"Maybe you can do here what you can't do in the cottage."

Iris squinted at her. "That is an odd idea."

"An odd idea may be what you need."

"I have no shape to focus my power."

"But you do." Della indicated the hollow.

Iris flushed. "Well then, sure, it be a sphere, too much for me."

"Try."

"I canna do it."

Kindly, Della said, "You won't know unless you try."

Iris feared to try, lest she fail yet again. But if she never took chances, she might as well live her life in a hole. She breathed deeply, centering herself, thinking of the round hollow. The waterfall shimmered with rainbows and blossoms hung from the vines, all colors, like mage spells—

Red.

Orange.

Yellow.

Green.

Blue.

Indigo—

With a great surge of power, her mind *opened.*

Chapter 2

Jarid

Darkness and silence filled his life.

Jarid was sitting in his favorite spot, a corner of his room. He preferred the floor, where he couldn't fall. Blind and deaf, he lived in an isolation eased only by familiarity with his surroundings. Stone, his foster father, had long ago stopped trying to make him use furniture; after Jarid had grown larger than Stone, he had simply refused to move when Stone tried to put him in a chair.

Today, he imagined shapes in his mind, beautiful spheres, glimmering and vibrant. Over the years they had helped him focus on Stone, until now he could sense his foster father's every mood. Lately, Stone worried that Jarid would become so immersed in his meditations, he would forget to eat.

Jarid sighed without sound. Meditation was his escape. These past fourteen years, he had neither seen nor heard, and he had never spoken. He knew about the rare visitors to the cabin only because their emotions differed from Stone's. His foster father loved him; others found him strange and disturbing. Mercifully, almost no one visited. He and Stone lived alone, cut off from the world, never communicating with it. From Stone's mind, Jarid knew he had no idea his foster son was heir to Aronsdale. Jarid wanted it that way. He strove to forget who he had been, because of what he had become. Never would he be king.

A vibration came through the floor, the tread of Stone's feet. The aroma of meat tickled Jarid's nose. He had distant memories of eating steaks from gold platters, but he wondered now if his recollections of loving parents and a grandfather who ruled as king were no more than a fantasy he created to fill the void of his life.

Jarid concentrated on the air currents, feeling them change against his face. He caught that blend of pine, wood smoke and sweat smells that defined his foster father. He thought Stone was kneeling in front of him; sure enough, someone took his hands and gave him a plate. Jarid smelled the meal so clearly, he could almost taste the meat, gravy and vegetables. He accepted the rough plate, but only to calm Stone. After his father left, Jarid set the plate on the floor. Then he sat enjoying the sunlight on his face. On these rare bright days, Stone opened the curtains, knowing his son enjoyed the warmth.

Eventually the sun moved on in its journey across the sky. Sorrow at its passing came to Jarid; so little in his life gave him pleasure. He rose and exercised, working any part of his body he thought needed training. It meant a great deal to him that he could do this without help. He worked out constantly, having little else to do but the simple chores he could manage. His only other diversion was sitting outside on those rare days when the cold, damp weather cleared.

After he tired, he settled on the floor again. Later he would go into the other room and weave more of the aromatic thatching Stone used to repair the roof. For now, he ate dinner. The meat had gone cold and the gravy congealed, but he didn't mind. Nothing much bothered him anymore. When he had first lost his senses, he had cried in silence for days, months, forever it seemed. He couldn't even feel the vibrations in his throat that would have come had he been making sounds he couldn't hear. Over the years, he had become numb. He locked away his emotions, protecting himself from pain. Now, full from his meal, he closed his eyes, more out of habit than for any need, and rested his head against the wall.

Shapes evolved in his mind.

He loved spheres. Even in that distant time he barely remembered, they had fascinated him. They'd helped him focus his spells. As a child, he had never understood why adults had insisted he couldn't feel the moods of other people, or that even a fully matured mage would have trouble doing what came so easily to him. They had also claimed he couldn't heal, though he had made his kitten better when it had the wasting illness. So he had stopped telling people, except for his mother, who believed him. She had encouraged him to play his shape games and helped him learn to focus.

Now he had nothing but those bittersweet games.

Jarid imagined cubes, rings, pyramids, bars, polyhedrons and especially spheres, all glistening in gem colors so lovely they made his heart ache. They were works of art he had been refining for fourteen years. He knew, from Stone's mind, that he could light up a room if he chose. It didn't matter to Jarid; he never saw the light—indeed, he had seen nothing since the night Murk had shattered his life.

Fourteen years ago Jarid had hated Stone, pounding him with small fists even as a blind and deaf six-year-old. Over the years, his hatred had faltered in Stone's unexpected kindness. Jarid knew he soothed his foster father just by his presence, and that he helped heal the emotional scars Stone had suffered in the lonely destitution of these rocky hills. But nothing could ease Stone's crushing guilt.

Jarid knew that guilt.

Stone felt it every time he looked at his young ward, every time he struggled to understand Jarid's needs, when Jarid could never ask or answer. If Stone had once been hard, these years had cracked his granite heart. Jarid didn't know how he could both hate and love his foster father, yet he did. It made no difference that Stone wasn't the one who had killed his parents; Stone had helped Murk attack the carriage. Yet since that day, Stone had been a compassionate guardian, at first out of guilt, but later out of love, an emotion he couldn't hide from Jarid. In spite of Jarid's intent to remain cold, he had come to love his foster father.

Isolated high in the Boxer-Mage Mountains, above even the most remote hamlets of the Tallwalk Mountains, they scratched out a living. Jarid helped as best he could, stacking firewood, digging, carrying heavy loads, making ropes and tools. Their poverty mattered little to him; all he truly cared about had died on that long-ago night. He was no longer whole. Stone had offered him a refuge where he could withdraw from humanity.

Jarid had no idea how he appeared to other people, but he thought he must be hateful and hideous. He had felt that way since his parents died. Stone seemed to find him tolerable, but in the harsh reality of their world, anything that wasn't actively lethal was tolerable. Jarid knew he should have prevented the crash, though *how,* he had no idea. His mother should never have died to save his life.

Moisture gathered in his eyes. Angry, he wiped it dry. Struggling to push away his tormented memories, he filled his mind with spheres. His thoughts easily expanded out from his center.

And yet...today something was different. A tension pulled him, *straining.* He suddenly remembered the sphere that had strained to protect him all those years ago against Murk's murderous cruelty. Jarid felt a similar sensation now, but gentle instead of desperate. The shapes in his mind blurred into a luminous rainbow fog.

Straining.

Reaching.

Seeking.

In his mind, a vine of shape-blossoms curled through the mist. Sweat broke out on Jarid's forehead. What invaded his solitude? He clenched the rough cloth of his trousers, resisting the presence that reached for him, unaware and unknowing, but coming closer, closer…

Leave me alone! The cry reverberated in his mind, and he felt foolish, reacting with such dismay to his own thoughts. For surely this "intruder" was no more than his own fevered imaginings.

But no…he still felt someone seeking, coming closer, so close. A green sphere vibrant with ferns appeared in his mind and a waterfall of light poured into a bright pool.

Beautiful sphere.

Sphere mage.

Rainbow.

And then he touched her mind.

"No!"

Iris's cry rang through the hollow. She mentally recoiled from the cold, silent darkness that had enveloped her.

"What is it?" Della was holding her shoulders. "I felt the surge of power!" She could barely contain her excitement. "What happened?"

"I—I touched his mind." Iris couldn't shake the overwhelming loneliness of that moment.

"His?"

"Another mage." Iris's pulse hammered. "A mage of power. But...but for this man, power has many forms."

"You know who you reached?"

"Yes." Iris stared at her, unable to believe this discovery. "Prince Jarid."

Chapter 3

Homecoming

His Highness, Prince Muller Dawnfield, paced in front of Iris, his boots loud on the parquetry floor. The receiving hall in the castle was much longer than wide and drenched in sunlight from its many tall windows. The walls and columns gleamed with gold, blue and white mosaics, tessellated patterns that had fascinated generations of shape-mages. Usually, Iris loved studying them, searching out patterns in the designs, but today she had no time for such games. She sat in an ivory-and-gold chair, her spine straight against its back, her hands folded in her lap.

"Are you certain?" Muller demanded for the fifth time.

"Aye, Your Highness," Iris said, also for the fifth time.

"But Jarid is *dead!*" Muller stopped and glowered at her. A slender man with white-gold hair brushing his shoulders, he was a full head taller than Iris when they were standing and nine years her senior. His cream-colored trousers accented the length of his legs and his gold tunic was designed in a futile attempt to make his narrow shoulders appear wider. Iris had always thought him beautiful, like a leggy and graceful wild animal, more suited to running in the forest than to the confines of his enchanting but inanimate castle. She doubted he would appreciate her comparison, though; he had always wanted to be seen as strong and powerful, not graceful and flighty.

Right now his changeable gray eyes reminded her of an overcast sky. He frowned. "My cousin, may he rest in peace, has been dead for fourteen years."

Della was standing by Iris's chair, one hand on its high back. "His body was never found."

Muller resumed pacing, adjusting his tunic to smooth out minuscule wrinkles. "The rescue party said he must have been thrown from the carriage when it rolled off the cliff. He could have fallen in any crevice. The caves and chasms in those mountains are a maze."

"It does seem impossible he survived," Della admitted.

"Nevertheless," Iris said. "He did."

Muller slapped his palm against his thigh. "If that were true, he would have come home."

"How?" Iris asked. "He was a little boy."

"Not anymore," Muller said. "So where is he?"

"I donna know."

His voice quieted. "You say he exists, yet you don't know where."

"I can find him." Iris had no wish to revisit the cold emptiness where she had found Jarid, but she would do it if necessary.

"Very well." Muller stood straighter. "Find him. Bring him here."

"Your Highness—" Iris hesitated.

"Yes, yes, speak up."

"Prince Jarid is the heir."

"I know that."

"He can claim the crown."

Muller waved his hand. "I doubt you will find him, but if by some incredible chance you do, he can have the title."

It unsettled her to hear him make such a proclamation. He was undermining his own reign before it began.

"Your coronation is in ten days," Della said. "That hardly gives us time to look."

Muller shrugged. "Then delay the coronation."

"I think it unwise," Della said.

"It's been months. A few more days won't matter."

"It's been too long already." Della exhaled. "Saints, Muller, you know the people are mourning King Daron. We've just come through a hard winter. They need the coronation as a symbol that life will continue. And Aronsdale needs a committed leader."

"The bishop canna coronate Lord Muller," Iris said calmly. "Prince Jarid is the heir."

Muller stiffened at her use of the word "Lord." Unlike in other realms, in Aronsdale only the heir to the crown had the right to the title of prince; Muller hadn't come into it until after Jarid died. Iris suspected he might find it harder to give it up than he claimed.

He drew in a deep breath. "If my cousin is alive, bring him to me."

Jarid sensed the threat even before he felt the vibration of too many footsteps. Usually he had to be in the same room with Stone to pick up his emotions, but today when his foster father became alarmed, his reaction surged with such strength that Jarid felt it from another room.

Lurching to his feet, Jarid pressed his back against the wall, his fists clenched as he prepared to face his silent, unseen enemy. A draft blew across his face: someone had opened the door. Unfamiliar and unwelcome scents assaulted his nose: dust, mud, wet wool, leather. Many people were entering his room, their emotions creating a muddle he couldn't sort. He fortified his mind against them.

Then he felt *her.*

It was the rainbow woman he had touched two sleeps ago. He had no real idea of how much time had passed since then; "day" had little meaning when he saw neither the dawn nor the darkling twilight. He slept when he was tired, but if his sleeps had any relation to the rising of the sun, he neither knew nor cared.

A hint of flowers scented the air. Was it her? Jarid waved his arms in front of his body, but he touched no one. He felt the tension of his visitors, but he couldn't tell anything more about them. Had he been inside one of the spheres he often imagined, instead of this boxy room, he might have focused better, perhaps enough to sort out their emotions.

Fingers brushed his shoulder.

Startled, Jarid swung his arm and his hand thudded into a soft surface. A shoulder? Whoever he had hit moved away. He struggled to subdue his panic. He didn't know what these people wanted, and he couldn't locate Stone clearly among their minds, though his father was definitely in the room.

Leave! He wanted to shout at the intruders, but he had no words. When he had first become mute, he had tried for days to scream, until he thought he would die. Tears had run down his face, but no sobs broke his silence. He hadn't even been able to cry aloud for his parents.

Again someone brushed his arm, softly. He reached out, searching, fighting to hold down his alarm—and then a large hand grasped his other arm and pulled him away from the wall.

Jarid snapped then, losing his battle for control. When the strangers tried to take him away, he fought them with the single-minded ferocity that had sustained him all these years. The physical strength and skills he had developed from his exercise regime served him well against his would-be captors, but every time he freed himself from one, another caught him. It only provoked him further. Yet no matter how well he fought, he faced too many of them—and they could see.

Three pairs of hands pressed him against the wall and someone put a damp cloth over his face. Jarid held his breath, but he couldn't do it for long enough, especially while he was struggling. A cloying smell overpowered him and his awareness ceased.

Iris sat by the bed, watching the man sleep. She had hardly been able to pull her gaze away from him since they had found him high in the north, living in a dilapidated shack that could barely keep out the rain let alone protect him from the severe climate of the Boxer-Mage Mountains. The range had taken its name centuries ago from a box-mage who had retreated there to finish out his days as a hermit. Only the desperate lived in those cruel peaks. Beyond them lay the wastelands of Harsdown. Iris had spent her entire life in fear of an invasion by the Harsdown armies, and she understood the need for a strong king to hold Aronsdale against them.

The man they had found in the shack now lay on a bed in a tower room of Castle Suncroft, on his side, his wrists tied to one post. She hated the bonds; if the soldiers had just given her time to allay his fears, she was certain she could have coaxed him to come with them of his own free will.

At least they understood her dismay at seeing him

bound. Who wouldn't recognize this man? He had the same dark curls as the man in the portraits of King Daron as a youth, the same handsome features and broad shoulders, and the Dawnfield long legs. Aye, he was like King Daron—but stronger, taller, even more fine of feature.

However, the resemblance ended there. The late king had been a sovereign of elegance and culture. This man was wild. His rough clothes were made from rags, all dull gray. A scar ran under his ear to his shoulder. His hair hung down his back in thick, matted tangles and stubble covered his chin.

Yet for all his untamed ferocity, he drew her the way a flame drew a moth. She wanted to touch the muscles that bunched under the thin fabric of his shirt. She flushed, embarrassed by the thought, especially for a prisoner they had taken against his will.

The man stirred in his sleep, his face contorting as his wrists pulled against their bonds. It violated Iris's sense of right to see this man, surely Prince Jarid Dawnfield, tied up like a criminal. She leaned forward and worked at the ropes. His bonds were tight, but she managed to free him.

Still sleeping, he pulled his arms down and rolled onto his back, one palm lying on his stomach.

Iris stroked a dark curl off his forehead. "Are you Jarid?" she murmured. "Can you be the mage I touched in that lonely place?" She didn't see how he had reached her from so far away, but even now, as he slumbered, she felt the luminous strength of his mage gifts.

A voice spoke tiredly behind her. "Muller has made the announcement."

Iris turned with a start. Della was standing in the doorway, leaning against its frame. Dark circles rimmed her eyes.

"He stepped aside for Jarid?" Iris asked.

Della said, simply, "Yes." She came over to sit in a chair next to Iris. "It is official. Muller accepts this man as the heir to the crown."

Even knowing what Muller had intended, Iris felt stunned. This had all happened too fast. She believed the man they had found was Jarid, but they had no proof. Nor was he in any shape to accept the crown.

"Will Muller help us with Prince Jarid?" she asked.

Della pushed back a tendril of her gray hair. "He plans to leave Suncroft. He thinks it best."

"But, nay! He canna just walk away."

"I'm afraid he can."

Iris didn't understand Muller's withdrawal. The king's advisors were keeping Jarid's condition secret from the people, but they had told Muller what they knew. Why would he leave this way?

"He must realize Jarid canna rule," Iris said.

"He says the king's advisors can help." Della sighed. "What can they say? Muller knew they expected to do exactly that with him. He says Brant is better suited to govern."

"Muller is angry."

"Perhaps. But he believes what he says." Della watched the man sleeping on the bed. "You shouldn't have untied him."

Iris spoke dryly. ‘‘What will we do, take him to his coronation in chains?’’

‘‘If we must.’’

‘‘This is all wrong.’’

‘‘Iris—’’

‘‘Yes?’’

‘‘I’m afraid there’s more.’’

Ah, no. ‘‘More what?’’

‘‘From the king’s advisors.’’

Iris didn’t see how they could advise a man who couldn’t hear. But then, in her experience, people rarely listened to their advisors even when they could hear. ‘‘What do they say?’’

Della spoke carefully. ‘‘We are all in agreement.’’

Well and sure, that didn’t sound good. ‘‘About what?’’

‘‘Only a sphere-mage could have reached across the great distance that separated this man from you.’’

Ah. Now Iris understood. ‘‘Aye, Della, I think it is true. His talent is incredible.’’

‘‘I didn’t mean him.’’

It took Iris a moment to absorb her meaning. ‘‘Well and sure, it couldna been me.’’

‘‘No one else.’’

Iris pushed her chair back from the mage mistress. ‘‘It was him who touched my mind.’’

‘‘I was there. You initiated the contact.’’

‘‘That canna be! Never have I even lit a room.’’

Della’s stern visage softened. ‘‘A room, no. But the trees and meadows, I think yes. The countryside stirs your power. That is why you have had so much trouble making spells. Inside the cottage, you didn't know how to reach the core within you."

Iris wanted to protest, but she couldn't deny the land had always called to her.

The man on the bed turned his head, restless, his dark lashes stirring. Iris leaned closer. "Who are you truly?" she murmured.

"Iris, listen to me," Della said.

Reluctant, Iris turned back to her. "Aye?"

"We have already spoken with Chime."

Hai! No wonder Della was so upset. "She must be devastated. I think she genuinely likes Muller."

"She and Muller still plan to marry."

"But she canna do that."

"Our greatest shape-mage must marry the king." Della had a strange quality to her voice now.

"Aye. Chime."

"No. Not Chime."

Iris suddenly felt as if the floor dropped beneath her. "Nay, Della! I canna be queen!"

"You must."

"Nay!" They couldn't expect her to marry this stranger—a wild, injured creature who didn't even know her name.

It couldn't be true.

Della had always found the counsel of Lord Brant Firestoke invaluable, but tonight, neither of them had answers.

"It is a disaster." Brant stood at the tower window, his gray hair brushed back from his face, accenting the widow's peak on his forehead. The night shadowed his austere features. As the ranking lord among the royal advisors, he had served the previous king for two decades.

He and Della gazed out at a nearby tower, where they could see into a room lit by orbs-bud candles. Iris sat next to a bed there, keeping vigil on their slumbering prisoner. The man might indeed be the lost heir of Aronsdale, but he couldn't act as king. Iris would soon have to shoulder far more responsibility than her nineteen years of life had prepared her for. Not only did she need to learn the duties of the mage queen, she would probably have to assume many of her husband's tasks, as well.

Della shook her head. "This matter of heredity reeks. We are asking children to do jobs that people twice their age would find difficult." Jarid was only a year older than Iris, barely twenty. Muller, at twenty-eight, showed little more desire for responsibility now than he had at their age.

Brant watched Iris with a brooding stare. "She has no idea what to do."

"She is intelligent," Della said.

"That isn't enough." Brant turned to her. "We cannot coronate that man tomorrow. What if he goes berserk during the ceremony? Our people are already discontent. If they think we are giving them a lunatic for a king, saints only know what will happen. Aronsdale is weakened, easy prey. Without strong leadership, we may fall to Harsdown."

Della knew all too well what he meant. Armies from the untamed lands of Harsdown beyond the mountains had long sought to conquer Aronsdale. They had power, strength and will to fight—but no shape-mages. Aronsdale held her own against Harsdown, despite being smaller and gentler, only because she had shape-mages. They could use spells to heal the wounded in battle, buttress the morale of Aronsdale soldiers and predict strategies of the enemy based on their emotions. Aronsdale needed a king to lead the armies and a queen to lead the mages. Theirs was a fragile realm; if their will faltered, they could fall to Harsdown.

"And if we cancel the coronation yet again?" Della asked. "What message does that send—that Aronsdale is such a mess, we can't choose a leader months after the death of our previous king?" She scowled. "We put off crowning Muller too long."

"With good reason. The boy was ready to bolt."

"Well, now he has bolted," Della said flatly. "The situation isn't going to improve. I say this—clean up this man, bring him out tomorrow, put the crown on him and let Iris rule."

Brant frowned. "She has no training."

"She has aptitude."

"That isn't enough."

"We can guide her."

He gave her an incredulous look. "And just how do we explain her husband? He may not even make it through the ceremony without losing control."

Della thought back to how they had found Jarid. "Bring his foster father here. He seems to calm the boy."

Brant's gaze narrowed. "No."

"Why not?"

"I don't want that man exerting any more influence on Jarid."

Della crossed her arms. "And just how long are your men going to hold him in custody, up there in the mountains?"

"It is better we separate Jarid from him. The boy needs a fresh start."

"And if Jarid wants him at the coronation?"

"We delay the ceremony." Brant didn't look persuaded by his own argument.

"We can't. You know that. We have waited too long already." Della suddenly felt tired. "Convincing Muller he wants the crown has become irrelevant. We must work with what we have. Waiting won't change that."

It was a long moment before Brant answered. Finally he said, "Very well." He gave Della a dour look. "Just pray we all survive the ceremony."

A touch disturbed Jarid's solitude. The hand stroking his forehead didn't belong to Stone; this one had longer fingers, with fewer calluses, and it was too small. A woman.

He caught her hand. As she froze, he became aware of another sensation. His wrists hurt. Why? What had these people done to him? Images of boxes formed in his mind, focusing his spell enough for him to pick up her mood. She was…in pain?

Startled, he realized he was gripping her wrist too hard. He let go and she pulled away her hand. Her scent came to him: woods, fresh grass, piney soap. He caught other smells, too; this place was cleaner than the cabin where he lived with Stone. The fragrance of orbs-bud candles filled the air, releasing a flood of his memories: the dinner chamber alight with hundreds of candles; his mother's wedding ring agleam, a gold circle inset with diamonds and amethysts; his father bidding him good-night and blowing out candles in his room.

What is this place? Jarid had no voice to ask his mysterious companion. Although he felt her mage power, he couldn't tell what she wanted from him. He wasn't certain she knew herself.

As the sleep cleared from his mind, he slid his hands over the quilt under his body, trying to understand. It had a finely woven feel to it, downy and well-tended, suggesting a prosperity unlike any he had known for many years. When he reached above his head, he found a post of the bed, its wood carved with shape-blossoms, their petals forming boxes, polyhedrons and orbs. The designs felt familiar.

Agitated, Jarid struggled into a sitting position. Stone would never have willingly let these people take him away from the cabin, and not only because Jarid could implicate him in the crimes of that long-ago night. Stone also feared what his young charge might do with his uncontrolled mage power.

But...Stone wasn't here.

Jarid searched with his mind, spinning orb images to focus his power. He found no hint of his father's emotions, only those of guards posted outside this room. They hadn't come in here because the woman hadn't let them know he had awaked, though they seemed to expect that she would alert them if he stirred. Her mind glowed, ruddy flames lighting his isolation. Warm. Inviting.

Go away, he thought, afraid of that warmth.

He knew when she moved because the air currents

shifted. Although he couldn't be sure, he thought she had come to stand by the bed. He wanted to strike out, as he had done with his attackers in Stone's cabin, but he hesitated. Her mood came to him like sunlight. She soothed.

Jarid gritted his teeth. He didn't want to be soothed. He preferred anger. These people had drugged him and torn him away from his refuge. He closed his mind to her mage gifts.

A hand touched his forehead and he jerked away, wincing as pain stabbed his muscles, which still ached from his fight with the strangers in the cabin. He slid across the bed, away from the woman, until he came up against a wall. Then he sat with one leg bent, his elbow resting on his knee, his hand curled in a fist.

The bed shifted, sagging with a new weight. Fingers brushed his arm and he jerked back, instinctively raising his fist. Then his mind caught up with his reflexes and told him that surely it was the woman who touched him, not a soldier. He lowered his arm.

She withdrew her hand, but after a moment she laid a clay tablet across his lap. Baffled, he ran his fingers over the tablet. Its disk shape helped focus his thoughts. He pressed the clay, noting its cool, grainy texture, making dents in it with his fingertips.

Her long fingers touched his hand, sending a chill down his back. That shiver had to be anger; her touch couldn't give him pleasure. He refused to let that happen. He would retreat into the fortress of his mind, which kept out pain.

The woman pressed her fingers into the clay, her hand moving against his so he could feel her actions. Then she brushed his hand over the dents she had made. It took Jarid a moment to understand; many years had passed since he had touched such shapes. Words. Pictures. She was writing to him.

Jarid shifted his weight, uneasy. It was true that by the age of six, he had learned some basics of reading. But he had done nothing since then and he recognized only a few of her symbols. The disk itself sharpened his mind, though, stirring memories. He traced one picture, a circle within a cluster of lines—no, an orb within crossed swords.

His family crest.

No! Jarid hurled the tablet away. He had no way to hear its crash, but he felt the woman scramble off the bed. He couldn't bear the truth she brought him, not after all these years—not after what he had done. His guilt was too big, the guilt he wouldn't say even in his own mind. But however much he fought it, deep down he had recognized the truth the moment he smelled the orbs-bud candles.

They had brought him home.

Chapter 4

The Dais

Iris retreated across the room, watching as Jarid slid off the bed and rose to his feet. The tablet lay in pieces, strewn across the floor. She knew Brant Firestoke would insist she bring in the hexagon lieutenants now that Jarid had awakened. But she didn't move. This wasn't the time to inflict more strangers on Aronsdale's heir. Jarid was standing next to the circular nightstand by the bed, his hand resting on its surface, his head lifted as if he were trying to catch an unexpected scent.

The creak of an opening door came from across the room.

Iris jumped, whirling around. Ah, no. Muller stood in the open doorway like a prince of light, radiant in his white-and-gold clothes. Whatever Iris might have said to him died in her throat, lost to the intensity of his concentration on Jarid. He slowly crossed the chamber, never taking his gaze off of his cousin.

Jarid remained utterly still by the nightstand. When Muller stopped in front of him, the only sign that Jarid realized he faced a person was the way his forehead wrinkled. He and Muller were the same height, with similar features. They stayed that way, frozen in a tableau, the golden lord and the dark prince, one splendid in his perfection, the other wild and untamed. Light and dark.

Muller waved his hand in front of his cousin's eyes—and Jarid didn't even blink. He stood like a wild stag mesmerized by fire.

"Can you hear me, Cousin?" Muller sounded as if he were wound as tight as a coil.

Jarid's hand stiffened into a claw gripping the table. Even now his eyes weren't quite directed at Muller. Iris felt certain he knew someone stood before him, but she had no idea if he could recognize his cousin.

"Won't you speak?" Muller asked him.

Jarid tilted his chin, but he made no other response.

Muller turned to Iris. "It is true, then. He has no sight. He hears nothing."

Iris nodded yes, disquieted by his fierce concentration.

"He has no voice."

"None," she said, sensing Muller's conflicted doubts. If he changed his decision now to give up the crown, and revealed why, it would throw Aronsdale into a turmoil. Yet who could blame him?

He gave Jarid a long look. Then he spoke in a numb voice. "May your reign be long and full, my cousin." With that, he spun around and strode from the chamber.

Jarid reached out to touch his cousin, but he found no one.

The Great Shape-Hall of Castle Suncroft gleamed like the interior of a sun's ray. Hundreds of candles flickered in chandeliers and candelabras, and orb-lamps on stands added their luster. The high ceiling gleamed with gold-and-white mosaics and starlight glimmered outside, beyond the tall windows. Hundreds of guests mingled here tonight, the gentlefolk of Aronsdale, glistening all, the men in fine tunics of ivory and gold, their trousers tucked into polished boots; the women in close-fitted gowns that swept the floor, each dress a single color, making a rainbow throughout the hall.

Iris felt like a fraud. She had no business doing this. She was no one. No matter what Della and Brant said, it felt wrong for her to stand here as if she deserved the title of queen.

Her new shape-maids had dressed her in a radiant yellow gown that clung to her body, and they had piled her chestnut hair high on her head, threading it with topazes. She stood now with Brant Firestoke and Della No-Cozen at the head of a reception line to greet their guests. She would have rather hidden in the stables.

Iris had balked when they had tried to put her in the blue silk of a sapphire mage. She had no right. A normal woman could wear any color she chose, but a mage dressed in the hue of her power. Iris couldn't wear blue when she had yet to light a room, the simplest spell. She felt foolish in yellow, but at least it was more realistic. Della claimed she had achieved a great deal more by reaching Jarid's mind, but Iris didn't even understand what she and Jarid had done in that incredible moment.

In a pause between greeting people, Iris glanced up and glimpsed Muller and Chime strolling hand-in-hand, glowing like sunlight. They paused to peer at themselves in a mirror and then went on, out an archway to the gardens. They seemed happier than Iris had seen them in a long time. She had secretly hoped Muller would challenge Jarid for the crown, but neither he nor Chime showed any inclination to reclaim the weight of responsibility that Iris's one flash of mage power had lifted from their shoulders.

After the last person passed through the reception line, Iris drew in a shaky breath. She glanced uneasily at the dais at the end of the hall. She had no idea if Jarid had understood what she had tried to explain earlier today with the clay tablet. She shuddered, remembering his wrath as he hurled away her tablet. This stranger she would soon marry had shown no sign he wanted anything to do with her. Why should he? In his darkness, he probably saw her better than all these people who might be fooled by her elegant clothes and the court manners she had learned this past year.

And yet...Jarid drew her. Beneath his tangled hair, his torn and disheveled clothes, and his scarred neck, he had a beauty that had nothing to do with outer form. It came from within. He reached her in a way she didn't understand, making her want to brush back his matted locks, to press his long fingers against her lips.

One of Brant Firestoke's men, a disk-captain, came up to them. The officer wasn't a mage; his title came from his position in the King's Army. Each military rank subdivided into shape-ranks, with triangle as lowest and orb as highest. All captains outranked all lieutenants, so an orb-lieutenant had a rank lower than a triangle-captain but higher than a triangle-lieutenant. Tonight the disk-captain wore a dark blue dress uniform with darker boots. He and Brant spoke in low voices.

"Prince Jarid is calm," the captain said. "But we aren't sure how long it will last. The major wants to proceed now, while we can."

Brant nodded. "Very well. Begin immediately."

Iris stiffened, barely holding in her protest. *I'm not ready.*

The captain bowed to them and took his leave. As Brant offered his arm to Iris, he gave her an encouraging look. "Shall we?"

She wanted to run, but somehow managed to nod instead. Taking his arm, she walked with him down the hall, doing her best to respond gracefully when people greeted them. As they reached the dais, the power of the great disk vibrated through her. For the first time since her gifts had awakened in the woods, she dared trying to focus her power. The dais gave less strength than the sphere formed by her hidden retreat in the woods, but it was enough to weave a spell of soothing. Whether or not her fumbling mage attempts would actually work, she had no idea.

They went to the center of the dais: Iris, Brant, Della and a military retinue. The Bishop of Orbs joined them, regal and tall, his white hair swept back under his miter. Two pages accompanied him, one carrying a tasseled cushion with two crowns. The gold circlets glittered, inset with diamonds and amethysts. Iris stood stiffly, aware of everyone in the Great Shape-Hall watching. All conversation had stopped.

The moment stretched out, seeming endless. Just when Iris thought surely they would all snap with tension, another retinue appeared in an archway at the end of the hall. With stately progress, they approached the dais. At first Iris didn't recognize the tall man walking in their center. Then she froze.

It was Jarid.

Two shape-soldiers walked on either side of him, guiding him with touches on his arm, their help so discreet that had she not known he was blind, she wouldn't have realized they were helping him.

Her breath caught. Jarid was resplendent, a well-built prince shining in the light from hundreds of candles and orb-lamps. His gold brocade vest fit snugly over a snowy-white shirt with belled sleeves, and his ivory-colored breeches tucked into gold boots. Gone was the ragged hair that had tangled down his back; now glossy black locks grazed his shoulders, trimmed and brushed. It enhanced the classic lines of his face, his straight nose and handsome features. His unkempt hair had half hidden his eyes before, but now she could see their dramatic violet color. They were larger than she had realized and framed by a thick fringe of black lashes. The scar that ran down his neck added an edge to his breathtaking appearance.

"Goodness," Della said at her side.

"Aye," Iris murmured. Jarid dazzled.

However, she doubted he felt as splendid as he looked. This whole business had to be disturbing for him. Concentrating, she used the dais to focus her spell. Jarid's emotions came to her, blurred and hazy; he was angry, bewildered, lost. He kept control of himself with an effort of will so great, Iris sensed it despite her inexperience as a mage. His inner strength was tangible, a strength that had carried him through fourteen years of a nightmare.

As Jarid's retinue joined hers on the dais, Iris felt as if she were a kite caught in a rushing wind, unable to stop her headlong passage. She and Jarid faced each other. He wasn't looking at her, but slightly to the side, his gaze unfocused. When Iris took his hand, his posture went rigid. She thought he would jerk away, but instead he clutched her fingers, his grip so tight it hurt. His confusion flowed over her; he had no idea who had brought him here. He wanted to fight his way free. He held back because he knew he was in his ancestral home, but his alarm and anger were rising, threatening to explode.

Iris offered him a spell of calming, like rain misting over flames. She tried a healing spell, too, but she had too little knowledge to make it work. Or perhaps whatever had hurt him went too deep for her to reach.

The Bishop of Orbs read the ceremony. Iris bowed her head, listening, while he spoke the ancient words in a resonant voice. The entire time she felt Jarid struggling to control his apprehension and anger. Strangers surrounded him, enemies who had taken him from his home by force. His grip on her hand never eased.

After the bishop finished, he asked Iris and Jarid to kneel. A hepta lieutenant on Jarid's other side reached out, obviously to guide the prince. Iris froze; Jarid might snap if a stranger touched him now. She shook her head slightly at the lieutenant, hoping he understood.

The officer hesitated, his hand above Jarid's shoulder. Everyone on the dais had gone still. Jarid tilted his head, turning toward the lieutenant, the tendons in his neck as taut as cords.

We are friends, Iris thought to her groom. *Friends.* She squeezed his hand and tugged downward.

Jarid drew in a sharp breath, turning toward Iris, his gaze still unfocused. She tugged his hand again, carefully, as if she faced that wild stag in the forest. He shuddered and took a deep breath—and then he knelt with her, his motions stiff and uncertain, the two of them in front of the bishop. Relief swept over Iris. She bowed her head, aware of Jarid doing the same, though whether it was from instinct or a memory of his past, she had no idea. He had probably absorbed some court protocol as a small boy, but he had never seen a coronation.

Iris heard rather than saw the bishop place the crown on Jarid's head. She could imagine it sparkling in the candlelight that filled the hall, but she couldn't bear to look, to see that final symbol of the upheavals that had disrupted their lives. Jarid's confusion swirled around her—and also his understanding of what the weight of that crown meant. An immense grief came from him for his grandfather's death.

She barely knew when the bishop set a crown on her own head. The words of the marriage ceremony swirled over her like fog.

Then it was done: she and Jarid had become the king and queen of Aronsdale.

Chapter 5

Shape Light

One candle lit the tower room with dusky light. It had been Iris's idea to bring Jarid here after the ceremony; now, alone with him, she felt less certain. She couldn't stay; at least one of them had to return to the Great Shape-Hall. Given Jarid's situation, that he had been lost for so many years, she hoped people would accept his withdrawing from the celebrations early. They would be less tolerant if *neither* of the newlywed couple attended their own festivities.

Although very few people knew Jarid couldn't see, hear or speak, it must have been obvious during the ceremony that something was wrong. All in Aronsdale were waiting to see how this strange twist of events would play out, whether it would result in a better age for the realm or the fall of the royal family.

No one had wanted to leave her alone with her new husband. She had needed a calming spell focused by this circular room to allay Brant's fears, and she suspected her success had been less than complete, given the way he had told the guards outside they must enter here if they heard the slightest sound. At least he didn't seem to realize she had used a shape-spell on him. Even knowing she had become mage queen, everyone—including herself—seemed to have a hard time thinking of her as other than the apprentice who had yet to learn even a lighting spell.

I belong here. Perhaps if she repeated those words enough to herself, she would come to believe them. Belonging. That hope seemed like a diaphanous floating bubble out of her reach.

It said a great deal about the lack of confidence the king's advisors had in the sovereign they had crowned, that they feared to leave him with his wife, lest he attack her. Iris knew Jarid needed this time to himself, without their interference; she felt him holding on to his control by a mere thread that could break. She didn't intend to subject him to any more strangers.

Jarid was sitting on the edge of the four-poster bed, still in his wedding finery, his face shadowed by the sweep of his hair. He held his crown on his lap, running his fingers over its edges and gems. The sight broke her heart; no justice existed in a universe that would trap such a vibrant man in a prison where he could communicate with no one, save by the nebulous touch of his mage gifts.

Iris walked closer to Jarid, and he turned his head as if he sensed her approach. She set her crown on the round table by the bed. She wanted to reach out to her husband, but she hesitated, unsure how he would react.

Jarid raised his arm, his palm facing outward toward Iris. He cupped his hand as if to grasp a sphere. Tilting his head, he closed his eyes and slowly turned his hand over until his cupped palm faced the ceiling. Then he extended his hand to Iris as if to offer her the invisible sphere.

Touched, Iris folded her hand over his cupped palm. A tingle went through her, as if he actually held a sphere of power. He stiffened, and she feared he would rebuff her again, as he had done earlier today when he had broken her tablet. But this time he only opened his hand, relinquishing the imaginary orb to her. Calm spread through Iris as if she had absorbed a spell of healing. Her loneliness and her longing for her home in the mountains receded. She didn't stop missing her home, but it became more bearable, not the anguish that had torn her heart.

"Thank you," she whispered, uncertain about this remarkable gift he had given her. Had he soothed her pain—or healed it? Only an indigo mage could heal emotional wounds and no verifiable record of any such mage existed. Legends claimed the indigo gifts had long been dormant in the royal line, but Iris suspected those stories were fables concocted to increase the Dawnfield mystique. Even if such a mage did exist, he would need a real sphere to focus his power, not one he imagined in his hand.

Jarid had turned toward her, though his eyes were directed to her right. He reached out until his hand brushed her skirt. Taking a pinch of silk, he rubbed it between his thumb and forefinger. For the first time since she had met him, a smile played around his mouth, easing his dark manner. It made her want to take him into her arms. For all that they couldn't converse, they somehow communicated. She didn't know how to define the way he made her feel; she had too little experience with these emotions he evoked. She only knew she wanted to be near him.

With care, Iris sat next to him and laid her palm over his other hand, where it rested on his crown. He tensed, but then he curled his fingers around hers. They sat for several moments, neither moving, Iris barely breathing. A blush warmed her face. Did he realize this was his wedding night? That she found him attractive didn't mean he felt the same toward her. How could he? He knew nothing about her, not even her name or age.

When Jarid moved, Iris thought he would withdraw. But he only set his crown on the bed. Her pulse quickened when he took her face in his hands and moved his thumbs along her cheeks. His skin scraped hers, rough with calluses he would have never developed had he lived the life expected of a prince and heir to the realm. She felt him struggling with his thoughts. He had returned home, lost his foster father, become king and married, all in a matter of days. It left him reeling.

Jarid exhaled, a breath she felt on her cheeks rather than heard. He touched her face, exploring, and she held still, letting him. His feather-light touch sent tingles up her neck. When his fingertip lingered on her lips, he smiled, just the barest curve of his lips, but the room seemed brighter.

Uncertain how to behave with him, Iris traced her finger over the dimple in his chin. With an inaudible sigh, Jarid drew her hand into his lap, running his thumb over her knuckles. When he touched the ring on her fourth finger, with its distinctive arrangement of gems, his grip tightened. He hadn't given it to her; the Bishop of Orbs had done it for him, sliding the ring on Iris's finger during the ceremony. Now she *felt* Jarid recognize the band. Yet he showed no surprise that she wore a wedding ring from among the heirlooms that belonged to his family.

Lifting her hands, Jarid pressed his lips against her knuckles. She inhaled, aware of the emotions tumbling within him, an engaging mixture of boyish wonder, sensuality, elegance, roughness and luminous inner strength. She also picked up the reason for his uncertainty; he had never touched a woman except as a small child, when he had hugged his mother. Iris had no experience with men, either, unless that peck on the cheek a valet had given her last year counted.

Iris slid her palms to his shoulders, wishing she understood him better. She could feel his moods, but nothing more specific. Softly she said, "I wish you could tell me what you are thinking."

Jarid didn't answer, didn't even seem to know she had spoken. He moved his fingertip around her ear, exploring, arousing her in the process of "seeing" her. Shy but curious, she laid her hands on his arms. His muscles felt firm under his rich garments. She wondered if he had any idea how fine he appeared. Unlike Muller, who knew his golden beauty well and expected everyone else to notice, Jarid seemed to have no inkling of the devastating figure he cut.

He caught her hand and touched her fingers to his lips. Then he mouthed one word: *queen?*

Iris's breath caught. Could they talk this way? Delicately, she put his fingers against her lips. "Yes."

He brushed his fingertip over her bottom lip.

"What happened?" she asked. "You spoke as a child. You saw. You heard. Why is that lost to you now?"

Although he still touched her lips, he didn't seem to understand. He drew her close, his arms around her waist, his embrace uncertain. When he rubbed his cheek against the crown of her head, his breath stirred her hair. He slid his hand down her back, and she sensed how much he liked her waist-length curls. She closed her eyes, pleased, and surprised, too, because she had always thought of her abundant curls as wild rather than beautiful.

Iris wanted to let him know she liked his touch, but she didn't know how to tell him. Tentative and unsure, she put her arms around his neck and rested her head on his shoulder. If only she could reach him through his darkness and isolation.

Try, she thought.

Just as she had done in the Great Shape-Hall, so now she formed a healing spell. An orange mage could sooth physical injury, but that only eased pain. It took a blue mage to heal wounds. Iris had never believed she had such abilities, but she tried to put aside her doubts and to concentrate, focusing through the cylindrical room.

Nothing.

She struggled with her frustration. This was exactly as it had always been when she tried spells. And yet...she *had* succeeded lately, a little, during the coronation tonight and even more in the forest. Drawing on those memories, she strove to reawaken the mental state that freed her gifts. She imagined herself surrounded by the sphere of greenery, her refuge in the woods.

Mage power stirred within Iris. Her spell became a waterfall, sparkling and bright—but instead of flowing into Jarid, it skittered off him like water splashing on rock.

Iris's head began to throb, warning that she was pushing too hard. She had to relax her focus and let the spell fade; otherwise she could injure her mind. Disappointment welled within her. She didn't know if her attempt had failed because she wasn't adept enough or because Jarid's defenses were too strong.

Jarid continued to stroke her back. He gave no sign that he realized she had tried a spell on him, but his mood had calmed, the last of his agitation subsiding. His mind shone, an inner radiance far more beautiful than the sunlight he never saw. Locked within his darkness, he had spent years developing his mage light, free of external influences, creating a purity of soul that graced her life.

Drawing back, she touched his cheek. "So beautiful, my husband."

His lips curved into a smile—a full smile, the first he had shown her—and it changed his entire face. Instead of a brooding stranger, suddenly he looked his age, a youth of twenty, hardly more than a boy. If she hadn't known better, she would have thought he had heard her compliment. Of course she would never tell a man he was beautiful if he could hear.

A thought jolted Iris; if she could feel his emotions, he was probably absorbing hers, too. Hai! That was embarrassing. She imagined a wall hiding her thoughts.

His smile widened. Then he drummed his fingers on the back of her hand.

Iris gave a startled laugh. "Aye, sure, I know that game. We played it all the time in my village." She turned her hands over so he was tapping her palms instead of her knuckles. That was the entire point of the game; to stop him from tapping the back of her hand. With a grin, Jarid flipped over her hands and caught her knuckles again.

Charmed, Iris tangled her fingers in his. It delighted her that a prince would play a commoner's game, but then, he had lived most of his life in mountains north of her home. He had probably learned the game from his guardian.

His hands stilled, his smile fading. He mouthed a word: *Stone?*

"Stone?" Iris brought his fingers to her lips. "What?"

He formed another word: *where?*

"I don't understand."

He mouthed, *Father.*

Sadness welled over Iris. "I am so terribly sorry about him, Jarid."

He seemed puzzled. She didn't understand why; surely he knew his father had died. A mage as strong as Jarid would have felt the loss intensely even at the age of six. It was hard to interpret his moods. If only she could breach his solitude. But his words were locked within him, trapped by his silence. Maybe one reason she felt so close to him, so soon, was that she recognized that sense of not belonging, of living with a crushing isolation from everyone else. She had known similar all her life.

Iris traced the gnarled scar below his ear. The accident that had killed his parents and caused this wound might explain his hearing loss, but it came nowhere near his eyes. She cupped his cheek, and he turned his head, pressing his lips into her palm.

"You have beautiful eyes," she said. "*Perfect* eyes. They have no scars, at least that I can see. Is it your emotions that were injured, never letting you see or hear or speak?"

Jarid gave no indication that he knew she had spoken. He embraced her as if she were an anchor in his sea of confusion.

"Hai," she murmured. If only she could help. She wanted to believe he possessed the legendary indigo gifts of the Dawnfields, but if he truly had such gifts, he could have healed himself. She pushed away the thought, refusing to acknowledge that her hope might well be useless. She had spent years unable to call on her mage light, unaware she even had such gifts; the same could be true for Jarid. Surely he might heal himself. She longed to see him regain what he had lost. She was grasping at mist, but it was all she had.

Jarid seemed to have no sense of his own radiance; he lived in the darkness of his loneliness and endured a shattering guilt she didn't understand. Why guilt? He had done nothing wrong.

Trying another healing spell, Iris used every shape in the room to focus: orbs on the bedposts, a half-sphere lamp with its flickering flame, star mosaics on the walls. Nothing helped. Her spell ran off Jarid like water.

"Why?" Moisture gathered in her eyes. "Why can I feel your emotions but I canna give you light?" She imagined his sight filling, his eyes opening to color and clarity: *Gossamer dawn, brighten his life; tenuous hope, unlock his heart.*

Nothing.

Iris buried her head against his shoulder and his vest soaked up her tears.

"Look who has deigned to rejoin us." Leaning against a pillar on the edge of the Great Shape-Hall, Muller raised his crystal goblet. "To our new queen."

Della followed his gaze. Across the hall, Iris was coming through an archway with her honor guard, a quartet of octahedron lieutenants. She glowed, from her yellow gown to the auburn curls tumbling down her back. But her eyes had darkened.

"And look at that," Muller added. "She's alone. Where could our new king be?"

His tone surprised Della. Here, with just the two of

them, he revealed a bitterness he had hidden before. Until this moment he had given her no reason to think he regretted his decision to relinquish the crown.

"It could have been your title," she said.

"I didn't want it." He was watching Iris intently.

Della studied him, trying to fathom his mood. Although she was a green mage, her abilities were more jade than emerald; at her best, she could feel only vague emotions from other people. She touched the jade pendant around her neck; polished into a five-sided pyramid, it represented the highest shape she could draw on. It was too small to handle much of her considerable power, but it focused her gifts with a finesse she couldn't achieve using a larger or simpler shape.

When she focused on Muller, a general sense of his mood came through; he genuinely didn't want to be king, but he had more conflicts about losing the title than he had let anyone see. She wished she understood why. She strove to deepen her awareness, but the pendant couldn't carry enough power. She tried to draw on the Shape-Hall itself, but it had six sides, too many for her. Pain jabbed her temples. She released her concentration and the pain receded, much to her relief; she hadn't pushed hard enough to injure her mind.

Iris was moving across the floor, accompanied by Brant Firestoke, the two of them stopping often to converse with the guests.

Della spoke quietly. "She needs your help, Muller."

"Whatever for?" He was clenching the stem of his goblet so hard, his knuckles had turned white.

"You've all made it excruciatingly clear you consider me unfit for the job."

She glanced up at him. "I've never said such a thing to you."

He tapped his long finger against her temple. "Ah, but you think it, my dear Mistress No-Cozen."

Della didn't know how to respond. Although she had questioned his suitability for the throne, she had told only Brant and Iris, and neither of them were likely to have repeated it, especially to Muller. He had to be guessing her thoughts, rather than sensing them with a spell; her strongest gift was the ability to recognize other mages, and she felt no power in Muller.

She covered her unease with silence. She couldn't lie to him, but neither did she want to alienate him or undermine his confidence. They needed him. And she had always liked Muller. She had known him since he was a sunny toddler running across the meadows, laughing and bright.

Muller lifted his goblet to Iris. "May her reign be long and fruitful."

He never mentioned Jarid.

Chapter 6

A Simple Radiance

She was gone.

Jarid lay on the bed, fully dressed, unable to sleep, battling his unwanted longing for the woman who had held him and then left him here alone. Someone else was in the room now, a guard, maybe two. He sensed their unfamiliar minds, and the smell of oiled chain mail permeated the room.

He couldn't believe these madmen had *crowned* him. Even if he had been whole, he would have been unfit to rule. He clenched the quilt with his fist. He had to escape. But to where? He felt like a man trapped in a cell, pounding the walls for an exit he couldn't see.

Jarid recognized the castle from hints here and

there: the turn of a hallway he had run along as a child; the feel of mosaics on certain walls; how the wind gusted in open windows; aromas wafting up from the kitchens. But this hadn't been his home for years. Its people were strangers. So far he had recognized only Brant Firestoke. Had he been able to see or hear, perhaps more of the people here would have been familiar, but as it was, they remained a threatening mystery.

He had no idea what they had done with Stone. Why hadn't his foster father come with him? Jarid needed him. That these strangers had cut him off from the one person he trusted made him want to strike out at them.

Nor did he know what to think of the woman. He tried to doubt her, too, but he wanted her to come to him. He loved the way she smelled, of fresh soap and wildflowers.

His wife. *Wife.* He had a woman.

She didn't seem to like him much, though, given the way she had left him alone on their wedding night. Not that he blamed her, having suddenly found herself bound to a violent stranger. And yet, incredibly, he felt no fear in her. She thought him radiant, of all the strange things. Perhaps she was deluded. Her emotions gave the impression of a gentle woman with a warm heart and strong character. He liked her for that as much as for the alluring curves of her body and the lovely heart shape of her face.

He wished she would come back. He wanted to hold her tonight. Touch her. The years had matured his body, tormenting him with a loneliness he didn't fully understand and a physical need he could never truly slake.

Jarid gritted his teeth. He detested this confinement they forced on him. He needed the hills and forest. He sat up, swinging his legs over the edge of the bed. When he tried to compensate for this mattress being larger and higher than his pallet in Stone's cabin, he overestimated and his boots came down hard, thudding on the floor. The vibration shook his legs. He felt a change in his guards, their somnolent thoughts jumping to attention.

Standing, Jarid reached for a bedpost to steady himself. Instead of finding support, his hand hit—what? Metal and leather. The chest of a man wearing chain mail? He wasn't sure; Stone had owned nothing resembling mail, but Jarid vaguely remembered it from his childhood. He jerked away and stumbled into someone else. Instinctively, he struck out, hitting another mail-clad chest. Someone grabbed his arm, restraining him. Agitated, he took the defensive stance he had learned from Stone, who had taught him to defend himself, an activity they could share that required no words.

When they tried to hold him back, Jarid fought his jailors, trapped within his darkness. He swung his fists, threw one man to the floor and slammed another against a wall. But in the end they prevailed. They bound his arms behind his back despite his being their king. Then they held him, one on each side, their mailed hands clenched on his arms. The emotions in the room had grown muddled and he was sure more people had entered, too many to distinguish individual minds. He snarled, his lip curling.

A hand touched his cheek.

Jarid froze. He knew that gentle touch, knew the soothing spell enveloping him. No! He wouldn't respond. He would be stone. Unmoved. Yet despite his intentions, his arm muscles relaxed, easing the pain from the ropes that bound his wrists.

Again her fingers came, brushing his lips. Jarid pulled back, embarrassed that she would touch him intimately in front of strangers. He wished he could pull her into his arms and enfold himself in her serenity.

Concern washed out from her mind, her emotions clearer to him than the moods of the others in the room. She ached to reach him, just as he wanted to hold her. She touched his lips again—and this time he held still, realizing her intent. Communication.

Jarid mouthed two words: *Free me.*

She lowered her hand. He sensed an argument among his captors, their determination to keep him bound. Another of the woman's soothing spells flowed over him, a backwash this time; she had directed this one at his captors rather than him. An odd weapon, using spells of calmness, but perhaps more effective here than fists.

Someone grasped his arms. Jarid held back the instinctual fear that drove him to resist what he could neither see nor know. He needed to stay calm. His wife was in the room. He didn't want her to see him go berserk.

A moment later he was glad he hadn't struggled, for they were untying him. As soon as he was free, he brought his arms in front of his body and rubbed his wrists.

The woman took his hand and led him forward.

A sparkle of stars lit the sky and the moon silvered the landscape. Iris walked with Jarid, who held the crook of her arm as they made their way down a slope outside the castle. The night was cool but comfortable. Six officers accompanied them, five decahedron lieutenants and one orb captain. Brant Firestoke walked a short distance away, respecting Iris's request for privacy but refusing to let her and Jarid out of his sight.

Her husband took each step as if he expected to fall into a chasm. Iris closed her eyes, trying to experience the world as he did, and she immediately stumbled on ground that had suddenly become unfamiliar and threatening, though she knew the land here well.

Opening her eyes, she murmured, "Would that I could light your vision the way Chime can light a room." She was speaking more to herself than Jarid, knowing he couldn't hear her.

Unexpectedly he stopped and faced her, his face gentling. It gave him a boyish quality, open and charming, the way he might have looked if he had lived a life free of such devastating losses.

He mouthed a word: *where?*

Iris had no idea where she was taking him, only that she had felt his need to escape the castle. She understood why he resisted its lifeless halls; she, too, preferred the forest and hills to the inanimate confines even of lovely Suncroft.

A wonderful idea came to her. She took his fingers and set them against her lips. "I will take you to a special place."

His forehead furrowed.

She spoke more slowly. "To the woods. A special place."

Jarid continued to look puzzled, but he nodded. He traced her lips, his fingers lingering until heat spread through her. As much as he stirred her, he also made her self-conscious, given how little privacy they had with the guards and Brant here. She lowered his hand to her side, intertwining her fingers with his. Rather than taking her response as a rejection, he squeezed her fingers. Then he set off again, walking carefully, holding her hand. It gratified Iris that he would trust her this way without any idea of where she meant to take him.

They entered the woods at the bottom of the slope, where the trees blocked the moon's glow. Iris paused while her eyes adjusted. Jarid waited next to her, his head tilted as if he were listening to the forest on a level beyond sound.

Iris made a decision then. She turned to Brant, who was standing by the moss-covered trunk of a nearby tree. "You must take these soldiers back to the castle."

He came forward. "Your Majesty, we cannot."

His address startled Iris; she couldn't think of herself with such a grandiose title. But she had no doubt about one thing. "My husband needs to know these soldiers are gone."

Brant showed no sign of relenting. "He has no way to know they are here."

She glanced at Jarid, who stood silent, his eyes dark in the moonglow that filtered through the canopy of branches.

"He knows," Iris said.

"We cannot risk it."

"It is'n my safety at stake, Lord Firestoke." Iris took Jarid's arm and he brushed his thumb over her knuckle. She caught a hint of his thoughts; he understood that she spoke on his behalf. Given that he had no way to hear her arguments, this trust he offered was a gift. It gave her a glimmering of how it felt to be accepted, making her wonder if she might have a place here after all. She hoped he didn't regret his choice to trust her.

"He must know he is not a prisoner," she said. "Well then, if we guard his every move, how will he feel free?"

Brant's face was shadowed. "We must guard his every move, lest he hurt you or himself."

"It is'n a risk." Iris willed him to believe her. She had no pure shapes to use here, only trees, rocks and ground. Her spells skittered around their incomplete forms and dispersed. But the woods and sky had an ancient power that called to her in a way the castle and its human-made shapes had never done. She reached to the moon itself. The disk wasn't quite full, and its face changed its contours, but it was enough.

Her power focused and the spell flowed through her with wonderful clarity. As it washed over Brant and his officers, she imagined soothing scenes, tranquil forest glades and burbling creeks.

Brant sighed. "Iris, you must stop trying to influence me with these shape-mage spells."

Hai! He had realized her ploy.

His stern visage gentled. "If I trust you, it will not be due to your spell, but rather because if you can calm me with such a strong spell, you can do the same for your husband." He glanced at Jarid, his austere gaze hooded. "I hope he appreciates his fortune in this marriage."

Iris thought of Jarid's inner light, his boyish mischief and his unspoken trust. "The fortune is mine."

"Ah, Iris," Brant murmured. "You are a jewel."

She stared at him, stunned. Never would she have expected to hear such from the formidable Lord Firestoke.

Then he became all business. "You must return to Castle Suncroft by morning. If you do not, we will come out and haul you both back regardless of what you say."

"We will be back before the sun clears the horizon," she promised.

"Are you sure you want to do this?"

"Aye, I am."

"The castle is a place of more...comfort."

She wondered why he sounded so awkward. "Jarid and I find comfort in these woods."

"You wouldn't at least like a blanket?"

Iris flushed, finally realizing why he thought she wanted to be alone with Jarid. "My thanks, but no."

He exhaled, but then he motioned to his men. They bowed to her and Jarid, and took their leave. Their minds receded as they returned to the castle, until she could no longer sense them.

The entire time, Jarid had stood without moving, like a stag in the woods when a human ventured into his territory. When they were alone, completely alone, he turned toward her, his expression questioning. Iris took his fingers and set them against her mouth. "They have left."

He stroked her lips. Then he bent his head.

She didn't realize what he intended until his lips brushed hers. A tingle went through her, but the kiss was so unexpected that at first she couldn't react. She thought his feather-light touch would vanish, but instead he deepened the pressure of his lips. With a sigh, she closed her eyes and leaned into him, her arms going around his waist.

Iris had never believed a person could really feel the beat of her lover's heart through his clothes, but it was true; his came to her, strong and steady. His hands roamed her back, catching her clothes and pulling her curls, making her even more aware of how he did everything by touch.

Eventually he drew back enough to press his lips on her forehead. When he lifted his head, she took his hand and spoke against his fingers. "I have a gift for you."

He hesitated, and she could tell he wasn't sure what

she had said. But he went with her as she led him deeper into the woods. They walked more slowly than before, Iris needing almost as much caution now as Jarid, with so little moonlight making it past the canopy of branches overhead. But in this forest she knew so well, she could have found the place she sought even if nothing at all had lit the way.

Spheres turned in Jarid's mind, spinning in an endless glistening dance. Never had he envisioned them with such clarity. Yet for all their beauty, even more than usual, they spun so fast that they gave him vertigo, which had never happened before. He shut them away, wanting to clear his mind of everything but the woman.

Breezes cooled his face, a change he craved after his imprisonment in the castle. He would have sung his joy at this freedom, if only he had the words. At Stone's cabin, he had known the land well enough to walk on his own as long as he didn't stray far. He had recognized all the many and varied scents of the mountains. He missed his home. He missed Stone. Surely he would know if these people had harmed his foster father. Jarid couldn't believe Stone would give him up so easily. No. Stone wouldn't do such a thing. The soldiers must have prevented him from following his son. Jarid vowed he would find a way to contact his father.

The woman guided him through a screen of heavy foliage. Branches snagged his clothes and he stumbled. He was surrounded, caught, penned in, imprisoned. *Suffocated.*

Just as Jarid started to balk, the woman pulled him free of the branches, into an open place.

Jarid froze.

Spheres!

They *jumped* in his mind, spinning, spinning, spinning, throwing off sparks of light. Dazed, he pressed the heels of his palms against his temples, trying to relieve the intensity of his reaction. Mist sprayed his face, hinting of a waterfall nearby. He smelled fresh water, a lake perhaps, more likely a pool, given the enclosed feel of this place. The fragrance of shapevines tickled his nose and he drew pure air into his lungs.

The woman was taking his hands again. She put his fingers against her lips, those lips he wanted to kiss until she groaned, though he would never hear her pleasure. He hungered for her, all of her, but lost in his darkness and silence, he couldn't find a path to her through the maze of his emotions.

She spoke against his fingers. *Jarid. Husband.* Her full lips tantalized his sensitized skin. The scent of fresh soap and flowers hung about her like a delicate perfume.

He mouthed two words. *Your name?* When puzzlement came from her mind, he tried again. *Name?*

Iris.

Iris. It made her more real to him, less of a mystery, a woman of colors he felt rather than saw: the ruddy warmth of her touch; the gold of her emotions; the sunlight of her intellect; her fresh serenity, like leaves unfurling in spring; the open spaces she gave him, as blue as the sky he never saw; and her indigo moods, the sadness that so often filled her.

Frustrated by his inability to speak and aroused by touching her lips, he pulled her close, harder than he had intended, speaking with his body, his confusion mixed with his desire until he couldn't separate the two. Love and anger, tenderness and rough edges: his emotions all tumbled together. The silken texture of her dress was foreign, like a rich dessert he craved. The unfamiliar softness of her skin excited him. He held her too hard and her alarm sparked, but he didn't want to stop. Not now. He needed her. He *needed.* He didn't know what to do with that need, how to make her want him.

Then her hands moved, stroking his arms. Her orb-spell flowed over him, and he took an uneven breath, struggling for control. Instead of fighting him, she offered this spell of trust. It bewildered him, for she had no reason to believe he wouldn't hurt her.

Moving stiffly, Jarid knelt on the ground, drawing her down with him. The grass felt cool and succulent on his skin when he braced his weight on one hand, and the heady fragrance of shape-vines tickled his nose. He wanted to clench Iris until he sated his driving hunger. When he pulled her forward, pressing her body to his, she tensed and put her palms against his shoulders, trying to push him back.

Jarid knew he should stop. He had frightened her. But it was so hard to let her go. He forced himself to ease his grip enough so she could jump to her feet and escape. To his unmitigated surprise, she stayed put. Instead, she relaxed in his embrace and moved her hands down his arms in a caress.

Let me, he thought to her, but even if he could have spoken, he knew none of the sweet whispers a woman expected from a man. They were strangers; this fragile bond they were forging could shatter if he let his true nature show. His guilt went too deep. That crushing guilt. He pushed it down, refusing to acknowledge it. For this one night, he wanted to forget.

Iris stroked his shoulders, his face, his chest. The sensuality of the way she smelled provoked him past reasonable thought, and the scrape of her skin against his, through a rip in his shirt, made his pulse leap. She tugged at his belt clasp and he would have groaned if he could have made a sound. Instead, he grabbed her wrists, his restraint crumbling. Pushing her backward, he unbalanced them both so that she tumbled onto her back in the sweetly scented grass. Before she could react, he stretched out on top of her, grasping at her small waist and full breasts.

When she stiffened under him, Jarid feared he had pushed too hard, too fast. But no—she was responding, caressing his back, tentative but without fear. He would have known if she acquiesced only because she was his wife. He felt her excitement. She wanted *him,* no one else. Realizing he kindled her desire that way aroused him more than any expertise on her part could have done.

Jarid kissed her neck, pressing his teeth against her

skin, aware of how it gave under the pressure and hard edges of his bite. He must be too coarse; surely a man came to his wife more gently. But he didn't know how to love her. He had lived a life more secluded than any hermit.

And yet she didn't find him repulsive. Her response flowed over him. That she would accept him now, despite everything, made him light, airy, almost happy, an emotion he had had little familiarity with these past years. Right now it made no difference that his world was dark; he saw her with his hands and felt her light-drenched moods. Nor did his silence matter; his touch spoke to her in a language that needed no words.

Her healing spells wove around him, released by the power in this forest place. She had tried her spells earlier, in the palace, but he had been stone. Here in this enchanted sphere, his defenses weakened. After so many years, they finally eased. Her spells were pouring over him, through him, *into* him, with tenderness.

So the two of them came together, protected within a sphere of life, misted with water. Her pleasure answered his, their moods blending as they loved each other.

Sometime later, Jarid lifted his head. He was lying on his side now, tangled in Iris's arms, warm from their earlier joining. She slept beside him, her mind tranquil, her body soft and tempting. He should have been happy, content, pleased—but he was *breaking* inside, the way the ice on a lake cracked after a long winter. His passion had surged through him in a catharsis, a great release of energy he couldn't control. He hadn't the words to describe what was happening; he knew only that he was shattering. He thought of Iris and the pain surged. This pleasure she gave him came at too great a price; she had breached his defenses and left him vulnerable. He would have cried out, but he had no voice.

Panic hit. Jarid yanked on his trousers and shirt and lurched to his feet. The spherical hollow vibrated with energy, focusing his mind until he thought he would explode with the power coursing through him. A memory came to him from a night long ago, his mother weaving her final spell: *the power of a life.*

No! Jarid strode away without even lacing up his shirt. He was dimly aware of Iris waking, of confusion replacing her contentment. He stumbled into the pool and slipped, falling to his knees. Angered by his inability to see, he scrambled to his feet, spraying water everywhere. Then he strode away, swinging his hands in front of his body as if he were fighting the air.

A branch jabbed his palm. Ripping the foliage out of his path, Jarid plunged forward into the bushes that surrounded this hollow. He thrashed through the barrier, unheeding of how it tore his clothes and gashed his skin.

Then he was free and striding through the woods, his outstretched hands scraping trees as he escaped the unbearable radiance of Iris's mind.

Chapter 7

The Power of a Life

Iris sank down on a large boulder by a stream. Jarid wasn't anywhere. She had searched for hours. The tears that had streaked her face were dry now, but nothing could ease her heart. Last night she had thought she reached him, but it had all backfired; now he was gone, without food, shelter or warm clothes, unable even to ask for help. She had done this, insisting Brant Firestoke and the guards leave; now she had to go back and ask for their help in finding her husband, their king. She doubted Jarid would forgive that betrayal of his trust.

Last night she had thought they discovered a place together, a place where they both belonged, where they could discover what love meant. Jarid reached out to her in a way no one had done before. It didn't matter to him that she had no name except those borrowed from the Larkspurs, a foster family that didn't want her, or that she was the illegitimate daughter of a mother who had deserted her at birth. She and Jarid lived in their own solitude, different, yet they each recognized the loneliness of the other, the kindred spirit, building their trust.

Now she had to ruin it.

The woods were lightening; soon dawn would come. Weary, she rose to her feet and trudged toward the castle.

Jarid awoke. It was hard to tell if he had nodded off for a few moments or slept soundly, but the air felt different from when he had collapsed on the mossy ground. The scent of night-blooming flowers had dulled. From the force of habit, he opened his useless eyes.

Green.

For a long time he simply lay, absorbing it. His darkness had turned green. For years he had seen no colors except in his mind, and over time those had leached into shades of gray. Yet now, everywhere, he saw *green*.

Gradually he became aware of details in that living tapestry: a twig, gnarled and brown, poking through moss; dark soil, rich and loamy under the ragged carpet of leaves; a red pyramid-blossom in the pearly light that heralded the approach of dawn; iridescent dew clinging to leaves.

Jarid slowly rose to his feet. A pressure built in his chest until he thought he would burst. He turned in a circle, unable to believe. If he could have made a sound, any sound, a sob would have caught in his throat. His world remained silent—but he could *see* it.

He could see.

Forest surrounded him, hoary trees draped in moss, with more shades of green, gray and brown than he could count. Shape-blossoms added yellow here, violet there, a splash of orange. Tilting back his head, he saw slivers of gray sky between the overhang of high branches. He went to a tree and pressed his palms against its trunk. Beetles scuttled away and a miraculous line of ants wound along the bark.

Jarid didn't realize he was crying until a drop of water fell onto his arm. Pushing away from the tree, he wiped his face with the ripped sleeve of his shirt. He wanted to laugh, to cry, to shout his astonishment, but no sound came. The emotions welled up inside him and spilled down his cheeks as tears.

His walk through the woods was a miracle. Every sight seemed touched with magic, every leaf, bird and twig. He climbed a knoll, making his way through trees until he came out onto an open slope. When he reached the hilltop, he could look over the countryside in all directions. Woods and meadows rolled away everywhere, and in the north the castle stood on a higher peak, draped in shadows, waiting for the rising sun to turn it gold. Memories welled within him and made his eyes sting; he had often stood on this knoll as a child, cherishing this view.

Then he spotted a figure; to the north, in a meadow, a woman in a yellow gown was trudging toward the castle.

Iris.

Apprehension and anticipation leaped within him. It had to be her. Iris had long, full hair and so did the woman below, her mane gloriously unbound. He remembered enough from his childhood to know that women at balls wore their hair up on their heads. But Iris let her curls hang down her back, another reason she captivated him.

Last night, he had retreated from her, afraid she would melt the protective ice around his heart. He had no defenses against her. He knew she could hurt him, but now he could think only of seeing her face. This morning, in the pure light of dawn, he fought against his fear. He wanted to live again, not just exist.

Jarid started down the hill, tripping on rocks because had so little experience taking himself anywhere. The world was too full of sights for him to absorb it all.

Birds chirped.

They sang everywhere, proclaiming the onset of morning. Grass crackled beneath his feet. As he gained confidence, he increased his stride, until he was running down the hill.

Iris heard the rustle just before the hand touched her shoulder. With a jump, she spun around.

''Jarid!'' Before her fear of rejection could stop her, she threw her arms around him. He enfolded her in a hug and they stood together in the predawn light, holding each other so tightly, she could hardly breathe. This wasn't like last night, when he had clenched her with desperation; now his embrace seemed filled with joy.

It wasn't until Iris felt sunlight on her arm, where her sleeve had torn, that she came to herself. Pulling back, she looked up at him. He stared back at her, his gaze caressing her face.

His gaze.

Iris's breath caught. He was *looking* at her. When she gaped at him, his lips curved in a smile. Then he mouthed, *You are beautiful, Wife.*

"Lord Firestoke, wait!"

Brant Firestoke turned from the search party gathering in the entrance hall of the castle. A triangle page was running toward him, his young face red from exertion.

"Yes, what is it?" Brant barely managed to hold his impatience in check.

"Come to the Star Walk, Gracious Lord," the boy cried. "Come see!"

Brant wanted to put him off; he was too edgy about Jarid to let anything distract him from the rescue mission. But he knew this youth to be a steady fellow. The page's unusual behavior struck him enough that he went with the boy.

The Star Walk topped the great wall that surrounded the castle. It took its name from its star-shaped crenellations cut into the wall. Archers hid here during battle and fired through the openings, and the castle healer used the star shapes to focus her power when she tended injured soldiers. Brant prayed they wouldn't soon need those stars to defend themselves against the armies of Harsdown.

The page took him to a section above a meadow. "Look, Gracious Lord."

Gazing out, Brant saw two people crossing the grassy field, walking hand-in-hand. Iris and Jarid.

Brant let out a long breath. "My thanks, young man." He wondered if the depth of his relief was as obvious to the boy as to himself. At times like this it was hard to maintain his veneer of impassivity. When Iris and Jarid hadn't returned this morning, his fear for Aronsdale had flared like mage-light. Nor was it only Aronsdale; over the past year he had grown fond of Iris, who reminded him of his daughter, and Jarid brought to mind the late King Daron, whom Brant had served with loyalty, respect and the love of a brother.

Brant headed back to inform his men. As he descended the stairs, the clangs and calls of the waking keep came up from below. At the bottom, he walked out into the entrance hall—and found Jarid and Iris already there, surrounded by the search party. The two of them looked a mess, their wedding finery torn and stained with grass. Iris had a leaf in her hair.

Watching the newlyweds, Brant smiled. They seemed oblivious to everyone but each other. Exactly why Iris had wanted to take Jarid into the woods, or why Jarid had wanted to go, he wasn't sure. The closeness of nature seemed to comfort them in a way the castle could never do. He had little doubt about the success of their nuptials, given the way they were beaming—

Brant froze. Saints almighty, they were *looking* at each other, both of them, Jarid as well as Iris. Servants bustled about the couple, clucking at their disheveled state, having no idea of this amazing event because none of them had known their new king was blind.

Muller's voice rang out. "Jarid, what is this?" He stepped out of the shadows at the other end of the foyer, near the great staircase.

The king jumped, his dark hair brushing his shoulders as he turned toward his golden cousin. Muller came forward, but stopped several paces away, his face stunned as Jarid met his gaze. The servants melted away, taking their cue from the tension in Muller's body.

"It can't be," Muller said. "You can't see."

Iris answered with joy. "It is a miracle."

Muller swung around to her. "How could this happen?"

"What do you mean?" Her smile dimmed at his dismay.

Muller seemed to struggle with his words. "As long as he couldn't lead Aronsdale, it would have been all right. But this—" His voice shook with emotion. "Now he can rule, but imperfectly. It is wrong. Wrong! It will destroy Aronsdale."

Iris stared at him. "How can you say such a thing?"

Jarid was watching them, his miraculous gaze going from Muller to Iris, his expression darkening.

"Fate must be laughing at us," Muller said bitterly. "No matter what decisions we make, no matter how lofty our intentions, we pay cruelly in the end."

"I donna understand—" Iris broke off as Jarid left her side and strode toward the great staircase.

By the time Iris caught up with Jarid, halfway up the stairs, she was running. She grasped his arm, pulling him to a halt—and in that heart-stopping instant, he spun around and raised his fist. But he didn't threaten her. Instead he stretched out his arm, pointing at Muller, who had come to stand at the foot of the stairs.

"My cousin is right." Jarid's deep voice rasped with disuse. "Ask Stone."

Their tread whispered on the pitted stone steps as they descended to the underground levels of the castle, Jarid and his guards on the narrow stairs ahead of Iris and Brant, with Muller and more guards behind them. Iris wanted to hit someone. It was wrong; she was a mage, a healer, a bringer of light, not a pugilist, but even so, right now she wanted to take a good, solid whack at Brant.

It was bad enough that he had never told them he had ordered his men to bring Jarid's foster father back here; even worse, they had thrown the man into the dungeon. Iris doubted Jarid would ever forgive them now. He had withdrawn into a place so deep, he would respond to no one.

She spoke in a low voice to Brant. "You had no right."

"I had every right." His gray eyes could have been granite. "That man kidnapped the Dawnfield heir."

"He took care of Jarid like a son."

Brant's voice hardened. "He murdered Jarid's parents."

Iris jerked. *"What?"*

At her raised voice, several people looked back. Brant frowned until they turned away again. Then he spoke quietly, words only Iris could catch. "You heard me."

"I thought highwaymen attacked the carriage," she said.

"That's right."

"Including Stone?" She spoke the name Jarid had used for his foster father.

"Yes."

"How do you know?"

Brant tilted his head toward the soldiers with Jarid. "This 'Stone' matches the description given by those two. They were the guards that the highwaymen knocked out during the attack on the carriage."

"You canna be sure this Stone is the same man, especially after fourteen years."

"He admitted it when my men questioned him."

Iris thought of Jarid's desperate loneliness. "Why didna you tell me Stone was a prisoner here? You let us believe he intended to follow us to Suncroft."

"I didn't want to upset the king." Brant spoke quietly. "You've had an empathic link with Jarid from the start. I couldn't risk your knowing. I'm sorry."

Iris sighed. "It surely is a mess." She watched the

rigid set of Jarid's back. Did her husband know his foster father had been involved in the accident? She guessed yes; Jarid didn't seem surprised by Stone's imprisonment. She couldn't fathom how he could have lived all these years with a man who had helped kill his parents. It must have been a nightmare.

At the bottom of the stairs they entered a rough hall lit with torches. The head guardsman took a hexagon of keys off a peg and led the way to a heavy door. While the guard unlocked the door, Jarid waited with several soldiers, his posture so stiff that Iris wondered he didn't crack. How would he respond, seeing for the first time one of the men who had destroyed his life? Stone may have spent fourteen years atoning for that crime, but nothing could give Jarid back what he had lost, neither his parents nor his childhood.

After the guardsman heaved open the door, two soldiers filed into the cell. Instead of following, Jarid turned to the people crowded behind him. When he held his hand out to Iris, her pulse leaped; it was the first time since Muller's outburst this morning that Jarid had shown any wish for human contact.

Stepping forward, Iris took his hand. His face was set with lines of pain he should never have had at his young age. His grief saturated her senses.

They entered a cell with rough stone walls. It was clean but bare, with no furniture or amenities except for a chamber pot in the far corner. Iris had thought they were underground, but the far wall must have been set in a slope on the northern side of the castle. Its barred window let in sunlight.

A ledge stretched along the wall to her right—and she recognized the man who sat there, watching them with the taut posture of someone who expected to soon face his execution. His mane of granite-gray hair swept down his neck and bushy gray eyebrows arched over his gray eyes. Stone. But this was no stone-hearted man. When he saw Jarid, he made no attempt to hide his joy. The six-sided cell focused Iris's mage gifts and she felt Stone's mood; he loved his foster son deeply—and he feared he had lost Jarid forever.

Jarid walked over to him, his face unreadable. Stone waited, his hands clenched on the edges of the ledge where he sat. And then, while everyone watched, the King of Aronsdale went down on one knee to a prisoner in his dungeon.

"What is this?" Stone spoke in such a low voice, Iris could barely hear him. "You kneel to me? Surely not." He was speaking to himself rather than Jarid; he obviously expected no response.

Jarid lifted his head. Then he answered in his rusty voice. "Surely yes."

Stone froze. *"Dani?"*

"Dani?" Emotion roughened Jarid's voice. "Is that what you named me?"

"I—yes, yes, I did." Wonder showed on Stone's face. "What miracle is this, son?"

Brant Firestoke spoke harshly. "Do not presume to call His Majesty your son."

Stone jerked up his head. "His Majesty?"

Saints almighty. Had they told him nothing about Jarid? It seemed impossible Stone couldn't have known. Only someone completely secluded after the death of Jarid's parents wouldn't have heard about their accident and the loss of their son.

And yet...remembering the desolate mountains where they had found Stone's cabin, many days' ride from any town, Iris realized it was possible he could have been that isolated, if Stone had chosen to withdraw from the rest of humanity. But why had he kept Jarid hidden for so many years? To protect himself?

Muller answered Stone, his voice icy. "Yes. His Majesty. That night you murdered the heir to Aronsdale."

Jarid rose to his feet. He started to answer, then stopped. Everyone remained silent, waiting while he struggled to do what most people took for granted—speak. Finally he responded, his voice rough. "Stone did not kill my parents. Murk was the one who drove us off the road."

"But I was there." Stone stood up next to him, watching the king with painful compassion. "I, too, am responsible."

Jarid raised his hand as if to touch Stone's face, the man who had taken care of him for so long. "Any sin you committed, even that Murk committed, was far less than mine."

His foster father answered in a low voice. "No."

"Stone—" Jarid's voice caught.

"Stone?" His father sounded subdued. "Is that how you thought of me?"

Jarid nodded. "For strength. A contrast to Murk."

"I don't understand," Muller said. "Who is Murk?"

Jarid tried to answer, then shook his head.

"Murk planned the robbery," Stone said. "He was the other highwayman."

"And you only *now* reveal this?" Muller demanded. "Better to protect your own, eh?"

Stone's gaze never wavered. "Aye."

"Nay," Iris murmured, using the cell to help her focus on Stone. "You did it for Jarid. You remained silent to protect him."

Stone blinked. "Jarid?"

"My husband. The King."

Stone's weathered face gentled as he turned to his former ward. "You have married this lovely young lady?" When Jarid nodded, Stone said, "It is a good thing." He hesitated, regret in his expression. "Jarid is your name?"

"It is," Jarid said softly.

"I am sorry. I never knew."

Jarid touched his arm. "Do not be sorry."

"What does she mean, you remained silent about this Murk to protect Jarid?" Muller asked. "What lies have you told my cousin?"

"Told?" Stone answered quietly. "I have told him nothing and everything. I spoke to him for fourteen years, Gracious Lord, and he heard nothing. What did I tell him? That the boy punished himself for something not his fault? Yes, I told him. He never heard."

Jarid spoke in a rasp. "I am no boy."

"Enough," Brant said. "Where is this Murk?"

"Gone," Jarid grated.

"Gone?" Muller's forehead furrowed. "Where?"

Jarid didn't answer. Instead he walked to the window and gazed past its bars to the meadows below. Iris wanted to go to him, to offer succor for his grief over his parents. But his need for separation surrounded him like a shield; to approach now would be an intrusion.

"I cannot take you to Murk," Stone told them. "I am sorry."

Muller's jaw worked. "You will tell us where your partner has hidden."

"I cannot."

Brant spoke, his voice like the wind that scoured the land in winter. "We have been patient with you, highwayman. But that is done now. You will talk."

Stone's face paled, but still he said nothing.

Brant motioned to the soldiers. "Take him to the interrogation room."

"No!" Jarid spun around from the window, unsettling in his intensity. "You will not."

"Why?" Muller asked. "*Why,* Cousin?"

"You know the legend of indigo mages?" Jarid's voice had jagged edges.

Muller blinked. "Of course."

Brant was studying Jarid closely. "No indigo mage has ever been known."

"My mother," Jarid said.

"That cannot be," Brant said. "We have no records of such."

A voice came from behind them. ''No. But I recognized signs of her ability.''

Iris swung around. Della stood in the doorway, her gray hair disarrayed around her face, her cheeks red as if she had run here through the wind.

''It is the legend of the indigo mages,'' Della said, coming forward. ''A mage's power is limited by the strength of her life. She can soothe, yes, but no more than she could soothe herself. She can heal only injuries she could recover from herself and feel only emotions she can recognize and endure.'' Quietly she added, ''An indigo mage would have the greatest power of all.''

''The power of a life,'' Jarid said, his gaze hooded.

Iris was beginning to understand. ''An indigo mage can save a life. But only one, for she has only one life.''

Della's voice softened as she addressed Jarid. ''Your mother saved your life in the crash, yes?''

His voice rasped. ''She died so I could live.''

''Nay, Jarid, it is'n your fault,'' Iris said.

''You must not punish yourself for their deaths,'' Della said.

''You should have brought him home,'' Muller told Stone, his voice edged with anger. ''How could you keep him in that hovel?''

''He didn't know who I was,'' Jarid said.

Iris watched her husband uneasily. There was more to this than his grief over his parents. But what?

Brant narrowed his gaze at Stone. ''You could have

made inquiries. You chose instead to protect yourself.''

''Yes.'' Stone met his gaze. ''I did.''

''Liar.'' Pain etched lines in Jarid's face. *''Liar.''*

''Son, don't,'' Stone said. ''Let it go.''

''Why?'' Jarid's voice grated as if it could tear his throat. ''They should know the truth.''

''What truth?'' Muller asked.

''About Murk,'' Jarid said. ''About me.''

''Dani, stop,'' Stone whispered.

''Whatever you're hiding,'' Brant told Stone, ''we will discover it.''

''Stop.'' Jarid was facing them, tall and imposing, his body dark against the patch of light made by the barred window at his back. He lifted his arms from his sides until his hands were at waist level, his palms cupped upward.

Then it began.

Light filled his hands, as if he held a glowing red orb in each. He had a haunted expression, his face stark, lit from below by the orbs. The rest of the cell darkened about him.

Della moved next to Iris. ''A red mage?'' she murmured.

Iris swallowed. ''I think more. Much more.''

Jarid continued to stare at Brant. The cell was growing hot, as if he held flames rather than light.

The spheres of light changed.

They turned gold—the aches and pains in Iris's body from her night in the forest vanished. When the spheres turned yellow, her grief for having never known her birth parents eased. The orbs turned green—and Iris knew, with a devastating clarity, the self-loathing that filled Jarid. But why. Why? The orbs kept changing, sky-blue now, and the scratches on her arms faded.

The spheres turned indigo.

Tears welled in Iris's eyes as she realized what he had achieved. Incredibly, Jarid had within him the power to cure even grief, at least that of people other than himself. Yet for all its beauty, she resisted his healing spell. She wanted to overcome her sorrows herself, not through spells.

The spheres turned even darker.

Violet.

"Saints above," Della whispered.

"The power of a life," Jarid rasped. "The power to give—or to take away." He extended his arm toward Brant, his hand filled with violet light. "I took Murk."

Brant stared at him. "I don't understand."

Jarid's words dropped into the air like stones. "That night when he murdered my parents, I reached out with my mind—and I killed him."

Chapter 8

Prince of Sun and Shadow

Della lit the candles in her cottage, one for each mage power: red, orange, yellow, green, blue, indigo. Iris sat at the circular table and touched the indigo candle. "In a rainbow, violet comes after indigo."

"So it does." Della wearily settled in a chair across from her. She seemed subdued, as if she had yet to absorb what had happened in Stone's cell today.

Iris spoke quietly. "Only a violet mage could have killed Murk. And Jarid was only *six*."

"Yes." Sorrow came from Della's mind. "His mother's spell on the glass ball probably helped him focus."

"I've never even heard legends of violet mages." Iris found it hard to comprehend such power.

Della shuddered. "It frightens me."

"He wouldna use it for evil." Iris wasn't sure if she was trying to convince Della or herself.

"All mage powers have their dark aspects. One who can heal can also cause injury."

"But it never happens."

"It happens, Iris." Della rubbed her eyes. "Shape-mages rarely abuse their gifts because it hurts the mage just as much as the other person. A healer who deliberately injures someone also experiences the pain herself. It is a powerful deterrent. But at the age of six, Jarid understood too little about his gifts—and the consequences of misusing them."

"He knows now," Iris said murmured.

"I'm surprised the spell didn't kill him, too."

"It came close, I think."

Della nodded sadly. "If he had truly wanted to use his power for ill, he could have done so long ago, instead of locking his mind away."

"Locking his mind?"

"He made himself blind, deaf and mute as punishment."

The thought threatened to break Iris's heart, all the more so because she knew Della was right.

Watching her, Della said, "With you, he has begun to heal."

"I canna do enough. We are shadows to his brilliance." Iris thought of the wedding gift he had given her, the invisible sphere, a spell of good will she had taken into herself. "I donna think he even needs actual shapes to focus. He imagines them. Real shapes help, but he can use those he sees only in his mind."

"And yet he hides from his own power."

Iris could see, in her mind, the tormented young king, his palms filled with violet light, his gaze haunted as he confessed to murder. "If only he would let me go to him."

"Is he still secluded in the tower?"

"Aye. He refuses to let anyone near." She grimaced. "Muller hasna been much better."

"I don't understand Muller. He practically begged Jarid to take the crown when he thought his cousin was incapable of ruling." Della shook her head. "Why is he horrified now that Jarid might actually rule?"

"Jarid killed a man with his mage power."

"Muller didn't know that until this morning."

Iris sifted through her impressions of the golden lord. "I think Muller sent us to find Jarid because he genuinely believed his cousin would make a better king. I donna know why."

"It makes no sense. Muller has spent years learning to govern. He had to know he was better prepared than Jarid." Della's face creased with lines that had deepened over the past few days. "You would think he would have fought for the title."

"He didna want it."

"I'm not so sure."

Iris exhaled. Neither was she.

Prince of Sunbeams, Iris thought. Muller stood at the top of a hill, facing away from her, gazing out over Crofts Vale in the valley below. Dressed in impeccable white trousers, gold boots and a gilded tunic, he glowed. The sun turned him radiant. Wind blew his hair back from his face, showing his regal profile, his features so perfect he never seemed fully real to Iris.

When she came up to him, he turned with a start, then relaxed when he saw her. He bowed deeply. "Good morn, Your Majesty."

This change of status between them unsettled Iris. Only a few days ago, she had bowed to him.

"Good morn." She gestured at the rolling green hills. "A lovely view."

"Like our royal family." Bitterness edged his voice. "Beautiful on the outside, rotted from within."

She responded gently. "That is'n true, Muller."

"Isn't it?" His fist clenched. "You heard Jarid. A shape-mage who can kill."

"He had provocation."

"And if he feels he has provocation again?"

"Saints, Muller, *look* what it did to him. It was'n his mother's broken spell that left him unable to speak, hear or see. It was *him.*" She searched for words that would do justice to what she had sensed in Jarid. "He felt Murk die. How could a six-year-old live with that? And he knew, even then, that killing opposed everything it meant to be a shape-mage. What if we hadna found him? Would he have spent the rest of his life atoning for being a terrified little boy who defended himself from the monster who murdered his parents and meant to kill him? He's suffered enough."

Muller answered in a low voice. "Before we knew anything about him, I had been so certain it would be best if I stepped aside. Then we discovered he was completely unfit to rule. Even that was all right for Aronsdale—you would do well in his place. But then he began to recover and suddenly we had a king who would rule, but imperfectly."

"Surely a flawed king is better than none at all."

His voice cracked. "Even then I didn't know the worst. He is an abomination. A mage who kills."

Iris couldn't sort his tangled emotions; she had no shapes to focus her power. She tried to draw on the sun, but it was too distant, too abstract. She felt as if she were using untrained muscles. She strained to concentrate—and then she had a sense of going over a barrier. Her spell blossomed and she felt Muller's deep-seated dread at the prospect of Jarid ruling Aronsdale. Even knowing how much perfection meant to Muller, Iris didn't understand the depth of his reaction, nor could she delve deeply enough to discover what caused his fear.

She spoke softly, "We are all flawed, Muller. Just look at me."

He lifted his hands, then dropped them, moving with the unconscious grace he never seemed to want rather than the warrior's power he longed to command. "Iris, it may not seem so now, but you *will* come into your own as a mage, at least a sapphire, maybe an indigo, greater than Della, greater than Chime, perhaps even greater than Jarid's mother."

She wondered why he hadn't answered her question. "In the past, Della said emerald was my limit."

"She was wrong. I told her so."

Iris felt as if he had just punched her in the gut. "You believed I had such power and you never told me?"

"Della didn't want me interfering. Besides, she thinks I have no mage power." He shrugged, trying for a nonchalance he obviously didn't feel. "She wouldn't listen."

"You should have told me." Suddenly Iris understood. "Except then you and I would have had to wed. And you want Chime."

He said, simply, "Yes."

"If I really am that strong a mage, surely you knew it would come out."

"Once Chime and I were married, it wouldn't have mattered. We couldn't undo the union." He looked toward the castle, high on its bluff. "And then you found Jarid."

Iris exhaled. "That is why you sent me to get him."

"In part." He swept his arm out as if to include the entire country. "But what I said before is true. Aronsdale needs you. I would only bring sorrow to our people."

"How could you give up so easily?"

Muller gave a bitter laugh. "You think I gave up?" Bending down, he dug up a chunk of rock. Then he showed her. "What shape is this?"

"An oval, sort of." A broken oval; the end had cracked off, leaving a jagged edge.

"An imperfect shape."

"Very."

"Can you use it for spells?"

Iris tried to concentrate on the rock, but instead of focusing her power, it dispersed her spell like a jagged seashore breaking up waves.

"Nay, Muller." She gave him back the rock. "It ruins the spell."

"As it would for any normal shape-mage." He concentrated on the rock, his forehead creasing.

"Muller?" Iris wondered at his intense focus. It was exactly the way Della looked before she did a spell.

Suddenly a spark jumped up from the rock, which turned red like a hot coal. With a grunt, Muller dropped the stone. It hit the ground and the grass sizzled.

Iris gaped at him. "What did you do?" The glow in the rock was only now fading.

"That," he said harshly, "is *my* mage power."

"But...but you have no—"

"No power? Aye, so Della believes. Why? Because she can't feel a 'gift' as imperfect as mine. I can only use flawed shapes." He kicked the scorched rock at their feet. "You want me to create light? That was the best I could do. My spells always come out twisted. *Wrong.* But I have the Dawnfield mage strength, green at least, maybe blue. It would devastate Aronsdale to have me at its helm."

"Hai, Muller." No wonder he had dreaded becoming king. In a realm that kept its freedom only because of its shape-mages, such a distortion of power from the highest authority in the land could debilitate the country.

Muller indicated the distant figure of a woman in a meadow. She was walking toward their hill, her white dress drifting on the wind. Like him, she was ethereally beautiful, almost unbearably so.

"My betrothed," he said.

"Does Chime know?"

"Yes. She helps me. Soothes me." Softly he added, "But we cannot deny the truth. She and I are flawed."

"Muller, nay."

His face was pensive. "You think she doesn't realize she has too much trouble understanding spells? She and I will never win acclaim for our gifts of the mind, but we complement each other."

Iris was beginning to see why he and Chime spent so much time making themselves beautiful. It helped them endure what they perceived as their flaws on the inside. She spoke gently. "Acclaim means little. A love that makes each of you feel whole is priceless." If only she and Jarid could find their way to such a gift.

"A pretty thought." Pain showed on his face, though he tried to hide it. "But idealistic."

"Sometimes idealism is all we have." Iris watched Chime climbing the hill. "Jarid and I know so little about our duties. All of us are flawed, Muller, but together, perhaps we can do what would be impossible for one of us alone." She turned to him. "Help us. Let me tell Jarid you will stay. He and I, we need you and Chime."

For a long moment Muller watched his betrothed. Just as Iris thought he wouldn't answer, he turned back to her. "I will talk to Chime." He gave her a wan smile. "But I don't know how much we can do."

"Thank you," she murmured.

In truth, Iris didn't know what she could do, either. Jarid had withdrawn from them all. She didn't know how to breach the barriers to his heart—and without him, Aronsdale would remain incomplete.

Jarid sat against the wall of the tower room, a curving surface tiled in gold mosaics. He felt like a figure in a round box. He could focus his power through the tiles, the room, the orb-lamp on its stand, even the stairs beyond the door. Power coursed within him, awakened by his wife and her damnably soothing touch, the healing she drew from within herself and gave to him.

Iris.

Pulling his knees to his chest, Jarid crossed his arms and laid his forehead on them. His mind kept replaying that moment from this morning when—for the first time in his life—he had seen his foster father. Stone. The man had a weathered face. A worn face. An aging face.

A beloved face.

Jarid had ordered the guards to free Stone and give him a guest suite in the castle, and he had made sure they did as he said. Then he had retreated here. Nothing would let him escape the truth. Now everyone knew: their king was an atrocity. All this day he had been reliving Murk's death; no longer could he deny the memory. That night, all those years ago, he had thought he would die himself. He was tainted. He would return with Stone to the mountains and live his life in isolation. He hated to leave Iris, but he couldn't let her stay with him. He would destroy her. He would destroy Aronsdale.

A knock came on the door.

Jarid ignored it, but silence no longer protected him. Nor could he shut out the compassion that flowed to him from beyond that portal. He shouldn't have been able to sense Iris so well with the door between them, but he did. They had reached each other across valleys and mountains and rivers, beyond the forest and beneath the bowl of the sky. It should have been impossible, but they had done it. Now she was a part of him, one so integral to his heart that he feared he would shatter when he left her.

The door opened. Jarid rose to his feet, his back against the wall, his posture defensive. Iris stood framed in the gracefully arched doorway. Guards loomed behind her, their hands on the hilts of their swords, ready to defend their queen against their king.

Iris stepped inside and turned to the guards. "You may close the door."

"Your Majesty," one began. "You shouldn't risk—"

"I shall see my husband in private," Iris said firmly.

When the guard still hesitated, Jarid spoke in his roughened voice. "You heard her."

With poorly disguised reluctance, the guard closed the door. Jarid told himself he should insist that Iris also leave, but the words deserted him. He wanted her too much.

Stop. He put up his hand, palm out, to push her away.

"You donna fool me," she murmured.

"You must go."

She came over to him. "Nay, my love."

"You cannot love me."

"You can say I will never be yours, but you canna tell me what I will feel." She spoke with compassion. "Give us time to learn each other, Jarid. With you, I feel a closeness I've never known before. It is as if we have a place in the world. A home. Perhaps neither of us knows how to love the other, but the seed is there. Let us give it a chance to grow."

Jarid wished he could give that to her: a home, a place, a husband to cherish her. She deserved all that and more. But his scarred heart had nothing to offer.

Iris besieged his defenses. He barely stopped himself from gathering her into his arms. His conflicted emotions bewildered him: his longing to believe her; his conviction he didn't deserve what she offered; his pleasure at seeing her, hearing her, feeling her. He felt her self-doubts and couldn't fathom why she considered herself undesirable. Her hair, so full and curly, gleamed gold, chestnut, red, yellow. Seeing her lush body, he remembered their wedding night and his pulse quickened. Her face glowed with health, her cheeks pink as if she had been running.

He spoke in a rasp. "I cannot promise you a life of the laughter and love you deserve."

Her voice softened. "I couldna bear it if you left."

It was too much. Even knowing he should push her away, he drew her forward, into his arms, and laid his cheek on the crown of her head. "Iris—"

"Is it truly so horrible, to be with the likes of me?"

"It is a miracle. But you destroy my defenses."

She rested her head against his shoulder. "It is a good thing, to heal."

"It's killing me."

"Nay, Jarid. Living hurts, but that is'n death."

"I must never forget what I am."

"You are Jarid Dawnfield, King of Aronsdale."

"I am a monstrosity."

"Nay!" She drew back to look at him. "You are a marvel."

His hands tightened on her back. "Muller is right. He is more worthy to be king."

"He didna say that."

"He doesn't want me to wear the crown."

"He wants it even less himself."

"He doesn't mean that."

"He means it." She set her palms against his chest. "Muller is also a mage, but his spells go awry. You fear you will kill because you have so much power within you. He fears he will kill because his spells twist out of shape."

He stared at her. "Muller is a *mage?*"

"Aye. He says I may tell only you."

Jarid leaned his forehead against hers. "He can learn to control his spells."

"He thinks not."

"I *cannot* accept the crown."

"You already have it."

"I will abdicate."

"Nay." Her melodious voice flowed over him. "What meaning would light have without darkness to define it? Goodness is'n the absence of evil, it is our ability to rise above the shadows within. If you had no such goodness, you would have never punished yourself all these years. That you have both light and shadows donna make you evil, it makes you human."

"I must go." He feared to accept the hope she offered him. "You must stay."

Her voice caught. "I would miss you forever if you left me."

Jarid pulled her close so he wouldn't have to look into her face. He couldn't speak his heart: *I fear to love you.* It would hurt too much, for to love meant to risk the anguish of loss.

Tenderness came into her voice. "We all leave this life someday. We canna let that stop us from giving our hearts. If we do, our lives have no meaning."

He told himself that his leaving would protect Iris, but when he tried to imagine a life without her, isolated in his mountain refuge, it was unbearable. Great ice floes were breaking within him, as his defenses cracked and split.

"Let them crack," Iris murmured.

His voice broke. "I don't know how to love you."

She cupped his cheek with her hand. ''Let us learn together.''

It was a long moment before he spoke. Then finally he said the words that both terrified and elated him. ''I will try.'' He took a deep breath. ''I will stay, my wife.''

Epilogue

Like sunshine sparkling on water, Chime ran up the hill to Muller, her husband. Sitting farther up the slope, Iris watched them. Off to her right, on the edge of a bluff, Jarid stood alone, staring out at the vista of green hills, meadows and woods. Although he wore rich garments now instead of rags, he still dressed simply in dark trousers and a white shirt. Iris had no idea what he was thinking now; even when she could feel his moods, she had trouble understanding them. But whatever thoughts occupied him today were calm.

Over the past months, during the spring and summer, his tormented moods had eased. Although she doubted he would ever let himself free of the guilt that haunted him, his days at Suncroft seemed to soften the jagged edges of his grief. He had asked

Stone to stay, providing him with farmland to the south of Crofts Vale.

Iris was coming to know her husband. In many ways, he was still the boy who had lost his parents. Although he learned at an incredible rate, he rarely spoke. His powers were unparalleled. Fourteen years of honing them through meditation had turned him into a mage greater than any known in the recorded history of Aronsdale. In the past, the queen had served as the mage for the realm and the king as its sovereign. Iris and Jarid were reversing those roles. He had little desire to govern, but he could easily spend all day developing spells. Together, they could give Aronsdale the strength to stand against Harsdown.

It wasn't an easy road, learning to govern, but to Iris's surprise, it suited her. She was also learning self-discipline. Incredibly, she had talents to offer Aronsdale, and she had a place here at Suncroft. She and Jarid spent most of their time learning their duties, with help from Muller and Chime, but today they had borrowed a few moments just to enjoy the sunshine.

As if he had heard her thoughts, Jarid turned to her, his dark hair blowing in the wind, and beckoned, inviting her over. Her mood warming, she rose to her feet and went to him, savoring the sight of this man who had come to mean so much to her. They sat together on the edge of the bluff, gazing at the countryside. In a distant valley, Crofts Vale slumbered in the sunlight. Closer, but still far down the slope, Muller and Chime strolled into view, holding hands.

Jarid spoke in a low voice. "They are happy."

"Aye." Iris wanted to ask, *And you?* But she held back. On the night he had agreed to stay at Suncroft, she had sworn to herself she would never push him. In the months since, she had done her best to keep the vow.

Jarid took her hand. "Iris—"

"Aye?"

He rubbed his thumb over her knuckles. "A lovely day."

"That it is." She wondered at his mood; he so rarely engaged in casual conversation.

He spoke softly. "It will never come easy for me."

"It?"

"Speaking."

She flushed. "Can you tell my moods that easily?"

"Not so easy. But some." He touched her cheek. "My silences leave a woman lonely, I think."

"Nay. You fill my life." She had never felt lonely since he had come here. Vulnerable, yes; if you loved someone, you risked hurting that much more if you ever lost them. But it was far, far better than loneliness. The emptiness she had known all her life was filling now.

"Silence donna mean absence," she said.

"It is hard for me to say what is inside."

Iris curled her hand around his. "It is you I want. Not words." She almost added, *Words can't love you,* but she held back. It was too much to ask him to return her love. They had wed as strangers. It was enough that he seemed content with their union.

Jarid turned her palm upward to the sky. He cupped

his hand under hers, as if they were holding an invisible orb. "Look."

A sphere of light appeared in her hand, glowing violet. His mage color. Her pulse quickened. The power of that simple orb could vanquish any mage in the land.

"It's beautiful," she whispered. "Terrifying and beautiful."

"Now yours."

"Mine?" No one knew yet her mage color.

His voice rumbled. "Watch."

The orb of light in her hand changed—into a rainbow. Every color swirled within the enchanted sphere, swirling in beauty.

Wonder spread through Iris at the exquisite sight. But she said, "It cannot be. A mage is one color, not all."

"You are like none other. You have part of all of us in you." He lifted their hands together, offering the orb to the sun, sky and land. Its light swirled and spun.

As she watched, marveling, the sphere rose from their hands, growing in size, translucent in the streaming sunlight. She could see the countryside through its glimmering surfaces. The orb bobbed on the gentle breezes like a giant bubble, rising higher, blown toward the village. It drifted across the land, pulling out into an arc against the sky. Farther and farther it floated, stretching out…

Then it was done—and a rainbow arched in the sky. It was impossible in the clear, sunny weather, without a raindrop in sight. Yet there it was, brilliant and pure, a great bow of color over the village of Crofts Vale.

"A gift to our people," Jarid murmured. "Light and the healing that comes after a storm."

Tears gathered in Iris's eyes. "It is truly lovely."

"It truly is." His voice had an odd sound. "A sight that I love."

Iris turned—to find him looking at her. Her breath caught. "That you love?"

"Aye." His voice gentled, falling into the cadences of the Tallwalk Mountains. He curved his hand around her cheek, his palm tingling with the power of the sphere they had held. "You."

For a moment her voice failed. When she found it again, she said, "And I you, my love."

So they sat together in the sunlight, watching the enchanted view, each a haven for the other, their hearts reborn in the gentle radiance of their shared gifts.

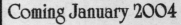

MIRA®